93

INTENTIONAL HARM

A NOVEL

INTENTIONAL HARM

STEPHEN L. GIPSON, M.D.

GUILD BINDERY PRESS
MEMPHIS, TENNESSEE

Published in Memphis, Tennessee,
by GUILD BINDERY PRESS, INC.

Library of Congress Cataloging-in-Publication Data

CIP
94-79629

Gipson, Stephen L.
    Intentional Harm / Stephen L. Gipson, M.D.
    p.   cm.

ISBN # 1-55793-050-3
Fiction

Printed in the United States Of America

1 2 3 4 5 6 7 8 9 10
First Edition

ACKNOWLEDGEMENTS

This is my first novel. It was written to entertain. If you find pleasure in reading it, then I have fulfilled my goal.

There are so many people to thank for helping me with this book. My wife, children and friends for enormous support. My office staff for their contributions and tolerance. Special thanks to those aggravating editors who helped make this manuscript better. I can't wait to argue over my next novel, which is half written by the way.

Special thanks also to Jill Steinberg, Suzanna Phelps-Fredette and Patricia Jennison for their extra efforts.

Stephen L. Gipson, M.D.

DEDICATION

I would like to dedicate this book to Dick Estell.
His program, *Radio Reader,* on National Public Radio,
has been an invaluable source of entertainment,
instruction and inspiration for my writing.

AND IN THE END,

WHEN ALL WAS FINISHED, MAN,

WITH RECKLESS INTENT,

HAD EATEN THE WORLD AROUND HIM.

CHAPTER ONE

A lone car made its way down Highway 61, a deserted north Mississippi route, one October night in 1981. Except for the bare-bulb porch lights of distant tenant houses dotting the farmland, the pitch-black night was empty. The car, an older Mercedes, steered straight at first, but began to swerve and wander as it cut through the still night air. Its driver had spent the day in Tunica and, once again, had had too much to drink. Shrouded in an alcoholic fog, he continued on heedlessly. A sudden jolt shook his car and brought him out of his stupor. He swerved again.

Slowly he pulled off the road and onto the grassy shoulder. Fumbling with the door, he struggled to get out — his feet were wedged under the dash. The car, still in drive, lurched forward. After the car came to a final stop he got out, straightened up and looked around; he leaned on the window, trying to focus his bloodshot eyes. The air felt cool and breezy on his half-numb face. Turning to his car, he noticed that the driver's side mirror was missing and the windshield wiper was bent backwards, sticking straight up into the air. Puzzled he looked closer; fresh blood was smeared along the hood and door.

Stumbling and unsure, running both hands across his face as if to wipe away the confusion, he weaved to the back of the car. There he unzipped his pants and took a long, much-needed pee. Relieved and rambling, he walked along the road treading down along the grassy ditch bank. Suddenly, he stumbled and fell flat on his face. He lay there a minute, stunned, and then, rising with some difficulty, he turned and looked behind him. In the dim taillights his eyes were slow to focus. Gradually, reality materialized in front of him.

"Oh my God. What have I done?" he gasped. His throat choked on his breath. What he saw made him retch instantly. Before him lay the motionless body of a young black woman. Face down, and two feet from her, lay the body of her small child. Death, delivered at the drunken hands of Philip Wilson.

Wilson never gave a thought to taking a closer look or checking the bodies for signs of life. Scared sober, he sped back to Memphis in shock. When he arrived at his Midtown home, he gulped two glasses of whiskey and swallowed several tranquilizers. Then, with trembling hands, he managed to call his family's attorney, Marion Kelly.

ᗡᗷ   ᗡᗷ   ᗡᗷ

MIDTOWN MEMPHIS
MARCH 14, 1993

The alarm clock rang out its usual 5:30 a.m. reveille. Marion Kelly kicked back the covers and rolled out of bed. In the bathroom, he splashed water on his face and then admired himself in the mirror while flexing his muscles. Within five minutes he was dressed in running gear. He sprung out the backdoor of his house and straight into his usual routine. The 10-minute warm-up followed by a five-mile daily run had been part of Kelly's life since Harvard

Law School. On bad-weather days he worked out with weights and machines. Kelly never missed his exercise. He was a highly disciplined man.

After his warm-up, Kelly bound through the familiar hole in his hedge onto East Parkway, the tree-lined boulevard that bordered the back of his house. At the corner of East Parkway and Poplar Avenue was Overton Park, which Kelly thought of as his own private track. The 140-acre virgin forest, a Midtown Memphis landmark, contained a zoo, an art museum, playing fields, a golf course and walking trails. Kelly ran along the trails that were usually quiet and deserted at this hour of the morning. While running, he visualized himself as a predator. Although it was well known that thugs roamed the park, Kelly considered himself dominant. He was a lion.

Kelly was a predator in his professional life, too, and his reputation at his law firm was well-earned. The law firm of Bensen Keller Gregory & Kelly was well organized. There were 42 senior partners, 27 associates, numerous paralegals, secretaries and support staff. Kelly managed the firm's litigation section and supervised 13 other partners and 10 associates. His section handled medical malpractice, personal injury, and criminal cases. Kelly advised his subordinates on legal strategies and other matters of concern to the firm. The underlings did all the work, but Kelly had the final say in all matters. Prompt at work every day by 7:00 a.m., six days a week, he did not tolerate sloughing off. "Get caught, get fired," was Marion Kelly's motto for his team of hand-picked legal talent — the best in Memphis. Under his guidance they were capable, aggressive, clever and merciless.

⚖   ⚖   ⚖

Becky did not want to ask, but she was in a bind.

"I don't give a damn what's wrong with your kid, just get your butt back to work," Marion Kelly shouted, slamming his office door.

Becky stammered: "But the nurse said ..." Overruled and intimidated again by her boss, Becky looked down at the floor. Her baby was sick. What was she supposed to do?

Becky Summers had lost weight over the last two years and hadn't taken very good care of herself. Her clothes were ironed, but not with care. Her hair, short and combed out efficiently, was not stylish. Her figure was still okay, but not really the way she wanted it to be. Her green eyes reflected the pain that had entered her life far too early for one of 29 years. Underneath, Becky was optimistic; she looked at the brighter side of things. But even she had to struggle to find the bright side of working for Marion Kelly.

Becky badly needed this job or she would have quit already. Juggling a full-time job as a legal secretary in a large downtown Memphis law firm and being the single mother of two boys, ages eight and nine, challenged her ability to cope. Her husband, Jim, had died a year ago from cancer, and Becky was forced to return to work. Her own father had been a lawyer, and she had worked for him during summers and in the years before she got married. Becky was desperate after Jim died, so she returned to the only work she felt competent to do. She applied for jobs in Memphis and was hired by Marion Kelly. Most of the people she worked with at the firm were nice enough, but somehow they all seemed cold and impersonal. And with few friends in her life, Becky often felt very alone.

When Becky came to work for the law firm, she planned to keep to herself — just earn a living and pay her bills on the $9 an hour she earned. She was assigned a cramped desk in a cubicle outside Marion Kelly's office. The drone of keyboards clicking filled the air continuously. It seemed to Becky that all lawyers did was turn out reams of paper after reams of counter papers. Stacks and stacks of work piled on each desk in a carousel of rewriting and stacking — stacking and folding — folding and mailing. Today, just when she had gotten a little ahead of the endless mounds of paper, the school called and told her that her youngest son, Jay, had the chicken pox, and she would have to come and get him right away.

"We can't keep Jay at school while he has a fever. You'll have to keep him at home until his temperature is normal for 24 hours," the school nurse preached through the telephone.

"But I'm at work, and it's hard for me to get away, even for a few minutes. Can't we do something?" Becky pleaded.

"We can't have him infecting the other children, you understand," the nurse said sternly. "You'll need to get him right away."

"Okay!" Becky said aloud, followed by, "Damn," under her breath. She felt the knot tightening in her stomach and tried not to cry.

After Kelly's outburst, Becky called her mother. "Mom, Jay's sick with the chicken pox and they want me to come get him right away. Can you help me?"

"Why sure."

"That's great, I've got tons of work to do and my boss is being a pig. I might even have to work late. I really appreciate it. I'll call to check on him later, okay? Gotta go!"

Becky returned to her dictation, opening the file marked Karen Hinkley vs. Paul Greson, M.D.

⚖   ⚖   ⚖

In an east Memphis medical building, Dr. Paul Greson sat behind his oak and red-leather-topped desk reviewing a stack of routine lab reports. The morning paper, left on the desk by his secretary, distracted the doctor from his work. A photograph of the crushed bodies of dead children dominated the front page. An earthquake measuring 7.2 on the Richter scale had buried a densely populated area of India during the night. Men, women and children were killed in one instant of terror as the earth's foundations shook and the walls of their homes crashed down upon them. That morning, 22,000 lay dead. "How absurd," the doctor thought, "to be sitting here worrying about someone's slightly elevated cholesterol."

Kim, the doctor's receptionist, appeared in the doorway trailed by a young man in uniform. Her knock startled Greson. "I'm sorry to disturb you, but the deputy here says he has to see you personally," Kim apologized and stepped aside, allowing the deputy to enter. The deputy was a young, handsome fellow — his dark hair and complexion in sharp contrast to his crisply ironed khaki uniform with hunter green trimmings and tie. He holstered a nine-millimeter Beretta, the typical younger deputy sidearm.

"Hey Doc, you've gotta sign for this one yourself," the bright-eyed lawman instructed, holding papers over the already cluttered desk.

"Yeah? What do you have?" asked Greson.

The deputy handed him a yellow summons from the Circuit Court of Tennessee for the 13th Judicial District at Memphis, Division 10 marked "Karen and Jack Hinkley vs. Paul W. Greson, M.D."

Greson looked at the summons, thumbed through the pages casually, and asked, "What do they want now, more records or something?" Being subpoenaed was customary for Greson's office. There was always an insurance dispute or some other waste of time.

The deputy paused for a moment, then shifted his stance and adjusted his sidearm. His leather holster creaked and moaned as he prepared a response.

"Naw Doc. This one says they're suin' you for malpractice."

Greson's whole body went numb when he heard that word. He stopped breathing for a moment, then looked at the deputy in disbelief. His face suddenly paled.

"You okay, Doc?" the deputy asked, worried that the doctor might faint. "Doc!" he repeated.

"Yes, yes. Of course I'm okay," Greson answered unconvincingly.

"Sorry. You seem upset. I spend all day givin' them out. It's just part of the business," the deputy consoled, making the best of an awkward moment. Without further discussion he turned and left, looking quizzically at the receptionist as if to ask, "What's the matter with him?" Kim, understanding the unspoken message, answered by shrugging her shoulders. Greson heard them mumbling outside in the hallway as he sat holding the papers, still trying to catch his breath.

Greson rose from his chair, leaned his knuckles on the desktop and stared at the summons. Twelve years of helping humanity without incident. Twelve long years with a sterling record, and now this. Greson was more than shocked, he was deeply hurt.

Alone after the deputy's departure, a wave of despair gripped the doctor. A patient had accused him of malpractice. "I don't believe this," he said in a state of denial. "I saved her life. How can she sue me for that?" Anger started creeping through the shock and despair. He knew in his heart he had done his very best for all of his patients. Sure, there were days when he could barely function. Often he was tired from staying up all night with a sick patient or one of his own sick children. There were times too when he didn't feel like hearing someone complain, but he had always done the very best humanly possible. No question. The very best.

Dr. Paul Greson was a gentle man of 41. He grew up on a Tennessee farm and learned the value of hard work early in life. His family was loving, but strict. He studied hard in college to make good grades, and worked nights and weekends to pay tuition. Those late nights were probably the cause of his prematurely gray hair, but he joked sometimes that his wife was the reason. A sharp dresser, Greson stood tall and handsome with striking blue eyes. His face was soft, and his mouth full and round. He exuded an air of confidence combined with humility. He spoke often, and lovingly, of his family and liked to develop close relationships with his patients and employees.

Greson became an oncologist partly because as a child he had watched his grandfather die from cancer. The old man had suffered a long, slow, painful death. When Little Paul had visited the country home of his grandfather, fear would paralyze him. Only a child, he didn't know what cancer was, but he knew it was scary. People around his grandparents' house whispered and talked secretly about the illness. "You're too young to understand," they would say when he asked them to explain. That had always angered him.

Little Paul loved his grandfather more than anyone. He watched as this great figure of a man weakened and withered day by day. During that long, horrible year, the five-year-old boy lost his favorite grown-up. Something he could not see or understand had taken him away, and when Paul lost his grandfather, he also lost his innocence. His life had been touched by death and nothing was ever again quite the same.

Dr. Paul Greson had come a long way in the 36 years since his grandfather had died. Now a highly respected oncologist 12 years into his practice, he had more than a few grandfathers in his care. Battling death was a hard, despairing business. Even after all these years, it seemed even harder to deal with, and Greson could feel himself beginning to tire.

CHAPTER TWO

HIGHWAY 61, NORTH MISSISSIPPI,
WINTER 1993

The ambulance arrived too late by anyone's calculations. The highway work-release crew from nearby Carlson
Federal Prison regarded the scene coldly. Their fellow
inmate's death had been quick and mysterious. None of the
prisoners or guards questioned by the sheriff could explain
how he had fallen under the giant machine. Someone said
they heard him pop as the two-ton asphalt roller squeezed
out his life. Otherwise, the metal monster had passed over
him without notice or hesitation. An imprint of the body
was left on the road after the ambulance crew lifted the
gelatinous corpse from its crater. The soft, hot asphalt was
stained orange by the inmate's uniform.

Back at the prison, members of the work-release crew
returned to their cells. News of yet another work-crew
death spread quickly. Several inmates remarked on how the
old-timers were never injured — how it was always the
new placements that seemed to have all the accidents.
Prison officials blamed the tragedy on the inmate's lack of
work experience. Most inmates and officials alike never
gave the matter another thought.

A state road crew completed repairs on the blighted section of Highway 61 the next day. An imprint of the body was still visible when they arrived the following morning. By that time, the closed casket of the accident victim was on its way by train to his hometown for burial, the two-line notice in the local *Advocate* his only requiem.

"Marion, this is Harry," exclaimed a clamorous voice through the phone. "We took care of that little problem down here. The Post Office is back in business and everything is quiet." The warden relayed the message while leaning back in his chair and propping his feet up on his desk. On the other end of the line, Kelly tapped a gold ball-point pen against his chin as he listened. The warden paused. Kelly had heard all he needed to hear and he hung up without a reply, a sinister smile slowly spreading across his face. Eighty miles away at Carlson Federal Prison, Warden Harry Fields sat propped in his rickety wooden chair and lit a Corolla cigar. The stench of hundreds of such cigars had permeated the office walls, turning them yellow-brown. Harry seemed to blend into the scene, like a hideous wallpaper.

⚊⚊　　　⚊⚊　　　⚊⚊

Dr. Greson entered the eighth-floor hospital room and closed the door slowly behind him. He had lost another patient to the Reaper. This one an old man who had reminded him of his grandfather. The patient had been friendly and gracious, and Dr. Greson had tried every trick he knew to slow the progress of the cancer. In the final hours the doctor had turned up the drip of dilaudid — at least he could try to make the old gentleman comfortable. Unable to recognize his family for days, the man now lay in bed with his eyes partially opened and his mouth blue and dry. His skin had turned cold, gray and clammy, and his heart was finally at rest, his chest motionless. He had passed through a door unknown to all those who now looked on in grief.

The small hospital room was crowded with waiting family members. The crying did not begin openly until Dr. Greson had felt the old man's withered neck and then turned to the family. "He's gone," Greson spoke softly. "I'm sorry. I did all I could." They had all known he was dead, of course, but now it was official. One daughter began to weep into her mother's shoulder. Paul stood back, looked at the old gentleman, and then stared at the floor thinking, "One day I hope I'll have something better to say at times like this."

In the hallway, outside the room, Greson turned to one of the nurses. "I never know what to say when I pronounce them dead. I mean, there ought to be words that comfort."

"I'm just glad we don't have to do it, that's all. I hate being around when the families hear the news," the nurse answered him softly.

All Dr. Greson knew was that he constantly battled with an inevitable part of life that is dying, and that he did what he could to make it a time of dignity for everyone involved. They didn't teach this in medical school and the church's answers were too ambiguous. He was on his own in this part of his practice.

Greson returned to the nurses charting area, secluded from the main station. He sat alone with his back to the door and wept silently for the old man. He hated to cry at work, but sometimes it was the only way to keep sane.

Paul Greson had been callous, to some degree, as a medical student and resident. He was taught to see patients only as owners of pathologic organs. "Don't get personally involved," his instructors said. After graduation, he began to see patients as a challenge to his growing skills and knowledge. Today, older and wiser, Dr. Greson saw patients as souls desperately seeking peace and comfort between the times of pain.

Greson found he had become more sensitive with the years, not more callous as many would suppose. The physician had become more in touch with his own humanity each time he witnessed another's pain.

Dr. Greson pulled himself together and continued his rounds. It was 8:30 p.m. and he wasn't even halfway through. Some days he wished desperately for a partner. He had had several in the past, but they never worked out.

He did not get home till past 10:00 that night. The children were in bed and his wife, Linda, had fallen asleep with the TV on, as she often did. He had missed another whole day in the life of his family, trading away the only thing he cherished. All for a day's work. There were many times he didn't get to see his five-year-old daughter, Jenny, chase fireflies in the garden at dusk. He didn't see her younger brother, Leland, help carry the jar, or Vanessa, the oldest, picking roses for her mom. Together they had caught 12 lightning bugs and put them in a big peanut butter jar. Linda had punched the obligatory holes in the top and the children's faces had shone brighter than the fireflies.

Linda would often tell Paul, when he got home, of the activities of the day. Upon hearing the beauty of it, Paul lamented his absence. Linda would explain how she had enjoyed it enough for them both. That offered him some comfort.

Paul had a deep-seated need to understand his feelings and the reason for his existence. He was once told that there are two important days in your life: One is the day you are born, and the other is the day you find out *why* you were born. Paul had not found the answer. He had searched in the eyes of his dying patients and in the faith that sustained them. He had searched in the halls of learning and in the books of scholars. Once he had gotten a glimpse of *why* in the eyes of his daughter. Perhaps the elusive answer lay somewhere in her spirit. Tonight those eyes were fast asleep and Paul had missed another chance, gone forever.

⚊⚊   ⚊⚊   ⚊⚊

Carl sat nervously in his family doctor's waiting room in East Memphis. He was daydreaming about Vietnam and the pretty nurse he met at the Naval Air Station in Millington where he recovered from his wounds in '67. Her name was Sandra. Carl almost married her. Maybe it was the confinement or maybe it was her uniform, but he had fallen completely in love with her. He wondered what would have happened had Sandra not been transferred to Maine.

Carl Wheat was a big guy with light sandy hair, green eyes and an easy smile revealing good strong teeth. He'd worked out with weights most of his life and maintained a strong, broad frame. His stomach, however, had begun to droop over his belt line. A Marine in Vietnam, Wheat was ambushed in some God-forsaken rice paddy half the world away from his Arkansas home. He took an AK-47 round in the left shoulder during the opening seconds of a skirmish and fell face down in muddy rice water where he lay for 26 arduous hours before being evacuated. During those long, unsettling hours — his buddies dying all around him — Carl had time to get close to God. For Carl, every day since then was gravy. That day had changed his life, and he would not forsake the promises he made in that rice paddy.

Finally, a medic had arrived and given him an antibiotic and a shot of morphine and bandaged his wound. Suddenly, before Carl could express his gratitude, the corpsman's head had disappeared, hit by a 20-millimeter round. Carl never knew his name. He had come to relieve Carl's suffering, even if it meant giving his own life. It had.

"Mr. Wheat!" the nurse called out through the doorway.

Carl stood and walked to the door carrying his three-month-old *Newsweek* without a response.

"Come this way," the nurse instructed, looking him up and down. "Are you here to see Dr. Bell?"

Carl affirmed with a nod followed by a quiet, "Yes."

She directed Carl to the first examination room on the left and told him to get undressed. As he returned to his *Newsweek* story, the door opened and the doctor walked in with his nurse in tow.

"Hello, Mr. Wheat. What seems to be the trouble today?" Carl looked up to the ceiling and then surveyed the overstuffed pocket of the doctor's lab coat. "Well, Doc, my back's been hurting quite a bit. I thought I'd just strained it or something, but it won't go away. It doesn't hurt all the time, but when it does, it can get fairly bad."

"How long has this been a problem?"

"About three months," Carl estimated.

"Any other symptoms?"

"No," Carl slowly replied.

"Hop up on the exam table and let me have a look at you."

Carl, like most patients, wanted to cooperate with his doctor so much that he became almost spastic on the examination table. He tried to breathe properly and jump when his reflexes were supposed to.

Dr. Bell examined Carl's stomach and then motioned for him to turn over. He examined the lower back for strain.

"You can get up now," the nurse said after Dr. Bell turned to the wash basin.

"Well, Mr. Wheat," Dr. Bell drawled, "let's get some lab and an X-ray, okay?"

Carl managed the blood letting and X-ray without major discomfort, even though he hated needles. Back in the exam room, he dressed slowly before returning to his chair and magazine. When the doctor returned, he was carrying two X-rays under his arm and seemed in a hurry. "The X-rays all look good. The lab is okay except a little blood in your urine. Have you had any trouble with your urination, like burning or going often, Carl?"

"No."

"I'm going to put you on an antibiotic for a week and then have you come back for a recheck. This will most likely clear up. Probably just a urinary tract infection, but I think since it's gone on three months, I would like to order an IVP. That's a kidney X-ray, Carl. The nurse will give you a prescription for the antibiotic and instructions where to go for the IVP."

"You're the doctor," Carl agreed without further questioning, still trying to be cooperative.

△△   △△   △△

Becky had returned to her typing when she recognized the name. Why had she not made the connection sooner? Dr. Paul Greson.

"Mary, this is Dr. Greson he's suing," Becky blurted.

"So, we sue lots of doctors," Mary said adjusting her glasses and peering at Becky.

"He was my husband's doctor. He was so nice to us. I don't know what we would have done without him," Becky said, suddenly regretting her participation in this assault on the physician. "I feel like Judas or something, and I'm just doing my job."

A black man passed Becky's desk and entered Kelly's office without an appointment or announcement. "Who was that?" Becky asked turning to Mary.

"I didn't see him."

Becky returned to her typing, and, after a while, gradually drifted into tears.

"What's the matter Becky?"

"Mary, I started thinking about all those trips to Dr. Greson's office with Jim. It seems like a lifetime ago already."

"I know, it must have been hard for you."

"We just stopped being a family when Jim got sick. Everything we did was centered around getting treatment or going for tests. Everything changed. The boys lost their daddy long before he really died."

"There'll be better days ahead Becky. I mean a young, pretty girl like you has lots of life yet. You'll find yourself another man one day."

"I don't know."

"Look this isn't 1900, women get remarried right after, you know, as soon as they feel comfortable. You'll finally get over him and be ready for love again."

"Who would want a widow with two boys?"

"It happens all the time these days. They call it blended families. Not to worry. If I were young and pretty like you, I'd be going out to catch me a man."

"Thanks for trying to cheer me up, Mary."

"You'll see. I'll be right. You'll see." Mary nodded her head in wisdom.

⏃⏃   ⏃⏃   ⏃⏃

Three weeks after the asphalt roller accident, Short Round, as he was commonly known, was released from Carlson Federal Prison — with a little help from Marion Kelly — for exhibiting exemplary conduct. Round and Kelly had known each other for more than 10 years, since back when Kelly was an aspiring junior partner. When Short Round returned to Memphis after his release, he paid Kelly a visit. After a 20-minute meeting, he emerged from

Kelly's office, tipped his John Deere cap at Becky and offered her a good look at his gold-crowned tooth.

Becky stood and walked to the hallway. "Who is that?"

She watched the visitor standing a little way down the corridor counting his money. It looked like a wad of $100 bills.

⚴   ⚴   ⚴

"Dr. Greson, there's a Ms. Stein on the phone to speak to you. She says she's an attorney. Do you want to talk to her?" the receptionist asked over the intercom system.

"Yeah, I suppose so," the doctor answered, wheeling his chair around to grab the phone.

"Dr. Greson, this is Diane Stein with Sullivan Shappley Bender & Marsh. I've been assigned by your insurance company to represent you in the malpractice suit filed against you by Karen and Jack Hinkley."

"Okay."

"The first thing we need to do, Doctor, is meet to discuss the allegations in the complaint.

Early in his career, Paul Greson was told by a close friend to clean out a drawer in his desk for nothing but legal documents, motions and letters. He had followed this advice. He pulled open the second left-hand drawer of his oak desk where the summons and complaint lay alone.

With a sinking heart, the doctor realized that the drawer would soon be overflowing with papers, letters and motions.

They checked their calendars and set up a meeting. "Don't worry, Doctor, we'll get you through this. I've handled many of these kinds of cases," the lawyer consoled.

Paul hung up the phone and thought a minute about what his new counsel had said. "Don't worry." Worry was about all a doctor could do. Doctors are trained to worry.

Worry about things you can't see, find or explain. It had made him a nervous wreck. Sometimes he couldn't sleep for worrying. Some nights he would wake up terrified by the fear of having prescribed the wrong dose of medication or having missed the decimal point.

Greson began to think back on his first encounter with Karen Hinkley. When she had entered Dr. Greson's waiting room, Kim looked up from her usual duties while handing her an information sheet. She immediately noticed the public figure.

"You're Karen Hinkley, I saw you on this month's, ah ..."

Karen did not smile, but offered a quiet "Yes."

"Hey, Karen Hinkley is here," Kim said turning to her office mates.

For the next 10 minutes, each female in the office snuck a peek at Karen and whispered to each other. Greson did not understand what all the fuss was about. His office was not accustomed to receiving celebrities like Karen.

It was almost two years ago that Karen Hinkley had been referred to him by her gynecologist after widespread cervical cancer was discovered during a routine checkup. Paul recalled that she was sitting on the examination table weeping into a wad of Kleenex when he entered the room. She was then 22 years old — a soft-featured blonde with a smile like piano ivory. She was a successful magazine model.

Paul also remembered his first glimpse of Karen's husband, who sat in a chair with his arms crossed, wearing an indignant expression. Jack Hinkley was more than twice her age and identified himself as her manager. What had surprised Dr. Greson about that first meeting was how it had started with Jack Hinkley blurting out, "How long is this going to take? She's got to be in LA by the end of this week to shoot a *Mademoiselle* feature. We haven't got time to waste. It will cost us thousands to be late."

It also surprised Greson to discover that Karen's tears were not due to her serious medical condition, but because she had been turned down for some TV commercial. At first, Dr. Greson thought that she simply didn't understand how serious her cancer had become, having spread to other areas of her body. But as they talked, he learned otherwise. Karen and Jack Hinkley had plans for the Big Time — films, Hollywood and the like. Cancer was not on the Hinkley agenda.

CHAPTER THREE

❦

Becky stayed in the bathroom for 20 minutes; her stomach was upset. Mary was sitting in the break room drinking coffee and having her second cigarette when Becky entered, looking pale and shaky.

"Are you all right?" Mary questioned, very concerned.

"I don't feel well. It's the stress," Becky reported, rubbing her abdomen.

"Why don't you take a vacation or something?" Mary suggested.

"Vacation! What's that? I haven't had a vacation in three years."

"But why?"

"Well, with Jim dying last year, I had to attend to him night and day. He couldn't even clear his throat at the end. After the funeral, well, I had to take care of the boys, you know and get back to work. Now I work full time and take on my second job at home."

"I know. I'm sorry." Mary understood, fell silent and lapsed into thoughts about her own tales of misery.

Becky returned to her desk. She picked up the file marked "Karen and Jack Hinkley vs. Paul W. Greson, M.D."

Curiosity prompted her to read the complaint and the

many notes clipped inside the folder in Kelly's distinct handwriting.

Uninterested when first approached, Marion Kelly had only half listened as one of his associates outlined the Hinkley allegations. However, as the story unfolded, he found himself becoming more and more intrigued.

"I've got a good one here," Richard Jackson, a junior partner, had said, shaking papers over Kelly's organized desk

"What is it? And don't bother me with the little stuff," Kelly mumbled, continuing to write across a yellow legal pad in small, even letters with a gold Mont Blanc.

"A model gets cancer, bad doctor, her hair falls out, Hollywood breaches movie contract." Jackson smiled like a pleased child.

Kelly looked up. "Let me see that," he demanded.

The Hinkleys alleged that due to negligent treatment on the part of Dr. Greson, Karen lost all her hair, including her eyebrows, none of which ever returned. As a result she not only missed out on glamour photo opportunities, but a prime Hollywood Productions contract was cancelled in what the Hinkleys considered to be a breach of contract. The movie turned out to be a blockbuster. Therefore, the Hinkleys allege that strictly due to the doctor's negligence, Karen missed her golden opportunity for stardom. In addition to suing the doctor, the Hinkleys wanted to sue Hollywood Productions.

It was the "Hollywood and hairless starlet" connection that caught Kelly's attention. He had always fancied himself as a big, national TV lawyer. A case like this was sure to get heavy media coverage if played right. Every aspiring celebrity lawyer had gotten hold of that one case that catapulted him to success, and this one just might be the ticket for Kelly. From that moment on, Kelly made the Hinkley case his very own.

"We can nail this doctor on malpractice by informed consent and get say $3, $4 million. Then we'll bust Hollywood on breach of contract and ask for $10, $20 million, plus expenses and punitive." Jackson eagerly outlined the scenario for his boss, who by that time was way ahead of him, winning the case and was watching himself on "Larry King Live."

"Yeah, they make headlines outta this kind of stuff," Kelly had agreed coolly, inwardly chomping at the bit to talk to the hairless starlet.

Becky finished reading the file. She recognized the Hinkleys' shtick — file anything to get a buck. "It's all about money, not justice," she thought wearily. Certainly, nowhere on Becky's birth certificate did it pronounce LIFE IS FAIR. For Becky, life had not been fair. It had come with its own set of terms and its own timetable. For one so young, Becky had a courageous nature and had become strong willed and intuitive as a result of her hardships. She didn't like people like the Hinkleys nor what Kelly was doing for them, but for now she would put it out of her mind. She closed the folder and returned to the endless pile of paper work that cluttered her desk.

⚖️   ⚖️   ⚖️

Carl Wheat was a straight-to-the-point kind of man. Big in stature, he was slow to anger and careful in his reasoning. Carl was outwardly friendly but felt uncomfortable in most social settings. He became nervous if someone stood near him for very long without talking. Although knowledgeable in many subjects, small-talk made him feel exposed and awkward. That's why he avoided parties and social gatherings for the most part. To Carl, a doctor's waiting room was a social gathering.

"Mr. Wheat," the technician called out, checking her

list.

"Yes, here," Carl reported in after having waited his turn for hours.

"Come with me please," the X-ray technician, a striking young blonde just out of college, motioned with her head.

Carl followed her down the light-green hallway towards the X-ray machine. Carl was embarrassed. The X-ray gown, with open back, caused him to "moon" the other patients as he passed down the hall.

"Are you allergic to dye?" her round, voluptuous lips spoke to Carl.

"No, I don't think so," Carl responded, not noticing her beauty.

"Okay then, I'll need to start a little butterfly in your arm for the injection after you get up on the table."

"You're here for an IVP, right?"

"If that's a kidney X-ray."

"Okay, the table's cold," the blonde warned.

"You bet it is," Carl exclaimed with an upward pitch to his voice.

Carl lay flat on the cold table awaiting the sting of the IV. The room was dark and cluttered with overhanging cables and machinery. There was a smell of vinegar or something that made Carl nauseated. It smelled like transmission fluid.

"Okay, I'm going to inject some dye and take pictures every few minutes. Don't worry about the noise and keep very still."

"Huh," Carl moaned.

Carl felt a warm, buzzy feeling all over his body as the iodine-based dye coursed through his veins around his heart and into his major arteries. Soon the dye would be coursing through his kidney vessels and excreted into his urine, outlining the kidneys and its collecting system.

The machine whizzed and clanked overhead. Carl waited. "That's it, all done," the tech said, thinking Carl was cute. "Go back to your changing cubicle and get dressed. The radiologist will send a report to your doctor in a day or so," she recited.

"Thanks," Carl said with a country nod.

"Sure thing," she purred, coming on to him with her eyes.

◿◺   ◿◺   ◿◺

Diane Stein had been raised in a family of eight boys. Her youth was dominated by overachieving men. As the only girl, she grew up feeling she had something to prove to her father, a stern, by-the-book man who raised his children to be competitive. Being the youngest, Diane was put down and beat up at every opportunity. Growing up tough was exceptional training if you wanted to be a good defense attorney, and a good defense lawyer was just what Dr. Paul Greson needed.

Greson was a dedicated doctor and family man who hadn't been exposed to those in society who intentionally harm others for their own pleasure and personal gain. Diane Stein knew those types well after an eight-year stint as a public defender. She had met just about every despicable character Memphis had to offer. She had gone into jails to interview rapists, murderers, armed robbers, child molesters and drunks at all hours of the day and night. Often, she was the subject of verbal abuse from her own clients. Her goal as an attorney was not to win, but to see justice applied. For eight long years she had worked in a system that she didn't approve of, and that, frankly, did not approve of her. But all that was behind her now. At this point in her career, she practiced medical malpractice defense exclusively.

What Diane now found most disturbing was the good-ole-boy network that operated openly and on a grand scale in the upright legal system. Judges, as elected officials, received campaign contributions from big law firms that contributed equally to all contenders, ensuring that their candidate would win. As a result, their clients received more favorable treatment in the courtroom.

Diane held such practices in contempt, even though it was the prevailing norm among her peers. To Diane, law was not a game. She wanted to do her very best and go home with a clear conscience. Diane Stein wasn't about to sell herself short for anyone, especially not a man.

⚖️ ⚖️ ⚖️

Dr. Bart Caperton arrived at his office, the Diagnostic Radiology Clinic, each morning at 7:30 a.m. He found that his most productive time was before the phones began ringing at 8:30. The doctor made a pot of strong coffee and sat down to begin his radiological reports. A pressure sensation occurred in his chest when he took the first big swallow, but Caperton passed it off and picked up a new set of X-rays to examine. "Oh yes," he thought to himself, "this is the patient I was going to get more X-rays on." He spoke into the Dictaphone. "Carl Wheat, IVP." He paused. Then he began to hear a buzzing sound. He couldn't breathe. Things seemed to be moving. The sound grew louder. His thoughts began to race. Panic erupted, and he fell out of the swivel chair and onto the floor. His face turned toward the wall. An image of his wife appeared before him and moved slowly away. It was his last thought in this world.

Dr. Caperton's left anterior coronary artery had been 97 percent occluded for several months with cholesterol plaques. That morning, while he had slept, a small fiber of protein stuck to the wall of his main artery just beyond the narrowing. Over the next few hours first one platelet, then another, began attaching. The cascade continued. In Caperton's office, just after that first swallow of coffee, the process had reached a critical mass. No blood flowed to the front of his heart. The heart muscle first became oxygen starved, then began to spasm. After a series of irregular beats, the muscle moved like a ball of wriggling worms. The irregular wriggling spread across the heart until no section of the muscle was contracting at the same time. Blood ceased to flow, and so did life.

△△   △△   △△

The alarm clock rang — 5:30 a.m. Kelly sprang from his bed and did a quick four sets of 10 one-handed pushups. He started his usual jogging routine, bursting through a hole in the hedges and onto the street by 6:00 a.m. While running, he focused his mental powers on visualizing a strong presence and a forceful presentation. Kelly had important meetings that day and these mental preparations never failed him. About halfway through his run, Kelly's thoughts relaxed and began to wander. He pictured the girl he had used the night before. How stupid she was. Wandering around his house in her tight little skirt, asking him for another drink every few minutes. He smirked to himself at the lines she had fallen for. She was the secretary for the bank president he was meeting today. In bed, Kelly had managed to gather very useful information and several names of people who frequently called her boss. He then linked those names to several shady business deals cooking around town.

Kelly needed to raise some cash for a short investment deal. His new, olive-green Italian suit, laid out in ritualistic fashion the night before, would help his presentation considerably. His most important asset, however, was a straight look in the eye without blinking, held for at least 30 minutes. Kelly had perfected this macho signal. Once he had timed himself at 46 minutes between blinks. No one could stand the pressure of his cold eyes. Kelly made sure of it.

CHAPTER FOUR

Carl squeezed a mosquito between his fingers. The blood it had been sucking — his blood — squirted in all directions. The jungle was sweltering. The air thick and humid. Each breath felt like a jet of hot steam. Corporal Marc Brown, USMC, was crouched next to Carl, pointing in the direction of a village two clicks away on the map.

They spoke in a sign language known only to Marine Corps snipers. Marc was Carl's spotter. He would be the one to guide him to his target, correct for wind or terrain, and set up the shot. Marc was from Kansas and used to arid, wide-open spaces. He was good at his job, but Vietnam suffocated him. It was like being in a sauna for 24 hours, he would say, breathing deeply and mopping his brow with his sleeve.

The village, a rural hamlet, consisted mostly of elderly farmers. The younger men had either been killed or taken to reorientation camps. Since the village was on the border zone, it was often visited by Viet Cong checking for enemy activity and intimidating the villagers to keep them cooperative. They would take rice, chickens and other farm property for their own purposes. They called it payment for defending the village. The villagers would stand in silence with clenched fists as their most valued possessions and the food they had worked so hard to obtain were taken from them. This war had gone on for half of the lives of most of these people. Many of them could not remember any other kind of existence.

"To the right, about 500 meters, is a ridge where we should be well hidden," Marc said, looking up from the topographic map and pointing. Carl acknowledged with a nod. The two Marines, skilled in concealed movement, crawled south through the dense jungle toward the ridge. They had matted fresh-cut vegetation to their clothing to conceal their silhouettes — extra camouflage and full-length clothing. Every pore of their bodies drained fluids like a sieve. They drank six liters of water and consumed 40 salt tablets per day to prevent heat exhaustion.

The men, with their faces pressed to the ground, could smell the decayed products of centuries of fallen foliage. It was a strong earthy scent, not like that found in an American deciduous forest — a musty, mildewy odor. Vietnam was an ancient country. The jungles had existed there unchanged for millions of years. The villages were the same today as they had been before the birth of Christ. Before the onset of this 20-year war, life in Vietnam had not changed in 2,000 years.

By mid-afternoon the snipers had reached their position on the ridge. It had taken six-and-a-half hours to crawl that 500 meters. Even though the ridge was overgrown, there were areas where the sun came through the forest canopy, increasing the already unbearable heat by 12 degrees. Marc had never felt such heat in his life. Carl had adjusted to the climate. In the jungle for six months now, he felt like a fungus himself at times. An observation post was established below the top of the ridge overlooking the village. They remained face down against the musty ground to prevent their silhouettes from being seen against the sky. Carl positioned his sniper rifle, a modified Styer SSG .308, that he had purchased himself and obtained approval to use in place of the regular-issue Winchester. Marc kept an M-16 at the ready on full auto in the event that they were surprised. Carl's sniper rifle was useless if things got tough.

The village lay about 200 yards to the northeast and slightly below by about 50 yards. Carl and Marc waited in silence. From a strategic viewpoint their position was excellent. Only those movements that were absolutely necessary for the mission were allowed. No unnecessary shifting, no talking, no swatting insects. They even urinated in their clothing.

Darkness approached, and the jungle changed into a creepy, crawly world. Shadows became bugs. With their strong, sweaty scents, the men attracted insects, buzzing their faces and penetrating the bare skin of their hands. Carl had slept on jungle missions about two weeks out of every month since being in Vietnam. He had stopped flinching at the bugs, and he no longer thought of a bed and shower as necessities. He didn't seem to notice much anymore, even when he began to stink. As the night wore on, the men divided up the watch — four hours each — until dawn. Carl didn't feel like he'd slept at any point.

About one hour after the sun came up, the village was disturbed by the arrival of three trucks of Viet Cong soldiers. As the trucks came to a stop, soldiers spread out and formed a line along the perimeter of the village. Carl's target, the Red Major, was sitting in the front passenger seat of an open-topped Jeep.

Marc studied the scene through binoculars. It should be an easy kill. They would have to move quickly afterwards because the VC would swarm down upon them if they could locate the direction of the shot. Usually, with just one shot, it was hard to tell where it had come from. One shot, one kill. That was the Marine sniper's motto. Carl raised his Styer SSG, which was covered with canvas to prevent reflection. He removed the lens cover from the Schmitt and Bender scope. He made himself a nest, arranging his body comfortably in his firing position, while Marc studied the scene. Now all they had to do was wait. The figures ran about below responding to the orders of the Red Major. The Marines could see him wave his arms in both directions as he bellowed in Vietnamese. They waited a long time, motionless, for the perfect moment.

"Distance: 210 yards. Windage: cross wind two knots — about eight inches. Elevation drop: 60 feet," Marc whispered. Carl made adjustments for distance, windage and drop. He placed a gold-tipped .308 round in the breech and smoothly closed the bolt. This was the moment they had come for.

Time took on unusual qualities at the moment of a kill. Slow and blurred. Carl adjusted himself again to make certain he was in perfect control. His finger reached for the set trigger. Through the scope Carl could see the back of the Red Major's head as he barked orders from his vehicle. He had earned the name Red Major because he would cut the throats of captured American soldiers in front of his men and drink their blood to display his courage and prowess. The Americans wanted him dead in a big way. Payback time had arrived.

The crosshairs came to rest on the nape of the major's neck. Carl drew a moderate breath and exhaled completely. His finger began to exert slow, even pressure on the tuned trigger. That was the mark of a great sniper — how evenly he could pull the trigger. That's what made the difference between a hit and a miss. A shot rang out. Carl saw the back of the major's head explode, and a great red river of blood and brains slid down the Jeep's windshield in front of him. His body jerked sharply and then fell listlessly to one side.

"Let's go, let's go," Marc whispered hoarsely, already

shimmying along the damp morning ground.

"Ah ..." Carl sat up in bed gasping for breath, sweat dripping off his body. Once again, he had the dream. At least twice a month Carl would go through the same mission as lucidly as he had 20 years ago. The same feelings, the same smells, the same fears, the same relief when he saw the major's head explode. Maybe he should see a shrink or something.

⚖   ⚖   ⚖

Diane Stein placed a call to the opposing counsel, Marion Kelly.

"I'm sorry, Mr. Kelly is in Key West," Becky reported.

"That must be nice. When do you expect him to return?" inquired Diane.

"Monday of next week. Can I take a message Ms. Stein?" Becky offered, thinking she sounded nice.

"Yes, tell him I want to discuss the Hinkley case when he returns."

Dutifully, Becky recorded the message. When she hung up she began to think about Dr. Greson again. She wondered how he was taking the malpractice suit and hoped he didn't know that she worked for Kelly.

Marion Kelly was in Florida meeting with two bankers who were representatives from the Land Development Corporation (LDC) of Key West. Kelly served as legal counsel to the business, as he came highly recommended by their people in Tunica, Mississippi. The LDC was a land holding and development corporation based in Key West, Florida. Its principal stockholders, the gaming industry, were from Las Vegas, Nevada and Tunica. The meeting now taking place had been scheduled to prepare a request for tax exemption and credits from the Department of Interior. Timing of this venture was fortuitous and not coincidental.

A newly passed law, which they had known of well in advance, offered tax credits and exemptions to owners of land that bordered many of the nation's wildlife preserves. Ostensibly, the purpose of Pub. Law 93X75 was to limit land development and encroachment into these critical habitat areas, citing the land bordering these areas as "essential to the ecosystem of endangered species." The Friendly Citizen Wildlife Bill had recently passed through the House and Senate without even a serious reflection.

This seemingly well-intentioned legislation gave government tax credits to landholders who agreed to suspend any form of commercial or residential development on these bordering lands for a period of 50 years. The tax incentives offered were sizeable. The Department of Interior was charged with regulation and enforcement of the law.

The LDC, under Kelly's guidance, was putting together a 6.3 million-acre proposal for exemption under the new law. The structure of the request to the Department of Interior was of utmost importance. The scheme was to submit map coordinates to the department that were obtained from a 1959 topographic survey of the Florida coast. Back then, the shore along the Everglades National Park in southern Florida stretched some 20 miles further out to sea. However, in contrast, modern satellite reconnaissance surveys would dispute the 6.3 million acres. In fact, modern maps would show the proposed LDC plan to represent only 0.8 million acres of land and the rest was the Gulf of Mexico. The key to making the deal work for the LDC was to have the Department of Interior pass the LDC application based on the 1959 surveys. The man who would make that determination was a newcomer to the department, Philip Wilson.

Philip Wilson was born into a wealthy Memphis family that made its money in the cotton business back when there was money to be made. His father had groomed Philip for a political career and continued to pressure him, even when he realized his president-to-be son was simple minded. Philip had always wanted to please his father, but had never had the mental or social capacity to pull it off. As a result of years of failure in the eyes of his father, Philip had developed deeply ingrained self-esteem problems. He had secretly sought psychiatric help to no avail and had become dependent on Xanax — a valium-like tranquilizer — along the way. He was unhappily married to a product of similar disappointment from another Memphis family. They had no children. The only person in his family that he could relate to was his grandmother, whom he often visited on her farm for comfort and solace.

Philip Wilson had served on the Memphis City Council for six years, and apart from the secret hit-and-run accident in Mississippi that had been so carefully handled by Marion Kelly, he had a clean record. That wasn't enough to get him elected mayor though, and after his own failed bid for higher office, he had acted as campaign manager for a Tennessee senator who later was elected vice president. As a favor, the newly elected administration appointed Wilson to a Washington post as Deputy Secretary of the Department of Interior.

Kelly, Wilson and the two bankers sat around the hotel conference table, each with a binder and a breakfast of eggs Benedict.

"Thank you for coming this morning, gentlemen," Kelly opened gracefully. "We have a few items to cover that shouldn't take long. Turning to page B-4, you will see the LDC's corporate register and financial report. Any questions?" Kelly surveyed the faces of the other men, who were leafing through their binders and sipping coffee, waiting a minute or two in silence.

"All right now, if you'll turn to C-2 where it says

Estimated Borderland Acreage, you'll see that I have broken this down into 26 different sections, showing each section to be represented by a different tax I.D. The figures listed in the right-hand column are the old survey coordinates. Take a moment to look over these if you will and see if there are any problems."

"These are the 1959 survey coordinates?" Wilson asked.

"Yes, and that's where you come in my friend," Kelly answered, turning his intense gaze to Wilson.

"Exactly what do you mean, Marion?"

"I have a list of map coordinates that will need correcting. You will enter them into the computer, replacing the new satellite coordinates with the 1959 ones. Once the calculations are made by the computer, then you can change them back. Simple." Kelly threw up both hands and smiled all around.

"How long do you think it will be before the credit codes are issued?" Jack Morgan wondered.

"By my estimates, four weeks, gentlemen," Kelly announced proudly.

"And what about the breakdown of credits to these 26, or whatever, sections. Will that translate back into the 6.3 million acres?" Harold Winner asked.

"The purpose of the breakdown is to squeeze in every possible acre. I needn't tell you gentleman, but this survey took some doing. We examined those maps backward and forward to get the most acreage possible. In addition, the breakdown allows us to route the tax credits in various directions, so it will be impossible to trace where all the money is going."

"Tell me what we're gonna do if someone finds out," Wilson asked sheepishly.

Kelly leered back at the spineless clod. "No one will find out, Philip, if you do your job like I tell you to. Understood?"

Wilson looked down at his plate of half-eaten eggs Benedict. "Yes."

"Now finish your breakfast and look over these files if you will gentlemen. I have to make a conference call. I should be back in 10 minutes," Kelly spoke in a commanding tone.

"Are you all right?" Morgan asked Wilson when Kelly had left the room. "You look sick."

"My stomach — I have ulcers," Wilson returned. His nerves were shot. Every time Wilson was around Kelly, he got nauseated.

Back in 1981, Kelly had solved a big problem for Wilson, and at the time he'd been grateful. But he'd been paying for the favor ever since. That night, Kelly had picked up the phone and called the sheriff of DeSoto County where the hit-and-run had taken place. He appeared to know him on a first-name basis and arranged a meeting. The sheriff was holding a charge of vehicular homicide — in Mississippi a 5-year minimum sentence — and eager to find somebody to pin it on. Elections were coming up and the sheriff saw a chance to kill two birds with one stone. First, he could ensure himself votes by catching the criminal, and second, he could ensure himself a sizeable contribution to his campaign fund by appeasing Kelly. The sheriff and Kelly agreed to have the incident tidied up by charging a local troublemaker with the crime, and the sheriff also arranged for certain witnesses to become available. The troublemaker he had in mind was already facing charges of grand larceny and selling controlled substances, so it wasn't difficult to convince a DA to add vehicular homicide to the list. Everybody won. A nasty little incident was nicely cleaned up for City Councilman Wilson, the sheriff got his votes and his donation, and Kelly got another pawn.

Throughout the years, Philip Wilson had remained quietly indebted to Marion Kelly, Esq., while his consumption of Xanax had doubled. Kelly had cashed in on a favor involving plans to build the Pyramid, a multimillion-dollar sports and entertainment arena that had been slated for construction on a tall Memphis bluff overlooking the Mississippi River. Mysteriously, the city council was persuaded to move the Pyramid off the bluff to the other end of the downtown area in a mosquito hole underneath the bridge to Arkansas. This lovely piece of swamp land was owned by none other than Marion Kelly. The profits of that deal were peanuts compared to the deal now coming to fruition with the LDC. Kelly knew that Wilson was still terrified of being found out as a murdering coward, and could be duped into doing anything to keep his secret.

CHAPTER FIVE

It was Easter Sunday at St. Mary's Episcopal Church and Becky was sitting in her favorite spot on the third row. She was wearing a navy blue dress with white trim and buttons, navy stockings and navy shoes. The boys were dressed in long, light-colored pants with short-sleeve white shirts. Their small, short, striped ties made them uncomfortable. Jay said it made him feel like a dog that was tied to a tree.

The church was resplendent with flowers and banners, and the priests had donned their Easter vestments. The air was alive with spring and the vocal harmonics of a well-rehearsed choir. During the service, when the congregation passed the Peace, Becky turned and said, "Peace be with you," to the man on her left.

"And also with you," the voice of Carl Wheat spoke softly back as he bowed at the waist. Their eyes locked onto one another. Carl passed the Peace with the boys and turned to complete the Mass.

After the service, Carl spoke to Becky. "My name is Carl Wheat. I've seen you here many times, but I don't think we've ever met."

"Oh, uh, hi. I'm Becky Summers, and these are my sons, Stephen and Jay."

"Nice to meet you boys," Carl grinned, leaning down. "Are ya'll gonna come to the church softball game this afternoon?"

"No sir," Stephen said, not really knowing.

"Why not?" Carl asked in a kid's voice.

Stephen just shrugged his shoulders and Jay said nothing. "Since their daddy died," Becky offered to explain, "I haven't had time to think about things like softball."

"Oh, I didn't know. I'm sorry," Carl said, realizing he had hit a nerve.

"Life must go on you know," Becky exclaimed nervously.

"I reckon," said Carl, not sure. He felt awkward like he always did when there was silence between people. He had to think of something fast. The silence was choking him. The room was closing in and the organ music had suddenly stopped. "I'd be happy to take the boys to the ball game this afternoon if it's okay with you."

"Yeah, Mom!" Stephen cried, jumping up and down.

"Yeah," Jay parroted.

"No, I couldn't ask this man to put up with the two of you," Becky said, looking down into the faces of her boys. They could get excited about anything now, having sat through what seemed like a 10-hour church service already.

"Oh, it'll be all right, Miss Becky. I've been around boys all my life and they just love softball, especially before it gets too hot. You know Janet and Robert Freeland; I'll be going with them and their kids to the game," Carl said in a country way that made him seem harmless and kind.

Becky saw how badly they wanted to go and knew that she was not able to give her boys the manly attention they needed. She had seen Carl at church over the past several years and believed she could trust him. She had even sat next to him in a Sunday school class about God and the environment. She remembered he had been excited about the idea of the church taking an interest in preserving nature. Her mind was already thinking, "Why not?" when Carl began to persuade her.

"Yeah, I know them. Well ... uhmm ... since you put it that way, I guess it wouldn't hurt. Well, okay, but just to the game," Becky said, thinking to herself how good it would be for the boys to be with a man for a while.

"Thanks, Mom!" "Yeah, thanks Mom," the boys said in succession.

"I'll pick them up about two this afternoon. We'll be going to Overton Park. Is that okay?" Carl asked with an upward pitch in his voice.

"Yeah, I guess so," Becky said, nodding her head in approval.

Carl wrote down the directions to her house and her phone number. As she spoke, Carl noticed that her smile and eyes had changed and that she had become warmer. Becky liked the soft, Southern way Carl spoke and how he had taken an interest in the boys. She had been so busy just getting through each day since the funeral that she hadn't thought much about another man or a relationship. She figured that no one would want a woman with two boys to look after. "Good grief, what am I thinking? He's just taking the boys to a ball game, and I could sure use a Sunday afternoon to catch up on my rest. I can read the Sunday paper and take a long nap," Becky reminded herself, wondering just how long it had been since she had experienced that simple Sunday afternoon pleasure.

Carl arrived at Becky's house right on time. The boys bolted out the front door of the modest Midtown residence with Becky trailing behind. When they reached Carl's older blue Suburban, he hopped out, opened the door, welcomed the boys on board and helped them fasten their seat belts. Becky stood back with her arms crossed in front of her chest. The old truck started with a little puff of blue smoke, the boys waved through the open window and Carl assured their mother that everything would be all right as he began to back slowly out of the driveway. Becky waved with a little uncertainty. She had clung to her children stronger since Jim's death. She felt the need to protect them.

ΔΔ　　　　　ΔΔ　　　　　ΔΔ

Diane Stein scheduled a meeting with Dr. Greson in his office after work. She had a number of items to cover and she liked to meet her clients in their own territory. It made them more comfortable.

Greson was just finishing the afternoon's paperwork when Ms. Stein appeared in the doorway with his secretary. After the introductions and obligatory small-talk, the lawyer went straight to work.

"I must say, this is one of the most absurd complaints I have ever read. I don't know what they are hoping to prove. I think we have a good chance to beat this one. Have you ever been sued before, Doctor?" the lawyer asked, reviewing her notes.

"No. This is a first."

"Well, the first thing we need to do is answer the complaint and prepare interrogatories. This is a set of questions designed to gather background information about the plaintiffs. It helps me in knowing what questions to ask at the depositions of the plaintiffs and at the trial. The other attorney will likewise send his interrogatory for you to answer. These must be answered within 30 days. I will send a first set of questions to you by courier. When you get them, look them over carefully and then call me. I want to know what you think of the questions and if you have any ideas about things I might have forgotten to ask."

"No problem." Greson hesitated. "Tell me about their attorney. What is he like? Is he any good?"

"Kelly? He's a difficult character." Diane paused and looked outside the window. "I've had cases against him before, and he's a formidable opponent. He likes theatrics and drawn-out legal ordeals. He will try every trick in the book and sometimes, in the end, he'll just drop the case. If he gets a chance, he'll try to stick his face in front of the TV cameras, too."

"So, we're in for a battle?" Greson asked unhappily.

"I would say so, but you never know for sure. We'll probably be dealing with one of his associates most of the time. Kelly usually doesn't do the work himself, but he almost always is at the trial. I've tried to call him to see what he is planning, but he's been out of town. I'll call again this week."

Diane and the doctor discussed the case and prepared the answers to the complaint. When they were finished the doctor asked, "What's the usual scenario in these cases?"

"We'll start with the discovery, which includes obtaining all of Karen Hinkley's medical and psychological records. Then I will take the plaintiffs' depositions as soon as possible. They will also want to take your deposition. And we will meet before then so that you will be well-prepared. I'll also need a list of possible experts who can testify on your behalf. That's about all we can do for today. If you have no further questions, I'll be in touch soon." They concluded their first face-to-face meeting with a firm handshake. Dr. Greson felt more at ease. He could see that his lawyer was capable and organized.

⚐   ⚐   ⚐

Becky found a note on her desk from Kelly, instructing her to bring the Land Development Corporation file to The Peabody hotel after work. She opened the file cabinet and removed the LDC file, tucked it under her arm, and grabbed her coat and purse. At the parking garage, she gave the attendant her stub and a $2 tip. "This garage will break me," Becky said to herself as she waited. The attendant wheeled around the garage corner like Mario Andretti. "Arrogant little creep," Becky said under her breath, wishing she could take the $2 back.

She turned her nine-year-old Toronado down Second Street, which was dark and wet from a recent rain. Becky had only lived in Memphis since Jim died. She had moved from Southaven — a Mississippi suburb about 20 miles to the south, but by now she knew the downtown area fairly well. At this time of day the working class scurried home to the east end of town and the old city turned into a parade of nightclubs, restaurants and tourists.

The Peabody, a Memphis landmark, loomed dark ahead. Becky passed the waiting valets as she turned into the self-park garage, where she stopped alongside a new Lexus. She thought how nice it would be if she could afford a new car. Maybe another year or two. But Becky knew she was kidding herself with two boys to raise on her meager salary. She made her way to the lobby, boarded the elevator and pressed the button for the 12th floor. Each passenger waited in silence and watched the numbers above the door as if they might appear out of order if not closely monitored.

The 12th-floor hallway had yellow wallpaper with tan trim. Becky found room 1222 and knocked. No answer. She knocked again and hesitated. She looked up and down the empty hallway. No one was in sight. She turned the handle, opening the door with uncertainty.

The room was dim. Reaching inside, she switched on the light. She entered slowly like a cat into sunlight. Stacks of legal papers, documents, letters and drinks were scattered around the suite. In the corner was a lunch tray with leftovers — it appeared to have been for four people.

The beds were made, but rumpled. Becky began to read one of the open files when suddenly Kelly's voice startled her.

"Hello, Ms. Summers. I thought you had forgotten," Marion Kelly spoke with a slurred voice that clearly had ordered too many drinks.

"Ah ... no. I had quite a bit of work to get done before the Bensen trial tomorrow," Becky explained uneasily. She turned and handed the file to Kelly. "Here's the file you wanted. I'll be going now."

"Thanks, Becky. You know, you have turned out to be an excellent secretary after all," Kelly said obstructing her exit. "I'm sorry if I've yelled at you. You see, this is a serious job, and I have clients that can't tolerate being disappointed. You won't disappoint me will you, Becky?"

"I really don't know what you mean, Mr. Kelly, but if that's all, I need to go now."

"Just a minute, Becky. I thought we could take a little time to get to know one another better. Relax and have a drink. I have a bottle of scotch right here," he motioned. "Let me pour you a drink."

"No thanks, Mr. Kelly. That's awfully nice, but I must be going. My children and my mother are expecting me." Becky was visibly uncomfortable.

"I bet it's hard taking care of those children by yourself. Terrible about your husband. You must get lonely, and with children it must be hard to find yourself a man."

"I really haven't been looking, Mr. Kelly. Thanks for the drink offer, but I really must be going." Tense but firm, Becky started around Kelly toward the door. As she passed, Kelly took her by the arm, drawing her close. Becky bit her lip. Kelly's hot breath blew across her nose with the strong odor of alcohol.

"Whad'ya say you and me have a little smooch ... uh Becky?"

"No, please, let me go." Becky struggled and turned away.

"Come on now baby, a sweet little thing like you don't need to be alone."

"Let meeee go!!!" Becky screeched, then realized she was in trouble. Kelly increased his grip. He spun Becky around forcefully and threw her on the bed. Becky fell silently; she seemed detached from her body, yet she was afraid he would hurt her. Kelly grabbed at her skirt and suddenly somewhere within Becky something said, "Enough is enough." She felt a wave of anger and force take charge of her actions. Rearing back her legs, she planted them squarely on Kelly's chest, cried out, and gave a great heave. Kelly flew backward off the bed and hit the dresser with a loud crash. Plates of food and drinks and stacks of papers fell everywhere. Kelly regained his balance and began to laugh.

"I like 'em spunky," he retorted as he wiped soup from his pants.

"Not this one you don't, you big jerk," Becky shouted back, angrily leaning forward.

Becky rushed by Kelly, giving him a shove on her way to the door. Secretly she was terrified he would grab her again. He didn't. "Don't be late for work tomorrow, baby," his voice echoed into the hallway before she could shut the door.

Becky didn't cry until she got to her car and locked the doors. It was the first time she felt safe. She placed both hands on the steering wheel and gripped it in fear and indignation. The tears started to flow. After a moment she burst out cursing Kelly's heritage. She sat there for some time — she didn't know how long — and let her feelings run their course. The drive home was a blur. She didn't tell her mother about the incident; it would only upset her.

CHAPTER SIX

Deputy Secretary Philip Wilson sat nervously on the plane back to Washington. He was worried that his ulcer was acting up. The Florida meeting had definitely left him with stomach pains. His palms were sweaty and cold. He had tried to take a nap, but that was impossible with all the noise in his head. Maybe a purple Xanax would help.

"Kelly has certainly forged a clever plan to conceal the discrepancy," thought Wilson. Technically, he would be able to demonstrate the LDC's proposed 6.3 million acres, but if anyone examined the surveys too closely, they would be able to see that the government had subsidized ocean water. If anyone discovered the truth, Wilson's career was ruined. But, he couldn't get the thought out of his head that there was no statute of limitations on murder.

Wilson knew that he was in no position to panic. "Just keep cool and no one will know," he thought to himself as he swallowed his Xanax and looked around for the flight attendant to order just one more before he arrived in Washington. After all, he was in charge of the Environmental Preservation section of the Department of Interior. He answered to only one superior, and preservation was not that person's area of policy interest. He just needed to keep cool, that's all.

⚖️　　　　⚖️　　　　⚖️

Marion Kelly had a breakfast meeting at The Peabody at 7:30. Even though he kept the room at the hotel, he'd spent the night at his home and gotten in his early morning run in the park. When he arrived at the hotel, he went up to room 1222 to get the documents he had left the day before. When he opened the door, he saw the mess from the struggle with Becky. For a moment he wondered if she would make any kind of scene. Otherwise, he had no concern regarding her feelings. No guilt, no remorse. His conscience had transcended those self-limiting sentiments long ago.

Kelly took the documents to the breakfast meeting downstairs at Café Expresso. He wanted to review the LDC proposal page by page with a fine-tooth comb before meeting Victor Jennison at his villa-style home at 9:30 a.m. Kelly and Richard Jackson ordered coffee as they sat down. Jackson laid his briefcase on the table and opened it to get his reading glasses. Kelly saw office files inside.

"Are those files in your briefcase escrow account statements? What are you doing with those?"

"I'm just looking over them for an internal audit," Jackson said.

"What are you doing with them in your briefcase?"

"Don't worry, I just wanted to take them home so I would have time to look over them. I'm gonna file them back today."

"I didn't hear anything about an internal audit."

"Not to worry, boss. I'll take care of it."

"Don't be horsing around with the escrow. The Feds watch those things like a hawk."

"Everything is in order. Let's look at that LDC application. Isn't that what we're here for?"

Legalized gambling had recently been approved in Mississippi, despite the heavy opposition from the Moral

Right. The solution had been to simply continue with "riverboat" gambling — the legal practice for 150 years or so. The trick had been deciding what constituted a riverboat, and the legislators were persuaded to approve any structure surrounded by Mississippi River water as such.

Thirty miles from the Memphis city limits lay the town of Tunica, Mississippi, previously Delta soybean land and one of the poorest areas in the country. A collective of Las Vegas gaming tycoons funded the Tunica Consortium, building 12 gambling casinos along a short tract of Mississippi mosquito flatlands. Each casino was constructed with its own levy to hold the Mississippi River at bay. Those levies not only held back the river but conveniently surrounded each casino with water, thus making them legal riverboats on which gambling could take place. The whole idea was such an obvious joke that no one really got it. The result of the joke had been the transformation of "Sugar Ditch" — as this county was labeled by the media when it was one of America's 10 poorest — into one of the top 10 per-capita income earning areas in less than nine months. The whole operation was cleverly handled by the consortium to create a new base of operations.

Locating these casinos in Tunica allowed all types of illicit activity to be conducted without the watchful eye of big-city law enforcement. This was a completely new game for the local law enforcement, as well as the gambling bosses. And, in keeping with the locale, the style of operation was more low-key than in Vegas. When the casinos were completed, they brought in $16 million per week. The money all came to rest in the same hands: the Tunica Gaming Consortium. Business was good. In fact, business was better than projected, so the consortium now planned to expand existing operations by adding six new casinos.

Without huge tax breaks, the Feds would syphon all the Mississippi profits. So the Tunica Gaming Consortium got involved in the LDC properties conspiracy. The ultimate plan was to build an offshore gaming island structured in such a way that it would be exempt from U.S. taxation. That was probably years away, but the cozy connection the consortium was now forming with the Department of Interior would be essential for the future. For the moment, the consortium needed relief from the new taxes recently legislated by the Clinton administration. The LDC connection could do just that.

The new taxes levied on gaming establishments had made the Tunica casinos the single-largest contributor to funding Clinton's much-publicized social reforms. His administration had proposed a high-percentage gaming tax, and besides a few, well-paid politicians and the gaming industry itself, there was little effective opposition. When the bill went through, the IRS started collecting 46 percent of the casino's daily take. The Mississippi state government had followed Clinton's example and added a state tax of 6 percent, pumping up the state's social reform revenues as well.

One of those well-paid Washington politicians, the best money could buy, had cleverly crafted a "back door" loophole for the gaming consortium to protect its profits from the Feds. Senator Bob Morgan, Democrat from Nevada, had proposed and engineered passage of the Morgan Bill, Pub. Law 97X75, also known as the Friendly Citizen Wildlife Bill. The good senator had carefully constructed his legislation to be the gaming consortium's salvation. The Tunica Gaming Consortium was the LDC. With the passage of this bill and the agreement with the Department of Interior made by the LDC, the Tunica Gaming Consortium could pocket $4.5 million more per week in earnings. Because of the way the LDC corporations were structured, an auditor would have to trace through four separate sets of books in order to notice the connection between the tax breaks and the casinos.

A thug by any definition, Victor Jennison had been with the Las Vegas Gaming Consortium for 12 years, and had learned the business well. Victor wore an acne-scarred face. He had cold, dark eyes and never smiled. He was chubby, gruff and grunted when he exerted himself. He looked physically uncomfortable in his suit, as if he would burst out of it like a kernel of popcorn if he got too hot. His teeth were constantly grinding — a habit that unnerved those around him. Victor had cultivated an intimidating appearance, and he enjoyed its effect. He looked as though he would kill without hesitation, and had personally done so many times on his way to the top of the criminal class. These days, as a comfortable senior member, he kept himself surrounded by a loyal group of outlaws, insulating himself from the dirty work.

Victor lived in an old section of Memphis near the gateway to its most prestigious golf course, the Memphis Country Club. Victor's house, on Goodwyn, was an Italian Renaissance-style villa with a red-tile roof, spiral columns and a flying buttress. The large, formal gardens were surrounded by a seven-foot iron fence and a security gate with cameras. Four professionally trained attack Alsatians prowled inside the fence. In addition, one of his goons was posted in the back guest house in case strong-arm tactics were needed.

As Kelly and Jackson eased their car through the slowly opening gate of the villa, they were keenly aware of the presence of two irascible Alsatians. Victor had cautioned them not to get out of the car until the guard arrived.

"Man, I'm glad I didn't try to break in here," Jackson said to Kelly, shaking his head. "Those dogs look like they could do some damage."

"Victor said to stay in the car until someone comes out," Kelly reminded him.

"I don't have a problem with that. I may not get out when they do come to get us."

Victor stood watching them from the doorway. "Gentlemen, come in," he called, waving his hand as the dogs disappeared.

"Those are interesting pets," Jackson commented as he climbed out of the car, attempting to ease his own fear.

"Not to worry, they wouldn't hurt a fly," Victor assured him and laughed.

As the two attorneys walked through the doorway, they were directed to a large living room with plush chairs, antique furnishings and a large table made of mombossa wood. "Gentleman, I would like you to meet Mr. Kelly and Mr. Jackson," Victor announced to the waiting dark suits. They stood and exchanged firm, brisk handshakes all around.

"Let's get down to business, Victor," the dark one with sunglasses demanded gruffly.

"All right gentlemen. The LDC plan is going to Washington this week. As you know, Mr. Kelly has handled this matter very professionally. This meeting gives us a chance to clean up the details and ask any last-minute questions. I'm very pleased with the way we have dovetailed the LDC with that guy Wilson at the Department of Interior. I think he will be useful to us in the future."

"My sources say he's a lightweight — not to be trusted," the man known as Doc said.

Everyone looked at Kelly. "I have that under control. He's not going to do anything I don't tell him to," he assured them coolly.

"I think we oughta go ahead and give him a million, you know, to keep him quiet," the dark sunglasses injected.

"I agree." Victor nodded and the rest of the men at the table grunted their approval.

"We need to move some money through your bank, Kelly. How soon can your man take care of that?" the fat one in a blue pinstripe questioned.

"I've taken care of those arrangements. We can start moving the money at $25 million lots about twice a week. The plan is to hide it in Federal World Delivery accounts. They're so big that no one will notice an extra few million. Then, we can wire it directly to Sao Paulo."

"That's good. I want to get started right away. We've got more coming in from Vegas than we can keep locked up. I have to hire 10 more meatheads every day just to keep up with it."

"What did you say about the Federal World Delivery?" sunglasses asked.

Jackson looked at Kelly, hesitated, and leaned forward. "Our bank, the Commerce Bank of Memphis — well, let's say the banking concerns — have a whole department dedicated to the Federal World Delivery Corporation. As you can imagine, they have a rather extensive account. Federal Delivery sends money all over the world to cover the expenses of their extended base of operations on a daily basis. We can piggyback your money on their wire transfers without attracting the interest of the Feds. Our money will look as clean as a surgeon's hands."

"Sounds good," sunglasses said. "How did you get that cleared through the bank?" He directed the question to Kelly.

"Let's just say I have a presidential friend who owes me a favor. He wants to keep the consortium's money and keep you boys happy. Why, they are tickled shitless just to count the quarters from the slot machines."

"Is he secure?" sunglasses questioned, leaning forward on his arms.

"He's secure," Kelly said firmly.

Victor stood and turned to the quiet one in the corner. "Okay, that about does it. Jackal, do you have anything to add?"

The silent man motioned "No" with his hands. Kelly surmised he was *the* Jackal, lord kingpin, big cheese of Vegas. The meeting broke up. No small-talk or pleasantries were offered aside from a comment from Victor about how Chernobyl, one of the Alsatians, had bitten off most of the arm of a recent gardener. Standing beside the doorway with the dog as the men filed out, Victor stroked Chernobyl, relating the gruesome anecdote on the front veranda. Five long, black limousines appeared, collected their fares and then slid out through the heavy iron gates.

△△   △△   △△

Carl came home from his job at The Sportsman's Center, a chain company that sold everything from tennis rackets to deer rifles. The work was not too glamorous, but it suited Carl's easy-going manner, and he still enjoyed working with guns. When he got home, he let his chocolate Labrador, Sable, run around the yard. It was a beautiful spring afternoon. All day he had thought of calling Becky, but hadn't decided on what to say when she answered. He picked up the phone and dialed her number. No answer. Oh well, at least he had mustered up the courage to make the call. He'd try again later. His back was hurting pretty bad again, and he decided to lie down for a while. Maybe he should go back to the doctor sooner.

Distance: 210 yards. Windage: cross wind two knots — about eight inches. Elevation: drop, 60 feet," Marc whispered. Carl made the adjustments. He placed a red-tipped .308 round in the breech and smoothly closed the bolt. This was the moment they had come for. Carl adjusted himself. His finger reached for the set trigger. Through the scope Carl could see the back of the

Red Major's head as he barked orders from his vehicle.

The crosshairs came to rest on the nape of the major's neck. Carl drew a moderate breath and exhaled completely. His finger began to exert slow, even pressure on the trigger. A loud shot rang out. Carl saw the brains of the major slide down the back side of the windshield.

Carl sat up, gasping and sweating. He had fallen asleep on the couch. His heart was pounding in his chest, and he thought he could smell the jungles of Vietnam. He shook his head and stood up.

CHAPTER SEVEN

Paul Greson and his attorney were scheduled for the plaintiffs' deposition at the office of Marion Kelly. Greson sat nervously in his car for a while before the meeting. He felt apprehensive at the thought of seeing Karen and Jack Hinkley face to face under these circumstances. He had saved Karen's life, and the thanks he got was a lawsuit.

Greson walked anxiously across the parking lot, scanning the downtown mall hoping to avoid the Hinkleys. Kelly's office building loomed ahead — a high-dollar architectural marvel that smelled of money. Kelly's was just one of several of the big law firms that occupied this building with offices overlooking the Mississippi River. The lobby floors were marble and the elevators were mirrored and thickly carpeted. Greson found the directory and located Kelly's suite number — 2200. As the elevator rose quickly and silently, he felt his tension begin to rise as well. By the time he exited the elevator, his muscles were tight and his head was beginning to throb.

Paul was not required to attend this deposition. His lawyer could technically handle the matter without the doctor being present. But he wanted to be there because it was important to him. He had never been accused of malpractice before, and he was taking it very personally. He had lost a lot of sleep over this matter.

When he entered the doors of Bensen Keller Gregory & Kelly, the receptionist was preening herself in a small, gold compact mirror. As he approached, she turned, snapping the compact shut, slipping it into the purse stashed at her feet, and offering a sexy, fake magazine smile. "Yes sir, how may I help you?" she asked, her freshly painted lips soft and pouting. Paul was in no mood to flirt. He was tense, angry, nervous, agitated and indignant. He felt like he had drunk a whole pot of coffee in the last half hour. His bladder refilled every 10 minutes.

"I'm Dr. Paul Greson. I'm here for a deposition with Mr. Marion Kelly."

"Yes sir. If you don't mind waiting here, I think the attorneys are running a little late."

"Okay."

As he waited, Paul reflected on the comments his patients had sometimes made about waiting for him. They were nervous, tense, agitated and indignant, too. The worst were the ones who had been in for a test the week before and were coming back to hear their results. Those people almost vibrated when they walked. Today, Paul felt like a heavy smoker waiting on a lung biopsy in a nonsmoking reception area.

When Ms. Stein came through the door, Paul felt at least two levels of tension leave his lower back and neck muscles. "Good morning, Dr. Greson. Sorry I'm a little late. I got held up by a train on Southern."

"No problem," Greson responded.

"Are we ready?" Ms. Stein directed her question to the receptionist, who was now checking out her flaming fingernails.

"I don't know where Mr. Kelly is, but you can go on into the conference room if you'd like. Come this way," she motioned, tugging at her skirt as she came around the sleek receptionist's desk.

Paul Greson followed Diane Stein like a chick following a hen. He felt safe as long as she was close. He guessed this was the way his patients felt in the ICU when he made rounds. Not that he was God, but they felt safer when the doctor was near.

Greson and Stein had gone over every inch of the hospital records, the office records and all other documents that were obtained by subpoena. She had filled a whole legal pad with notes, and had reviewed them with the doctor. Together, they formulated questions to pose to the plaintiffs. The discovery deposition of the plaintiffs was critical to the case. In it, the factual foundation was set and future testimony was frozen. The primary intent today was to set the plaintiffs' testimony in stone. If they tried to change their story during the trial, the deposition would be available to check the validity of the courtroom testimony.

They waited. The oak-paneled room had no windows, and the large oak table made Paul feel small. Just as he leaned over to speak to Diane, the door opened and Marion Kelly paraded in followed by his clients, Karen and Jack Hinkley. The tension was palpable. Paul had told himself he would look them in the eye. He was not going to cower, even though he was scared.

Kelly heaved a large folder up on the table, pulled back a chair and seated himself. The folder was marked "Hinkley vs. Greson" in large letters. Paul looked at Karen with thoughts of hate in his mind. She looked back at him with a smugness that made him want to jump across the table and throttle her.

"Okay, let's get started," Diane Stein opened, surprised that Kelly himself was present at the deposition. She had expected a junior partner.

The court reporter had set up her nest near the upper corner of the conference table. She used a stenography machine and two tape recorders, which she now double-checked to make sure they were functioning. Diane sat directly across from Karen Hinkley, and Paul was across from her husband. Kelly sat at the head of the table with his huge file in front of him.

"Do you solemnly swear the testimony you are about to give is the truth, so help you God?" the reporter recited with a raised right hand.

"I do."

"State your full name."

"Karen Louise Hinkley."

"Ms. Hinkley, I'm Diane Stein, and I represent the defendant Dr. Paul Greson in the suit you have brought before the court. I will ask you some questions. I would like you to answer them completely. If the answer is yes, say "Yes," and do not nod or say "uh-hum." If you don't understand the question, ask me to repeat or rephrase the question. Is this clear?"

"Yes."

Paul sat motionless. He was determined not to slump or squirm during the deposition. Instead, he held a steady, ice-cold stare on Karen Hinkley. Unable to believe her lies, he found it difficult not to stand up and shout, "I saved your life, you little bitch." Hinkley had distorted and twisted every aspect of his treatment and care.

"If I had known I would lose my hair, I would have rather died anyway," Karen whined in a prissy voice. "I told that doctor that I was a star and I had to look good. I can't take medicine that makes me break out or has a bad effect on my skin. Next thing I know, I'm picking up enough hair out of the bathtub to make a wig. Before too long, there isn't anything left. I look like Mr. Clean! He told me it would come back. Well," she moaned, pulling the hat off her head and revealing her hairless skull, "it didn't!"

"Did Dr. Greson inform you of the side effects of the medications you were taking?" Ms. Stein asked calmly, ignoring the dramatic display.

"He told me." Karen looked at Greson and leered. "He said that sometimes your hair could fall out from the treatment, but if I would have known it would be like this, I would have never taken the stuff." She slapped herself on top of her bald head as she spoke, and then tried to fit the hat back on unsuccessfully.

"Did he not explain the complications?"

"If I had known what he meant by complications, no, I'd never have taken that stuff."

"Did you understand that you had a very serious form of cancer that normally results in death?"

"That's what he said, but I didn't know I would look like this. I'd rather be dead."

"How is this possible?" Greson kept asking himself throughout the entire two hours Karen's deposition lasted.

Jack Hinkley was then questioned for about 40 minutes. At one point during his deposition, he stood up and shook a fist at Dr. Greson, shouting, "Until that son of a bitch right there touched her ..." Paul remained motionless. He wanted to throttle the husband, too.

"She had a contract for layouts in six top magazines, plus the Hollywood Productions contract for the movie and several TV appearances. She could be making about one-hundred-thou a month if that quack hadn't made her hair fall out," the manager/husband complained.

"How has this affected your career, Mr. Hinkley?" Ms. Stein posed. "Do you have other clients?"

"My career, Counselor, was my wife. I lost my whole career when she saw that quack."

"Are you referring to Dr. Greson?" Diane corrected.

"Yeah, that quack Greson. I would have had it made — we would have had it made if it hadn't been for him," Hinkley said, pointing a shaking finger at Greson.

"Did you understand that your wife had a serious, and

most likely fatal, illness?" Diane questioned.

"Yeah I understood, but I'm like her. I'd rather she were dead than lookin' like she does now."

During the depositions, Ms. Stein remained focused, cool and direct. She watched for evasive answers and repeated questions five or six times in different ways to get what she wanted. She was very good.

Marion Kelly seemed uninterested, although he took more than five pages of notes. At the deposition, Kelly had learned for the first time the particulars of the case. He never once gave a thought to the possibility that it was all frivolous. He didn't care. He was only interested in getting his 33.3 percent. He didn't give a damn about anything else. The doctor and his insurance were commodities. Period.

By the end of the session, Dr. Greson wanted to choke somebody, and he could have. He had felt hate before, but not in many years. Not only was he feeling hate for the Hinkleys, but he found himself loathing every breath Marion Kelly took. Greson found himself plotting to murder him. He began to entertain ideas that before this moment were unthinkable to him.

Marion Kelly said little, but when he did, he sounded self-righteous and pious. He spoke as if all this detail was beneath him, even though he was its primary architect. Kelly kept a cold smirk on his face and saw Diane Stein as an inferior in a man's job. Ms. Stein could feel his chauvinistic attitude from the outset. It was consistent with her previous dealings with him, and she had expected nothing more from him. The look on his face was the same arrogant grin she had endured from her father and her brothers, and this made Diane Stein all the more determined. Secretly, she wanted to kick Kelly's butt, big time.

△△   △△   △△

"Becky? This is Carl Wheat. How are you?"

"Fine, and you?"

"Okay, thanks. Are you going to church today?"

"No, Jay has a bad cough, and I thought it best to keep him home in this weather."

"Yeah, good idea," Carl fumbled. "Ah … I was calling to see if maybe you wanted to go to a movie this afternoon?"

"Well … I could use an outing. That sounds okay, but I'll have to call and ask my mother to watch the boys. I'm sure she won't mind."

"Great, I'll see you about two this afternoon then," Carl said and hung up the phone. He noticed that his heart was racing and his palms were sweaty. It had been a long time since he'd asked a woman out.

Carl arrived at Becky's house a little early. He approached the door and paused. He hated first dates — who didn't? He knocked. Becky appeared, swinging the door wide open. "Come in and have a seat," Becky welcomed. "I'm just about ready." Carl sat nervously, searching the room for a conversation piece. Becky returned from the back of the house and sat down beside him. He was starting to get uneasy with the silence when Becky asked, "Would you like to see the new Eastwood movie? I just love his movies."

"Yeah, sure," Carl answered, relieved that she had made the suggestion. "I like them too."

"Great, I'm ready to go." Becky rolled her exposed round shoulders as she smiled at Carl and got up from the sofa.

Carl led Becky down the sidewalk to his restored 1966 Corvette. He opened the door as if it were the Waldorf Astoria.

"Nice car," Becky remarked.

"It's my pride and joy. I've worked on it for years now, and I have it just like I want it. I'd like to get a Hurst shifter, but otherwise it's a real beauty. My Suburban is just for running around town, but this is my hobby."

"Oh, you have a four-speed T-handle!" Becky observed.

"As a matter of fact I do. It's a four-speed Borg-Warner. How do you know about that?" Carl asked with a puzzled look.

"Oh, my brothers used to be eat up with that stuff. I couldn't help but learn about it 'cause that was all they ever talked about." Carl smiled to himself. He had never met a girl who knew about transmissions, even if it was from her brothers. He really liked her. She seemed down to earth. As they sped off down Becky's street, Carl explained the various parts, restorations and details of his pride and joy. Becky smiled as she nodded and listened.

ΔΔ   ΔΔ   ΔΔ

Victor Jennison placed a call to Kelly at 8:30 sharp on Monday morning.

"Yeah, Victor. My secretary will be working on those documents today. I hope to have the final approval by Wednesday. I've scheduled a flight to Washington on Thursday. Everything should be in order to submit the LDC plan to the Department of Interior by Friday morning."

"After Wilson gets the papers, how long will it be until we have the ball rolling?" Jennison probed.

"He told me he could pass the documents through the filing process by Tuesday of next week, so the review would begin by then. The exemptions won't be effective until a few weeks later when the department has issued our tax and subsidy credit code. Of course, it will be retroactive," Kelly assured.

"Good. The gathering here is anxious to move that money into other concerns once the Feds have taken their mitts off it. So you're sayin' we will have some free assets by the end of the month, right?"

"Should be no problem. I spoke with Wilson over the weekend. I have also reviewed the Friendly Citizen Wildlife Bill. The way it's written, once the money starts flowing, it'll keep moving."

"We don't want anything to go wrong with this deal. The concerns in Vegas told me this Wilson fellow is not very smart. They think you better have a good backup plan set up. The worry is that Wilson is too stupid to be depended on to fix a problem," Jennison lectured.

"Not to worry, Victor," Kelly recited like he was reassuring a child. "This document will stand solid before any scrutiny. The Department of Interior will audit the deal using Wilson's computer references, which are the ones we agreed on. There will be no reason for anyone to review the base data. They're just numbers in all that bureaucracy. Once the deal gets through the audit department, they'll issue the account number and we'll get Key West to start deducting money from Uncle Sam's bill."

"We're all countin' on you to put this thing through right. Better not screw it up or there'll be hell to pay." Jennison went off the line. Kelly checked his E-mail for messages. A message from Key West appeared on the screen.

"Becky, get Mr. Jackson on the phone. Tell him I want to go over my calendar with him. I have some work for him to do."

"Yes sir." Becky could hardly stand the sound of Kelly's voice. But she knew if she got fired, she would not be able to get a job in any law office in town.

For several days, Becky had been typing the rewrite of the LDC application. She had never heard of getting tax rebates for swampland before. The whole thing seemed like some kind of joke to her. Her suspicions began to grow after she took time to read the entire file carefully. Becky suspected that Kelly was up to something illegal. She secretly began to keep track of all information that crossed her desk regarding the LDC.

CHAPTER EIGHT

Becky had hit the snooze button for the fourth time when the crying and screaming erupted down the hallway. The sound of running, chasing footsteps grew louder. Jay and Stephen burst into her sleep, fighting, screaming and pulling at each other.

"Boys, boys," Becky managed in a gruff early morning voice, "Stop that right now."

"Mom, Stephen won't let me have my Batman. He says he won't let me play Power Rangers if I don't give it to him," Jay said, whining and pouting.

"It's not your Batman, it's mine," Stephen rebutted. "You already gave it to me."

"You two ..." Becky grumbled. "Give me that Batman and stop fighting. Go get dressed for school." She needed coffee badly. It was times like these that she wished their father was here to help. She still missed him very much. "Oh well," she consoled herself out loud, "no time to get misty." She forced herself to start the daily routine — get coffee, get a shower, get dressed and get the boys to school. It seemed to Becky she never woke up soon enough, and if she managed to leave the house on schedule, traffic always seemed to put her behind.

Becky drove to work preoccupied with a second notice

from the phone company. She felt inadequate because there wasn't enough money to take the boys to McDonald's or a Disney movie. She wrinkled her forehead when her car sputtered at a traffic light, hoping something wasn't going wrong with it, too.

Carl and Becky had been dating for several weeks. Carl had fallen for Becky from the beginning, but Becky was more reserved. She told herself that it was good for her to get out more, but they were only friends. Once in a while the thought crossed her mind that maybe they would develop more than a friendship, but for now she was happy around Carl just because he was so nice to be with.

Becky hadn't been at work long before Carl called. He had mustered the courage to ask her away for the weekend.

"My, I'm surprised to hear from you so early in the day," Becky responded pleasantly when she heard his voice.

Carl spoke awkwardly, "How would you like to go rafting this weekend? The Ocoee River near Chattanooga is lots of fun. We can camp out nearby."

"Camping?" Becky asked with surprise. "I don't know. The boys and, uh, well ..." Becky stuttered.

"The boys can go too, they'll love it," Carl injected. "It'll be great to have them."

"It does sound like fun," Becky heard herself saying, "When would we need to leave?" she sounded as if she were won over.

"Friday at noon if you can get off work and the boys can leave school a little early," said Carl cautiously at first, not wanting to seem too eager. "We'll take the Suburban — there's plenty of room for the gear and stuff. We'll be back Sunday afternoon. There's a campground nearby that is great for fishing." Carl was getting excited now. It seemed like she was going to accept.

"Oh, the boys really would love that, and the thought of getting away from here does sound good." Becky paused for a minute. "Sure, we'll go," she suddenly agreed to her own amazement.

"Great, I'll call you later this week with more details. Sorry to call you at work, but I wanted to give you plenty of notice."

△△   △△   △△

Marion Kelly arrived at Dulles Airport and took a taxi to the Grand Ritz Hotel. He carried with him the LDC documents for Philip Wilson. Kelly was proud of the way he had arranged the LDC scheme. "Plenty of deals are snaked through Washington," he thought, "but this one is really slick." He was proud of how tightly he had designed this scheme. The LDC plan was virtually foolproof if Wilson did his job right, and he was here to make sure that happened.

Kelly met Wilson at a deli near Georgetown for lunch. They sat at a corner table underneath a blaring TV.

"Well, Wilson, how do you like the big city of deals?" Kelly opened.

"It's a lot different from Memphis," Wilson said, shaking his head. "I mean, the deals never stop. Meetings, meetings and more meetings. I've been run ragged since I've been here."

"It's good for you Wilson. Maybe a little work will put some color back in your face," sneered Kelly as he poured his sparkling water into a paper cup. "Okay. Let's get down to business," he directed, wiping the table with a paper napkin and placing his briefcase in front of him. "I have the documents for the Department of Interior. Everything is outlined, labeled and in order. Just do as you've been instructed and nothing will go wrong." Kelly made certain that Wilson knew, line by line, what he was supposed to do, and concluded his briefing by assuring Wilson that this deal was foolproof. Wilson had listened intently, except for the occasional interruption for a potato chip.

"I have a briefcase in the car," Kelly said as they got up to leave, "with a little gift from Memphis inside."

Wilson sat back down in his chair and looked nervously at Kelly. "Ah, I don't know 'bout that Marion. I'm worried enough about the LCD deal without throwing gifts into the deal."

"Don't worry, Philip, it's all right. The Tunica Consortium just thought you should be paid a fair wage for your good work." Kelly wanted Wilson to take the money. It would give him that much more leverage. Anyway, payola was standard operating procedure for Washington — like any good lobbying deal. Kelly pressured Wilson until he agreed to accept.

The two men walked to the parking lot, where they stood talking by Kelly's rental car. Kelly opened the trunk, producing a new, red-leather briefcase. The weight of the case was greater than expected when Wilson reluctantly took charge of the handle. They parted with a firm handshake. Wilson scanned the parking lot nervously and placed the briefcase in his trunk under the spare tire. He was jittery and sweaty. Inside his car he swallowed several Xanax without water, as he had done so often before. It took more and more these days to affect him.

When Philip Wilson returned to the Interior building, he placed the files in the hands of the department clerk. The clerk acknowledged Wilson's instructions and took the documents as a matter of routine. Returning to his office, Wilson closed the door and sat motionless in his chair. He was scared he would get caught. Thoughts tumbled around his head. What if? He felt choked by Kelly's manipulation. Maybe ... if Kelly wasn't around. Maybe he could use the money. No. He needed to get rid of the money. If he suddenly turned up with a lot of cash, he was sure to raise sus-

STEPHEN L. GIPSON, M.D.

picion. He didn't want the money. The money just added to his anxiety.

Wilson remained in his office until late in the evening, waiting for everyone to clear out so he could alter the computer data. When he completed the job, he sat back and began to consider how to get out of Kelly's grip. He figured that the LDC plan would go through without a problem, and even if it was discovered, he probably wouldn't get caught — but he wasn't certain. After all, he was only carrying out a request according to the official application. Wilson's mind raced. If the LDC deal went through without a hitch and he got rid of the money that linked him, the only thing left to do would be to get out of Kelly's clutches once and for all. A favor was a favor, but Kelly had cashed in on this one for the last time.

◊◊   ◊◊   ◊◊

Friday afternoon came quicker than Becky could believe. Every night before bed the boys had begged to go over the plans for the weekend, and each night their excitement grew. Becky found herself almost as excited as they were. Carl had gone over every detail of the trip, listing all the equipment they would need and making certain they had all the necessities to protect them from mosquitoes and ticks. He and Becky had talked on the phone every night, and the boys wanted to ask him a million questions.

Thursday night when Becky finished talking to Carl, she told the boys of the last-minute details. She hadn't noticed at first, but Stephen's mood had been changing gradually, and he had become quiet and withdrawn. Becky reached down to him and lifted his chin with her finger. His little face, usually bright, looked back at her now with tears welling up in his eyes.

"I miss my daddy," Stephen whimpered, swallowing his

— 68 —

tears.

Becky looked at him and broke down herself. They sat on Stephen's bed, holding on to one another and crying softly. They had done that from time to time since Jim's death. She guessed they weren't finished yet. Becky never knew when it would happen again.

⚖   ⚖   ⚖

A black cloud rolled over the Memphis skyline from the west. The air traffic control tower was kept busy as planes lined up nose to tail on the runway. It seemed as if the passenger jets were in a rush to outrun the clouds. The rain started with large infrequent drops. Just in time to avoid the turbulence and wind sheer, a Northwest Airlines M-80 with 200-plus souls on board landed at Memphis International Airport. Marion Kelly was among those souls — if he actually had one. Kelly had arranged a meeting with Victor Jennison as soon as he came in from Washington. Jennison wanted to be briefed on the filing of the LDC documents. Not wanting to waste time, Jennison had agreed to meet him at an airport bar where Kelly assured him that all had gone well and that Wilson had taken the money.

After the meeting, Kelly went by his office to review records for a deposition that was scheduled for Monday with Dr. Greson. Kelly noticed that although the doctor had documented all his treatments well, he had failed to document proper informed consent. Kelly sneered to himself triumphantly.

The phone rang. His private line. "Kelly," he answered and sat back in his chair, tapping his chin with a letter opener.

"This is the warden. We've got trouble down here," warned Harry Fields. "One of the inmates is trying to make a deal with the Feds. He's gonna talk about the Post Office. We need to do something."

"What's his name?" asked Kelly, tapping away at his chin and looking out the window as a barge drifted by on the river below.

"Jack Kempner. We don't know how much he might have blabbed. He's met with two marshals from the U.S. Attorney's office a couple of times already."

"I'll need to make some calls," Kelly said. "What are your ideas?"

"Down here, people have a way of disappearing if necessary, but we ain't sure he hasn't already thought of that and planted a postmortem surprise for us. We need to find out who he's got on the outside, so we can make our move. He's been seeing a woman regularly, but we don't know anything about her yet. We need a new inmate. Can you arrange that for us?" Harry questioned.

"Let me check on a few things and get back to you. I'll call by tomorrow."

The Post Office deal was one of Kelly's special "consultant" projects that he had developed with Warden Fields at Carlson Federal Penitentiary. For many years now, a counterfeit workshop, which they called the Post Office, had been operating smoothly at the prison. Legitimate $10 money orders, mailed in by outsiders, were counterfeited into $100 money orders and sent back out. The quality of the workmanship was impeccable and the returned cash was used to buy influence, lawyers, drugs and favors. The prison officials, who profited from the scheme, turned a blind eye. The warden had reason to be concerned. The U.S. Attorney had his eye on the governor's seat, and that would surely lead him on a witch hunt. This Kempner guy could supply him with good political mileage from a "dirty cop" indictment against the warden for his part in the counterfeiting scheme. "Damn politicians," growled Harry, puffing away on his cheap cigar, "always go snoopin' around when it's time to climb up the political heap."

It was late. The lights on the bridge reflected in the dark waters of the Mississippi River as Kelly left a message on Becky's desk. "Cancel deposition for Monday." By the time he got in his car and headed for the High Rollers Casino in Tunica, it was 11:30 p.m.

△△　　　　△△　　　　△△

Carl was reaching far under the hood of his '66 Corvette, replacing the fuel pump. It was a beautiful, late-spring day with blue skies and mild temperatures. He was drinking an IBC root beer, his favorite drink.

"How in the hell do they think you can get to this SOB down here?" Carl shouted at the manifold. "This damn thing ... Ouch! ..." Carl cursed. A 5/8's inch open-ended wrench in Carl's grip had slipped off the bolt, slamming his hand, wrench and knuckles into the engine chassis. The familiar thud was followed by a slowly growing pain swelling up across Carl's knuckles. He had busted his knuckles before. Carl stood up suddenly, feeling a sharp pain in his back that ran around to his groin. He grabbed his side and doubled over. The pain was so severe he stumbled back and fell on the grass.

At that moment 47 cancer cells broke through a capsule that had formed in Carl's right kidney around a growth that lay between the kidney and a long back muscle. The growth was renal cell carcinoma — kidney cancer. As Carl strained, the capsule ruptured into a blood vessel. Fifteen of the cells clumped together and raced first through the renal vein, then through the right side of the heart, stopping in the middle right lobe of his lung.

Another clump of 30 cells made a similar journey and came to rest in his right leg muscle. The remaining two cells passed through the lungs and heart and travelled upward into the carotid artery, jamming to a capillary located in the brain stem.

Carl was not aware of any of these clandestine events that later would be so important. In fact, he began to feel better and finished off the root beer in a few quick slugs. Due to the damaged capsule around the growth, the blood flow to the remainder of the tumor was weakened. The main kidney tumor mass, growing at a rapid rate, would require an ever-increasing flow of blood, but with this recent damage, the tumor would outgrow its limited blood supply in a few short days.

Carl returned to his mechanic work. He wanted to finish and get ready for the camping trip. He had taken the day off to be sure everything was ready when Becky finished work. Another 20 minutes and the job would be completed. The pain in his knuckles and side had passed by the time he dropped the hood. Carl squeezed out some orange glop into his hands and watched it dissolve away the greasy coating. The nail beds were harder to clean. He made his way to the shower and stepped in.

In the shower, Carl sang along with a Beatles' tune. Carl loved the Beatles and knew every word to every song. His voice was not quite like Paul's, but it sounded pretty good in the shower. Freshly showered and dressed, Carl packed his gear into the Suburban and checked the list he'd made. He was excited about the weekend. Even though he had been to the campgrounds before, this time would be different.

When Carl arrived at Becky's house, the door flew open as Jay and Stephen ran out to greet him. Their excitement was electric. Becky followed them with armloads of stuff. She laughed and chattered about their plans, absently dropping one of the blankets on the ground in front of her feet. After she stumbled over the blanket, Carl took over the packing, and under his expert supervision the Suburban was soon loaded.

The drive down Poplar Avenue on the way out of town was slow due to Friday afternoon traffic. The boys bounced around in the back of the truck like Mexican jumping beans, and Becky, flushed with the idea of spending a weekend out of town with a man, even if the boys were along, smiled happily. After they turned onto I-40 leading to East Tennessee, it all seemed a blur to Becky. She was astonished when they arrived at the campgrounds and it was almost dark. Though the drive had taken almost six hours, the conversation and the company had made the trip fly by.

The campsite was in the Appalachian National Reserve Park along a slow-running stream bordered by a rock cliff. The spot was incredibly beautiful and almost deserted. They unloaded the truck and started a campfire right away. The boys ran this way and that, exploring every pathway within the light of the fire and screaming with delight at all their discoveries. The two adults sat together talking and drinking coffee made over the open fire. The night took on magical qualities for Carl and Becky.

CHAPTER NINE

Marion Kelly called Obadiah Morgan, owner of the Old Time Billiard Parlor on Third and Vance. The billiard hall was a downtown hangout for older black men and the occasional respectful younger boy from the 'hood. Its wooden floors hadn't been properly cleaned in 50 years. The pictureless walls were an unknown dark color, and the windows were painted over with thick, black housepaint. The only available lighting hung over each of four pool tables that bore the scars of many years.

The crowd that hung out at the Old Time had all been regulars for years. They came by every day, except Sunday, drank a beer, chewed tobacco and talked of other times. The old "security guard" of the billiard hall was as scarred as the pool tables. He wouldn't allow the project thugs in. Obadiah liked things the way they were. It was a place where no stranger was allowed in unless accompanied by someone of known standing. True, some shady business was conducted there, but no drug dealings or messing with families was allowed. Obadiah kept a lead pipe with a bicycle handle on the end underneath the bar. If someone got out of hand, he would give him a headache and dump him out back, allowing the victim to recover at his own leisure.

Marion Kelly was looking for Short Round, a short,

crazy black man about 50 years old who had been involved in every sort of crime invented and a few that were patent pending. Another of Kelly's pawns, Short Round had been helped out of many predicaments and even more jails by the scheming attorney. He had a rolling tab with Kelly, who called upon him to perform burglary, intimidation and surveillance as dealings required.

"Naw sah, I ain't seed him today, but if'in he come back, ah, hold on ... here he is now, hold on a minute." Obadiah laid the phone down on the grimy bar. "Short Round," Obadiah shouted out. "The Man wants to talk to ya'."

"Yeah?" replied Short Round, who, having recently been released from jail, was not expecting any calls.

"Short Round, it's Kelly. I've got a little job for you. I'll be out front in a few minutes. Get in the car."

Kelly stood waiting impatiently for the elevator on the 22nd floor. When the doors opened, he saw a blonde, about 20, leaning against the corner. She wore a dark-red skirt that revealed her long slender legs and a sweater that outlined her curves. Kelly let his gaze wander from her high heels to her round, full buttocks. He could smell the sweet fragrance of her hair. He was just about to deliver one of his standard opening lines when the door opened and she vanished. He grinned to himself and brushed back his hair.

As the garage attendant wheeled his shiny, black 580 Mercedes to a stop, Kelly made a mental note to find out who that girl worked for. Perhaps she could offer him some valuable information. He drove the Mercedes down Adams Street to Danny Thomas Boulevard, cutting across a gas station corner to avoid the traffic light. He passed along Vance Street, where the prostitutes used to hang out on the corners. Times had changed. The sidewalk was no longer decorated by high-stepping black women, dressed to satisfy and eager for business. Kelly missed the show they used to put on when they saw his Mercedes cruising the street.

He pulled up in front of the billiard hall. The building sat alone in a rundown block with grassy lots and broken asphalt in the parking spaces. He sat in his car with the air conditioner running. Short Round swung open the ratty screen door and walked to the car while scanning the streets with his eyes.

"What's up?" Short Round opened, as he settled into the car, turning the air-conditioning vent in his direction.

"Seems we've got a stool pigeon down at Carlson who wants to let the cat out of the bag about the Post Office operation. Some of the boys are concerned that he may have talked already or even planted an envelope to be delivered should he turn up missing. I need you to go in there and find out what he has planned and who he has talked to," Kelly spoke as if issuing orders.

"Carlson! You gotta be crazy." Short Round frowned. "Man, I can't be goin' into no prison! I jes' got out. You gotta be crazy." Short Round was sweating. "How you gonna get me in there — an mo' impo'tant, how you gonna get me out? Man. You gotta be crazy," Short Round ended with his mouth open, looking at Kelly from the side.

"Listen, Short Round, I can get you sent in and out with no trouble. I got a judge that can take care of all that, and the warden's crew is working with me, so there won't be any problems while you're on the inside. We need that information so we can decide how to take care of this guy."

"What's his name?" Short Round asked as though he might know him.

"I forget now, but I can get you all the details in a day or two and have you in the bunk next to him by the weekend."

"I ain't gonna have to kill him am I?" Short Round hesitated, looking across at Kelly.

"No, just find out what he's up to and come out."

"How much you gonna pay me?" Short Round asked, getting down to business.

"Five-thousand dollars for one week's work. That should be enough time to get the scoop, and enough money for your time," Kelly answered, quickly looking at Short Round.

Short Round rubbed his cheek and gazed down the street. He thought the part about going into prison was crazy and a little scary, but he trusted Kelly. Kind of. Round was in a little trouble anyway and could use a few days off the street. There were some boys with nasty reputations from the 'hood looking for him.

"When do I go in?" Short Round asked.

"Wednesday or Thursday."

"Okay, I'll do it," Round concluded. "But I could sho' use a little down payment."

"I'll see what can be arranged," said Kelly. "I'll call and leave a message at the pool hall tomorrow with the details."

"Okay, you the Man," Short Round responded with a nod, climbed out of the car and shut the door.

As Kelly drove away, Short Round lumbered back into the pool hall doorway and disappeared into the darkness. The screen door took 30 seconds to swing closed.

⚊⚊   ⚊⚊   ⚊⚊

"Are you up?" Carl asked Stephen.

"Yeah," he replied sleepily.

"Let's get things going for your mother's breakfast," Carl said. "You get the wood gathered for a fire and I'll get the coffee ready."

In a matter of a few minutes Carl had rekindled the fire. The old Coleman stove was rusty and took a little fiddling to get going, but once the fire was hot enough, Jay helped Carl start the bacon and eggs. Carl really loved to cook outdoors — the food always seemed to taste better for some reason. As he broke the eggs into the pan, the mist from the nearby stream crept over the campsite and surrounded the tent in the early morning light.

The birds were performing the second movement of their morning chorus when Becky came out of the tent, shifting her shoulders and arms and groaning with the first stretch of the day. "Ah," she said, walking over to the fire, "that bacon smells wonderful." Carl looked at her and she at him. He was thinking how beautiful she was, even first thing in the morning after sleeping on the hard ground. A natural beauty. He loved that about her. Becky smiled and put her arms on Carl's shoulders. Carl bowed his back, inviting her closer.

The boys wolfed down their breakfast and then ran to the stream, where they threw rocks at the trout hiding behind the big stones. Becky stood with her hands on Carl's shoulders watching the boys disappear down the bank. She was beginning to have warm feelings about Carl, and she wanted to kiss him. She leaned over toward him and took his face in her hands. Searching his eyes for permission, she gently placed her lips on his, then again a bit more intently. Carl pulled her onto his lap with his strong arms. He wasn't finished. They fell into each other, kissing and wrapping their arms more tightly. Stretching his leg out to balance himself, Carl knocked over the bacon, but no one, save the ants, took notice.

The trip down the Ocoee River was magnificent. The rafting experience now over, the weary crew returned to their wooded camping site, wet, tired and happy.

"Where has the day gone?" Becky directed her question to Carl.

"Time flies when you're having fun."

"I want to thank you for taking such good care of Jay today. He used to turn to his daddy when he got scared. I'm glad he's got you to be there."

"He's really a sweet boy."

"That rafting trip this morning was more fun than I've had in years. I've never done that before, but I'll be back for sure."

"Isn't it awesome?"

"Yeah, just when you think you're gonna tump over, it straightens out again and off you go. Did it really take three hours for the trip?"

"Yep."

"I just can't believe it. Thanks Carl."

"For what?"

"Thanks for showin' me how to have fun again. I really needed this."

"Oh! It's nothin'."

"Looks like the boys are off to go fishin'."

"Hey, boys," Carl shouted.

"Yeah."

"Ya'll keep back on the bank real good and don't be horsin' around and fall in."

"We won't."

"Will they be all right by themselves?" Becky asked.

"Yeah. That pond isn't three-feet deep. They'll have a lot of fun playing with the fishing gear. How about you and me goin swimmin'? There's a nice, clear pool not far from here."

"Okay. Sounds good." Becky winked.

When she emerged from the tent in her bathing suit, Carl tried not to look straight at her figure, but he couldn't help himself.

"Whoa, nice suit," Carl admired, scarcely disguising his admiration for Becky's body.

"Oh, thanks," Becky replied nervously, "I haven't worn it in a long time. I'm afraid it's not very stylish."

They began wading barefoot in the clear water at the edge of the stream. Soon, Becky reached out for Carl's hand. The stream narrowed, running cold and shallow. Half a mile downstream there was an eddy deep enough for swimming. Carl dove in the water. Becky hesitated for a moment, worried that the water was too cold. Carl laughed, splashing her and telling her she would get used to it. She took the plunge, shivering and laughing. Soon they were swimming and diving carelessly in their own private lagoon.

Becky said to Carl, "Hey, I really like the way you helped Jay this morning when he got sick."

"I really love him. They're both really good kids and I'm sure they miss their dad a lot. I know I would. I'm not trying to take his place, but I feel kinda' like a big brother to them," Carl said as he slowly backstroked.

"You're just so patient and caring. I wonder, could you, I mean, do you think they could accept another man being with their mom?" Becky said before she realized the full meaning of what she was asking.

"It happens all the time. I don't see why not," Carl answered, wondering what she was thinking.

They swam apart, each thinking about the other. Each coming to the same conclusion. The day became quieter. Becky turned away knowing somehow what was about to happen. The tips of her hair were dripping, her skin taut and goosefleshed. He moved closer behind her. She felt his presence, but didn't turn. Carl's hands fell softly on her shoulders, beckoning her skin with slow, sensuous motions.

He had such a longing for her.

Tenderly, he moved his hands under the loose straps of her top and let them fall down over her round shoulders and began to caress her, his hands gentle yet insistent.

Moving to the ancient rhythms of desire, she turned to him, her bare skin pressed against his chest — her body delicate, oscillating, inviting.

As their lips touched, Becky's breathing became erratic and heavy. She gave into him — moving against him as he moved her -- guiding, turning, his mouth and hands exploring her body.

Short Round passed by the 7/11 on Second Street, headed for his sister's house. He had decided to lay low there until he heard from Kelly. As he walked past the vacant lot at the end of the street, he saw three figures appearing out of the darkness from behind an abandoned car. At first, Short Round gave them little notice, but then he realized they were headed directly toward him. As the three black youths approached, Short Round spun on his heels to retreat, only to meet face-to-face with two others.

"Listen nigger, you been ghostin' us ain't ya?" the big one said.

"Naw, I ain't been doin' nothin'," Short Round insisted.

"We seen you over to the warehouse last night. What did you see, nigger?" the light-colored one pointed a finger in Short Round's face.

"I ain't seed nothin'," Short Round said, beginning to back up.

"You're lying nigger. We gonna bleed you, real quiet like, an' leave you here," the darker one said.

"Naw, man I don't know nothin' 'bout what you boys been up to, I ain't seed nothin' to tell nobody," Short Round said, looking around for an escape.

"Den what you doin' talkin' to that uppity white lawyer for?" the big one charged.

"I ... I been seein' him for a long time 'bout gettin' me outta jail, an' trouble. He's been my lawyer when I went before the Man," Short Round said, rubbing his palms.

"What's a uppity honky doin' defendin' a nigger like you Round?" the dark one questioned.

"I been doin' him favors, you see I ... I do thangs for him on the side an' in return he keeps me outta the lockup."

"He's lyin'," the big one said. "Let's bleed him 'for he gets a word out on us."

The big one stepped forward and ran an eight-inch blade into Short Round's chest between the sixth and seventh ribs on the left, missing his heart, but piercing the left lower lobe of his lung, letting air escape. With each breath, more air entered Short Round's chest, and his lungs became smaller. The big man twisted the knife, withdrew it, and thrust it in again, this time into Short Round's stomach where the knife passed through his spleen and into a loop of the large bowel. Gas escaped from the stomach. Short Round bent over and let out a long, silent cry.

A city police car rounded the corner. The gang moved together, holding Short Round close to them. When the car had passed without even slowing down, they dropped Short Round to the pavement, looked around and walked swiftly away. Short Round lay bleeding in the dirt. He could feel his shirt getting heavy and wet with blood. Then everything went blurry and he passed out of consciousness.

⚠   ⚠   ⚠

Carl stepped into the shower and leaned into the warm watery stream, releasing the tension is his neck. It felt so good. He squeezed Prell from the bottle and watched the green gook squiggle onto his palm. The shower was his sanctuary where all bad thoughts and pains were washed away, "Except for this damn poison ivy," Carl grumbled, still itching even under the warm soothing water. Ever since the camping trip, Carl and Becky's relationship had grown much faster than anticipated. This was partly due to their strong physical attraction, but also to the ease and comfort they felt in one another's company. For Carl, Becky was like a favorite pair of old blue jeans — warm, soft and relaxed.

Carl had planned a big night out — dinner at the Butcher Shop and dancing afterward at Automatic Slim's

Tonga Club, a chic restaurant located across from The Peabody. He had grown to like dancing again since meeting Becky. She had been able to help him relax and be himself. He was looking forward to a great night out and then coming home and making love until the wee hours of the morning. The anticipation of the evening made Carl giddy. As the water ran over his face and neck, Carl realized that he was in love.

CHAPTER TEN

Diane Stein took her yellow legal pad from her brief-case and looked at Dr. Greson. He was on Marion Kelly's hot seat, ready for questioning. They were meeting in a large conference room in Diane Stein's office. This time there were windows. The light was welcome, as was the panoramic view across the tall, downtown Memphis buildings. Barges could be seen passing under the Memphis-Arkansas bridge. On the previous afternoon, Diane had explained the "rules" of deposition to the doctor and coached him on how to answer questions. She explained the basic legal principles and told Greson to speak the complete truth, but say no more than was necessary. "You're not in a deposition to argue the case," she reminded him. "You're just there to answer questions. You'll get your day in court."

Marion Kelly looked up from his notes after the stenographer completed the swearing-in process. Before he began to speak, he took an exceptionally long pause, deliberately designed to increase the good doctor's tension.

Kelly tapped a pen against his chin. "Now Doctor ... tell us where you were born." Kelly opened the questioning. Greson at first remained calm and answered directly, but as the personal questions wore on, he thought it very odd that it was necessary to ask about his upbringing, brothers and sisters, mother and father, and the details of their lives.

"What does my father's occupation have to do with a malpractice suit?" Greson shot back after one of Kelly's questions.

"Just answer the question, Doctor. What was your father's occupation?"

Greson looked at Diane who nodded at him to answer. "He was a farmer."

"Have any members of your family ever been in jail?"

"Ms. Stein, do I have to answer this nonsense?" Greson asked, turning to his counsel, searching for some relief.

"Let's take a break," Diane said to the stenographer. She led him into the hallway. "You have got to answer the questions. Kelly has the right to ask anything he wants to."

"But what does my family have to do with it?" Greson pleaded, visibly upset.

"Nothing, I'm sure, but you just give him short, complete answers to whatever questions he asks. If he asks something that is out of line, I'll object, but this is a deposition and you will still have to answer. I'll bring it before the judge later. Keep your cool and don't worry."

"She said 'don't worry' again," Greson muttered under his breath.

"Now Doctor, are you feeling better?" Kelly asked Greson with a grin and turned to the stenographer. "Proceed."

"Yes," Greson answered as he returned and adjusted his chair. He looked at Karen and Jack Hinkley sitting across the table, rocking and posturing in their seats, and felt their constant, projected anger. The room was tense, and Greson turned away a moment to look out the window and watched the boats glide peacefully along the Big Muddy. It was like a different world out there.

"Now Doctor," Kelly held a long pause, "have you ever

engaged in homosexual activities?"

Silence followed.

"I will repeat the question, Doctor. Have you ever engaged in homosexual activities?"

"No."

The pointed and sensitive questions continued for a total of four hours. Greson was getting very punchy; he lost his cool several times over inquiries about his sister's involvement in a religious organization. When questioned about his father's death in a automobile accident he nearly broke down. Kelly had structured the questions to imply some type of foul play. The subject matter never turned to the actual treatment of Karen Hinkley.

Diane Stein interrupted the process when she could see that Greson had buckled from the stress. She and Kelly argued over the relevancy of the questions and more than once there were discussions of taking a walk to the court-house to see the judge about the disputes. Kelly had played his cards well and kept a poker face throughout the ordeal. He had learned that long delays followed by rapid questions would throw defendants off. Kelly had figured Greson to be self-righteous and pious like most doctors, and relished the idea of breaking the man down. He tapped a pen on his chin throughout the whole deposition.

A continuation was scheduled for the following week. "More hours of accusations and innuendo," thought a tired and nerve-racked Paul Greson. He had come to hate Marion Kelly. He hated him so much that he could picture him dead.

△△   △△   △△

Carl continued to have intermittent back pain. Becky noticed his complaints but, like Carl, thought his pains were from straining underneath his car. One Saturday morning when Carl had slept over at Becky's, she got out of bed very early, went to the bathroom, closed the door and switched on the light.

"Carl … Carl!" she said, opening the door. "Did you use the bathroom last night?"

Carl still half asleep mumbled, "I think so."

"Carl, there's blood in the toilet. It must be from you. Are you feeling all right?"

"What? Blood in the toilet?"

Carl got up to see for himself.

"Call the doctor, Carl," Becky insisted.

"But it's Saturday."

"Call the doctor." Becky spoke firmly, like a mother.

Carl did not like to bother anyone on their day off, but he did as Becky asked and called Dr. Bell's office, reaching the doctor's exchange. Dr. Bell, after hearing the details, told Carl to meet him at the Baptist Hospital East Emergency Room.

△△   △△   △△

Short Round was wheeled into trauma room two at the Elvis Presley Trauma Center, known locally as The Med. His clothes were quickly cut off and large intravenous catheters threaded into his femoral veins. Bags of plasma expander were pumped into him at a rapid rate. The trauma RN reported no detectable blood pressure. The EKG was flat. A first-year intern was pumping his chest as another tried to intubate his trachea. The intubation was difficult due to the heaving motion caused by the CPR. An endotracheal tube was successfully passed, and pure oxygen pumped into his lungs. The resident anesthesiologist took charge and noticed the lungs were hard to ventilate. He called to get a stat. chest X-ray. The team worked through the X-ray procedure, being exposed to the rays themselves, but knowing that the patient needed continued life support. These were young, dedicated professionals.

The chest X-ray showed a collapsed lung. The senior surgery resident quickly made a two-centimeter incision under Round's arm and grabbed a large tube with a pair of hemostats. He shoved the tube and hemostats into the incision, and a loud crunch was heard as it penetrated the chest cavity. The tube was connected to a vacuum, and Short Round's left lung expanded as did his blood pressure. These residents were good. They had all done their training there at The Med, one of the country's busiest Level One trauma centers. Every day the "knife and gun club" of Memphis had supplied the training doctors with every possible challenge.

Within eight-and-one-half minutes after reaching the Trauma Center, Short Round had his blood volume doubled, his cardiac output increased ten-fold, his left lung inflated, and precious oxygen flowing through his brain. His blood chemistry was already restored to half of normal and detectable signs of life were returning.

"Yeah? Whatcha got?" the attending physician asked, answering a page.

"John Doe, male, black, knife wounds to the chest and abdomen, found on street corner, pulseless, no vital signs. Estimated blood loss, four pints. Chest X-ray shows pneumo, probable air in the abdomen. Intubated and ventilated with improving vitals. Cross-matched six units of whole blood — two units of O negative running now. Blood gases, okay. Chest tube in place. Surgery needs to explore abdomen for perforated bowel. Chemistry is sent to lab. No evidence of drugs or alcohol," the chief trauma resident reported to his senior attending physician.

"Get the OR ready for an exploratory abdominal, and get the chest guys here to check his lungs," the physician barked.

Short Round heard distant voices and struggled to cough on the endotracheal tube. He passed back into unconsciousness. He thought he was still on the street in the hands of his assailants.

△△   △△   △△

Dr. Bell got up from his breakfast, folded his napkin and finished off a second cup of coffee. He had planned to work in the garden this morning. Instead he would have to go to the hospital. He drove his Jeep to Baptist Hospital East and parked in the ER lot, where there always seemed to be construction going on. Every time he left his vehicle there, he would return to find it covered with a layer of red dirt. He liked to have a clean car. He entered the emergency room and checked the roster. He found Carl in C-14 cubicle.

"Doctor, I'm sorry to get you out today, but Becky insisted," Carl apologized.

"You need to get this checked out, Carl. Tell me how you have been feeling."

"This morning we got up and there was blood in the toilet. Becky got all upset and that's about it, Doc."

"Carl, didn't you come into the office recently?"

"Well, yeah, about three months ago. You said I had some blood in my urine and sent me for X-rays. I called the nurse and she told me they were okay."

"So you didn't keep your last appointment?"

"Well, no, I thought everything checked out, and I've been busy lately and just didn't get around to it."

"I'll get a urine specimen and some blood work and see if I can round up those X-rays," the doctor said, turning and leaving Becky and Carl alone in the cubicle.

Carl squeezed Becky's hand. "Don't worry, sugar. It's nothing serious."

⚖️   ⚖️   ⚖️

Dr. Greson swung his legs out of bed and stretched his back. He felt terrible. He had never felt so tired. The stress of the malpractice suit had really gotten to him. He found himself awake many nights thinking about the accusations and the testimony and what might happen. He felt drained and sometimes hopeless. His malpractice insurance only covered $1 million, and the Hinkleys had sued him for $4 million. The thought of working just to pay them off made him both furious and depressed. In his despair he imagined that he would have to quit practicing medicine and file bankruptcy. He was not about to work for the Hinkleys.

"Paul, what's the matter?" Linda inquired.

"Oh, nothing, same ol' same ol'."

"It's Saturday. Maybe we can take the kids to the zoo. The meerkat exhibit opens this weekend, and I hear they are darling."

"Yeah, well okay, but I'll have to do rounds first. I'll probably be done by 2:00 p.m. if I get going."

Paul stepped from the shower and found his favorite coffee mug full of hot, black coffee on the sink top. On the mug was a picture of flying ducks. He had drunk his morning coffee from this mug for years. Somehow coffee wouldn't taste the same without it. He dried off and wrapped the towel around his waist. He lathered up his face and began the daily ritual of shaving, hated by most men, but tolerated by all.

Paul thought back to his early adolescence when he had wanted to shave like his father. He wondered why his father never taught him how to shave — or if other boys' fathers had taught them how. Wasn't that a rite of passage into manhood? Had they all passed this test alone with the cold steel of the razor as their only companion? "I'll teach my son how to shave," he thought. Not now, of course.

Leland was only four and not even pretending to shave. So deep in thought was the doctor that he hadn't noticed the boy slip into the bathroom. Looking down, to his surprise, he saw Leland standing there, watching him shave, his eyes big as the morning. Paul grinned.

◬   ◬   ◬

"Well Carl, you've got blood in your urine and your lab is showing a low blood count. The X-rays you had taken several months ago do show a problem. I don't understand why you weren't notified. I wish you had kept your appointment, Carl." Dr. Bell tried to be careful and diplomatic as he spoke, wary of a malpractice suit. He knew there had been a mistake made with Carl's X-rays. Carl clearly had a mass on the kidney. Why it was not followed up was not clear, except that it had been around the time Dr. Caperton died. Probably the confusion surrounding his death had caused Carl's report to fall through the cracks. Dr. Bell was careful not to come out and say there had been a mistake, but he wanted to be straightforward with his patient as well.

"We'll have to admit you to the hospital, Carl," Dr. Bell informed.

"Today?" Carl raised up in disbelief. "What do you mean, am I really sick or something?"

"Carl, you have blood in your urine, your blood count is low, and there are signs of abnormalities in one of your kidneys. I think you should go into the hospital and get this thing worked up so we know what we are dealing with. I don't think it can wait."

"Well, Doc, I guess you know what you're talking about," Carl said. Trying to conceal his panic, he turned to Becky. "Could you get some things for me at the house?" he requested. Inside, he was scared.

"Sure, sweetheart," Becky responded lovingly.

"I'll write some orders, call admissions and send Becky around to fill out the necessary paperwork," Dr. Bell informed. "I'll also have Dr. Johnson come by to see you. He's an excellent urologist and a real nice guy, too."

Becky took Carl's wallet, and he pointed out the various worn-out insurance cards and instructed her on how to check in. His words served as a smokescreen to hide his nervousness. He didn't like being in the hospital.

Becky was cool throughout the whole ordeal. She had taken her late husband through many hospital admissions and at least 20 emergency room visits. She felt like a seasoned professional support person, and she was. For the moment, Becky had her emotions on hold. She could feel herself pushing back anger and tears, but for now she needed to be strong and help Carl.

At the admissions desk, there was a problem with the obligatory call to verify insurance information. "They say you have to get a second opinion for admission," the clerk said, shaking her head.

"What do you mean? The doctor said he had to go in today," Becky said, not understanding.

"I'll call Dr. Bell and tell him, but Mr. Wheat's insurance company says he has to get a second opinion, and I can't admit him if they won't waive that requirement," the clerk said in a prerecorded, monotone voice.

Dr. Bell was still in the ER waiting for the lab results when the admissions clerk called to report the holdup.

"Give me the damn number," Dr. Bell growled.

As he dialed the insurance company, he could feel the anger swelling up inside his chest. His job was hard enough, and he hated the added irritation of dealing with insurance companies. A seasoned practitioner, he knew the tricks of the insurance industry. Make everything enough of a hassle and the doctor will give up. Result: cost containment. He also knew he would be talking to a 20-year-old high school graduate who would recite the company policy of "say-this-when-they-ask-for-that."

"This is Dr. Bell in Memphis. I need the pre-cert clerk, Janice Watkins." "One moment, sir."

"Hello, Janice Watkins here. May I help you?"

"Ms. Watkins, this is Dr. Bell in Memphis, and I have a Mr. Carl Wheat, a policy holder of your company, who has a kidney mass, urinary bleeding and is anemic. I want him admitted today to Baptist Hospital."

"I've talked to admissions, sir, and his policy states that unless he is in immediate danger of life, a second opinion must concur regarding any admissions," she shot back.

"Look miss, I don't give a rat's tail-end what his policy says. I'm his doctor. I'm on the front lines every day and I get up in the middle of the night for my patients. I went to school for half my life while everyone else was living it up, and I say he's going in. I don't care what your company thinks and I don't care if they don't pay — but he's going in, and I'll be the first to testify at the trial that you personally were the one that caused him to die," Dr. Bell spoke without halting to draw a breath.

"I'm no doctor and I don't make medical decisions, sir. I'm telling you what the policy says," Ms. Twenty came back as she was programmed.

"You're damn right you're no doctor, but you are making a medical decision," Dr. Bell blustered, turning red.

"Well, sir, I guess this is an emergency, in which case I'll authorize three days," Ms. Twenty consented, deciding this hill wasn't worth dying on.

"Thank you so very kindly," Bell said sarcastically.

When Dr. Bell hung up the phone, he felt tired. His conversation reminded him of the misdirection medicine was taking. He longed for the days when he was in charge of what happened to his patients. After all, he was the one who delivered them as babies and followed them through puberty and into adulthood. Now those damn bureaucrats in Washington had decided that they could answer medical questions better than a patient's doctor. "If you like public housing, you'll love public health care," he thought to himself.

Becky returned to the emergency room where she found Carl waiting. "Okay hon, I've got everything sorted out. They're going to put you on the third floor. I'm going home for a while. I'll call your room before I come back to see what you need." Becky looked into Carl's worried face, doing her best to hold back her own feelings. She was still on automatic — something she had learned how to do when Jim was sick. She hadn't thought she would need to resurrect those skills again so soon.

"Okay, babe," Carl replied as an older black attendant wheeled him from the ER down the corridor.

Becky looked upon the scene she knew so well, watching Carl being rolled out of sight down the same damn hospital hallway they had taken her Jim only a year and a half before. "How is this possible?" Becky turned to the wall and asked God. She pounded her fist against the hard tile surface and lost the ability to hold back her anger. She turned toward the ER doors, her purse and jacket wadded under her arm. As she approached the electric doors her emotions burst upon her full force.

Becky ran into the daylight, her tears blinding her. "I can't do this again! Do you hear me? I can't do this," she sobbed.

CHAPTER ELEVEN

Philip Wilson phoned Marion Kelly at his office. He lost what little cool he possessed when he started to explain that the auditors had begun a review of the LDC request. Wilson was particularly concerned about one of the younger auditors who had questioned the quantity of acreage. The auditor had suggested to his supervisor that a review be made since it represented such a great sum, not only of land, but of tax credits as well. His supervisor, an older man who had worked in the government for years and really couldn't care less these days, shrugged it off, saying it wouldn't be necessary. "The general accounting office will review all the figures after we're through here. Let them do all the hard work. Finish up and let's go," he had told the eager young man, checking his watch and noticing it was close enough to 5:00 p.m. to call it quits.

"I don't think we need to get in an uproar at this point," Kelly assured.

"I don't know, Kelly. This is the one thing that won't stand up to too much scrutiny. If they start looking at the surveys, they'll start investigating my department, and somebody is going to be in big trouble. Maybe I could retrieve this application and let you resubmit it using the correct surveys. It would still represent a significant tax credit." Wilson was practically begging at this point.

"No, Wilson! Don't you do any such thing. Is that clear?" Kelly barked. "Look, nothing is going to happen, okay? So just chill out and keep your mouth shut. I don't want any suspicions aroused by switching applications. These investigations are routine stuff. There's not going to be a problem. It's standard operating procedure, that's all. Now you keep quiet and don't do anything stupid. You know I've kept your little secret all these years, and I don't want anything happening to jog my memory. Understand?"

"Yeah," Wilson said, sweat pouring from his forehead, and hung up the phone. He felt a panic attack coming on. He had taken 10 Xanax today already, but he still couldn't get a deep breath. He didn't have the guts to say no to Kelly, and he didn't have the brains to make an alternative plan of action.

Kelly hung up the phone in disgust. "What a spineless ass," he said aloud. Maybe it had been a mistake to give him all that money. Wilson was so stupid he'd probably deposit it into his checking account. It occurred to Kelly that Wilson might be more of a liability than an asset at this juncture. As soon as these routine inspections were finished and the documents were approved, he no longer would serve any real purpose. Kelly leaned back in his chair, tapping his chin with a letter opener, watching the sun go down over the flatlands of Arkansas. He had some thinking to do about this insignificant screw-up.

△△   △△   △△

In the warden's office at Carlson, a quiet meeting was under way. The warden and three top-level deputies were discussing the problem of inmate Jack Kempner while waiting for him to arrive. They had called him in for a "chat" after two marshals from the U.S. Attorney's office had visited Kempner and talked for more than two hours. Attempts to get information from the U.S. Attorney's office had completely failed, and now it was time to do a little fishing with Kempner.

"Jack, come in. Make yourself comfortable," the warden said, lighting up one of his cheap cigars and blowing the smoke across the desk. "We've been discussing your case the past few days, and me and the boys here think that your request for early release to the U.S. Attorney's office has merit. We've been in close communication with his office, of course, and he says everything is looking up for you. We want you to know that we support your efforts to appeal. What can we do to assist you?" the warden asked, fanning himself with a file folder.

"I don't think anybody here can do anything else for me, but I appreciate it anyway," Kempner responded with surprise.

"Well, Jack, as you well know, the other inmates sometimes get upset when a fellow prisoner starts getting somewhere with an appeal. We've seen them get rather nasty at times, haven't we boys?" The warden looked over at the three deputies, chewed on his cigar and leaned back in his chair as the other men nodded in agreement. "Maybe if you told us a little more we could help keep the hostility down." The warden now spoke in a fatherly tone, placing both feet on the desk corner.

"I better not say."

"Now Jack, we're here to help, but we can't if we're not part of the deal."

"Yes sir, I understand, but I don't think I have anything to say right now, sir." Kempner was being careful.

The warden sensed that he had better not press the issue any further lest he alert Jack to the possibility that they were worried. The warden was unsure whether Jack knew that prison authorities were involved in the Post Office scheme.

"Jack, there's a light work detail that goes into Tunica every day to help with the new road project. We thought it might do you good to get out a little. It's low security, but I don't think you want to screw up your chances for an early release by doing something stupid. I'm going to trust you on this, okay?"

"Sounds good to me," Jack said with some delight. He was tired of the prison walls and hadn't been out since last year's trip to the hospital to have an abscess lanced.

"Okay, Jack. You remember to let us know if there's anything we can do to help you out. You can go now."

"Thank you, sir." Jack nodded all around and left the office, somewhat confused by the meeting.

△△   △△   △△

The control desk phone was answered by Charles, a location camera man for Action News Five.

"Okay, thanks. We'll see what we can do." He replaced the receiver and turned to Margo, a newscaster. "We aren't interested in a press conference by an attorney named Marion Kelly, are we?"

"Oh, yes we are! He's the one who got Judge Hathaway off murder one charges in the death of his wife a couple of years ago. If he's going to the trouble to call a press conference, you can bet he's got something. What's the scoop?"

"That was his office. They just said he would be holding a press conference this afternoon at 5:00 at The Peabody."

Margo looked at Charles in disbelief, "That's it? That's all you know? You didn't get any details?"

"Well, I didn't think that you would be interested."

"Knucklehead."

By 4:30 that afternoon there were three white vans parked outside The Peabody with various news numbers scrolled along their sides and large satellite dishes affixed to their roofs. The roar of their portable generators added an additional groaning to the sounds of the rush-hour city. Inside, reporters from the newspapers, radio stations and television news shows were interrogating one another trying to find out more about the upcoming conference, but nobody had a clue.

At 10 minutes past 5:00 p.m., a white stretch limo pulled up to the curb at the entrance to the hotel. A uniformed driver leaped out of the front to open the door, and Marion Kelly stepped out in a black pinstripe suit, adjusted his tie and surveyed the scene. He was followed by one long slender leg in an elegant high heel shoe and then another. They were legs that caught the attention of every eye. Next, a deep-red fedora emerged from the dark depths of the car into the bright sunshine, hiding the face of the slender but shapely woman who accompanied Kelly. She did not lift her face to the bewitched crowd until she had stood to her full height, a head taller than Kelly. She reached up and touched the flaming-red brim of the hat delicately with one white-gloved hand and placed the other glove lightly in the crook of Kelly's arm. Recognition of the beautiful model rippled through the crowd like a puff of wind. "It's Karen Hinkley!"

On the other side of the limo, barely noticed by the chauffeur, stood Jack Hinkley, rolling his shoulders in his new Italian suit and fidgeting with his jacket buttons. Kelly placed his hand on the small of Karen's back and guided her through the entrance of The Peabody as two doormen stood smiling, holding the doors open wide. Jack Hinkley trailed behind with relatively little fanfare.

In the conference room on the mezzanine overlooking the lobby, the news types were getting antsy, when someone shouted, "He's here and he's got Karen Hinkley with him!" Kelly and Karen Hinkley, taking full advantage of the photo opportunities offered by the mezzanine, had chosen to walk up the steps instead of taking the elevator, giving the cameras a chance to start rolling before they even arrived in the conference room. They ascended the stairs like royalty. When they arrived at the doorway to the room, Kelly stepped aside, allowing Karen to steal the attention of the waiting crowd as she paused briefly and delivered one of her million-dollar smiles for the cameras.

Karen glided into the room as if she were walking down a runway. She wore a pearl-colored silk dress that draped gracefully over one shoulder and around her thin waist, turning before touching her knees and floating back up again to encircle her other shoulder, which was partially bare. Her makeup was flawless, her hat stunning. She knew that all eyes were following her, and she took full advantage of the opportunity to display her beauty. She broadcast another cover-girl smile and catwalked around to the back of the conference table. Kelly appeared precisely on cue to draw back her chair, and Karen floated into it like a princess. Kelly took the center seat in front of five microphones and three tape recorders, clasping his hands in front of him. Jack Hinkley entered and seated himself on the other side of Kelly, almost unnoticed.

Kelly paused and surveyed his domain with arrogance. "Ladies and gentleman. I want to thank you all for coming today," he began, silencing the crowd. "I called this conference to inform you of a highly significant lawsuit that will be fought right here in Memphis."

Three fat cameramen in blue jeans were positioned with their bright lights focused on Kelly. The newspaper reporters all held their obligatory small spiral wire notepads ready, and the radio people fidgeted with their cantankerous pocket recorders.

"Today, I have filed a lawsuit on behalf of my clients, Karen and Jack Hinkley, against Hollywood Productions of California. This suit is for breach of a movie contract. In addition, we recently filed a medical malpractice suit against Dr. Paul Greson, a practitioner from Memphis, in relation to this cause."

"Can you give us more detail?" Margo shouted from the side.

Kelly smiled. "I was just about to. My client, Ms. Hinkley, was offered a starring role in a Hollywood Productions movie. Perhaps you have seen it — *Pretty Woman II*?" Heads nodded in confirmation across the room. "Well, Ms. Hinkley became ill some months before shooting was scheduled to begin, but recovered in time to meet her contractual obligations. When she arrived in Hollywood, the movie people decided she was no longer suitable for the role and canceled her contract. Since this contract was executed here in Memphis by a local firm, I have filed the suit in Tennessee."

"What about the malpractice suit, Mr. Kelly?"

"Ms. Hinkley was sent by her regular doctor to see Dr. Paul Greson, a Memphis oncologist. Dr. Greson treated my client with drugs that caused her grievous consequences resulting in the loss of Ms. Hinkley's movie contract. We charge that Dr. Greson, due to his gross negligence, intentionally harmed my client even though she made it plain to him that her appearance could not be altered by any treatment. However, precisely as a result of the doctor's treatment, my client lost all of her hair, which, unfortunately, ladies and gentlemen, has never returned."

The crowd all looked at Karen's hat in confirmation as Kelly finished his spiel. "And that is what led us to sue Dr. Paul Greson for malpractice."

"*Memphis Daily*, Mr. Kelly. What are the amounts of the suits?"

"We're asking for $4 million in the malpractice litigation against the doctor. As far as the Hollywood suit goes, we want $8 million in compensatory damages and $10 million in punitive damages."

There was a loud reaction as questions rang out from all sides of the room. "Ms. Hinkley, has this ended your career as a model?"

Karen took a tiny cotton handkerchief from her purse and blotted away the tears at the corners of her eyes. "Yes, it has. Completely."

"Are you saying the doctor gave you something to make you lose your hair even after you specifically told him you didn't want your appearance altered?"

"Yes he did. He's a monster and a quack," Karen whimpered. "He made me take that awful stuff, and the next thing I knew, I was brushing my career right off my head." As Karen spoke, she reached up with both of her white-gloved hands and dramatically removed the red hat, revealing the taut, shiny scalp that would later be referred to in the tabloids as her "crown of glory." The onlookers were shocked. Kelly, pleased with his staging, decided that it would be a perfect note on which to end.

"That's all for today, ladies and gentleman, but don't worry. I'll keep you up to date on the developments."

As the cameras followed the trio out of the room and to the waiting limo, Jack Hinkley, husband/manager, thought to himself, "Now this is more like it! What a show."

Forty-five minutes later Dr. Greson sat watching the evening news with his wife. As the news brief ran the color drained from his face, but he said nothing. "Paul? Paul are you all right, darling?" asked Linda. Pale and shaken, he rushed to the downstairs bathroom and threw up.

CHAPTER TWELVE

Marion Kelly called Obadiah Morgan at the Old Time Billiard Parlor looking for Short Round.

"He ain't here, suh, he in da hospital," Obadiah reported.

"What for?" Kelly asked, irritated by the inconvenience.

"He done got his'self cut up by 'dem boys down to the 'hood. He gonna be all right though, I think," Obadiah said, stroking his scruffy chin and gazing at the tattered ceiling.

"When did this happen?"

"'Bout three, fo' days ago I reckon. His sister say he was pretty bad at first, but 'dey brought him through. Say he needed 16 pints o'blood."

"Which hospital, Obadiah, do you know?" Kelly asked briskly, hurrying the small-talk.

"Yes suh, he at The Med," Obadiah answered solemnly, as if speaking of a hallowed institution.

"Thanks, Obadiah."

"Yes suh," Obadiah spoke into the receiver after Kelly hung up.

Kelly placed an immediate call to Carlson Prison.

"We got a problem, Harry. My mole got himself cut up and he's in the hospital. I don't know of a replacement off hand who would do this kind of a job."

"Hell! What else can go wrong?" the warden growled.

"I think we're going to have to wait a few days on this one unless you boys can handle it down there," Kelly said, trying to pass the buck.

"We've talked about the situation, but we don't want to make any sudden moves until we know what Kempner has told the Feds."

"Okay, I'll see what things look like up here and get back to you when I find out our options. I might be able to find somebody else."

"Well, I'm sitting tight for now, so hurry up and figure this one out," Harry prodded. "Two boys from the U.S. Attorney's office were here today, and we're gettin kinda' itchy about this thing."

"Just relax, I'll come up with something."

△△ △△ △△

Kelly made a visit to The Med where Short Round had been moved to the step-down section of the surgical intensive care unit. The Med, a teaching hospital, had been constructed one building at a time over a 50-year period, and recent attempts had been made to connect the structures with large, tubular, plexiglass hallways suspended on stilts. The futuristic maze of passageways reminded Kelly of corridors on the Starship Enterprise. More than once, he found himself looking for someone to ask directions. As if that wasn't irritating enough, the hallways were packed with the less-than-fortunate patients and their families. The whole place seemed like a homeless refuge to Kelly, and he hated having to stand so close to those "dirty indigent pigs."

When Kelly finally located the right sector, he demanded immediate attention. "Nurse. Nurse! I'm Marion Kelly, the attorney for one of your patients. He goes by the nickname Short Round." As he spoke, he looked the woman up and down.

"Let me see, ..." the nurse replied helpfully, bending over the counter to review the patient roster.

She was young and very attractive, her curves apparent even in the shapeless blue scrub shirt she wore. From his angle, Kelly could look down her shirt and see her tender young breasts cradled in a passionate purple bra. He maneuvered himself to get a better view. She looked up and caught him. Kelly continued to undress her with his eyes.

"He's in 1102, bed B. Anything else, sir?" the nurse said, straightening up and backing off a little.

"Actually, yes." Kelly became suave. "Did anyone ever tell you that you have beautiful breasts?" Kelly grinned.

"They certainly have. But you, sir, have seen all of them you're ever going to," she responded, looking Kelly straight in the eye. Then, flipping her long hair, she turned and walked coolly away. Kelly grinned as he watched her figure glide down the hall.

"Short Round, it's Kelly." Kelly shook his shoulder. "Short Round, wake up."

"Can I help you, sir?" A resident physician appeared in the doorway.

"Yes, I'm Marion Kelly. I'm this man's attorney, and I need to talk to him."

"I don't think he's up to much right now. He's had a pretty rough go of it."

"Are you his doctor?" Kelly asked, taking his hand off Round's unresponsive shoulder.

"I'm one of them, and until he's transferred to rehab, I'll be his primary physician." The resident shifted his stethoscope, looking beyond Kelly to the monitors.

"How long do you think it will be before he's out of the hospital?" Kelly asked, turning back to the sleeping figure.

"Several months I would guess. It's going to be a big adjustment. I'm afraid he's been extremely handicapped."

"What do you mean?" Kelly was surprised.

"He suffered a stroke from the shock of his injuries, and he's going to have to learn how to do everything all over again."

"Oh," said Kelly, uninterested now that he realized Short Round would be of no more use to him. Kelly pushed past the resident, leaving him standing in the doorway. The nurse with beautiful breasts was standing at a medicine cart reviewing the medication sheets. Kelly walked down the hallway toward her. He held out his left hand as he walked by and let it slide along the outline of her derriere. The nurse jumped forward and glared at the sight of Kelly walking away, trying to burn a hole in his back with her thoughts. Kelly kept walking without ever looking back, a big smirk on his face.

△△   △△   △△

Dr. Johnson stepped up to the viewer, removed his glasses and squinted at Carl Wheat's X-rays. After a moment he flipped the view box off, replaced his glasses and lumbered down the hallway to room 3241, where he lifted the vitals chart from the door pocket and entered.

"Good morning, Mr. Wheat. I'm Dr. Johnson, your urologist. Dr. Bell asked me to come by and have a look at you. I've reviewed your X-rays, and I think we need to do an arteriogram of your kidneys. That's where the radiologist injects dye into your renal arteries and takes pictures to outline the blood supply. It should be done by this afternoon. After the arteriogram I can tell you a great deal more about your problem."

"Ah, what do you think is the matter, Doc?"

"We'll have a lot better idea after today's test, so I'll set that up now and then I'll see you tomorrow. Okay?" the doctor said as he turned and left.

"Okay," Carl replied after he was already out the door.

⚡   ⚡   ⚡

Becky was sitting by Carl's side holding his hand when the orderly came with the gurney. They had fallen silent. Carl was afraid, but he believed that he had to be a man in such matters and not let his feelings show. After all, he was a Marine.

The door opened, breaking the silence. "'Scuse me Mr. Wheat, but I got to take you on down to X-ray now. Sorry miss, but I'll bring him right back." The attendant pushed the stretcher in slowly. He was an older black man with salt and pepper hair; his voice was gravelly but soothing.

"Now if you can, just get on up here on the stretcher."

"No problem," Carl exclaimed as he helped himself over. Becky took his hand and squeezed it tightly, and as the attendant began the labor of rolling him through the doorway, she bent down and gave Carl a quick, upside-down kiss.

"I'll be here," she reassured. "I'll say a little prayer for you."

"He'll be fine, miss. I'll be bringing him back before you know it." Somehow his voice comforted Becky as she stood in the hallway watching Carl like she had watched Jim so many times before.

"My name is George, Mr. Wheat. If you ever need anything you just call George and he'll come fix you right up," the attendant said and then began to hum softly one of the old spirituals in perfect rhythm to his steps. George's appearance reflected a life of manual labor carried through without resentment or bitterness. He was from the generation of blacks who took pride in themselves regardless of their situations, and who suffered hardships with dignity and integrity. The younger blacks who lived in his neigh-

— 107 —

borhood called him "Rastus" and didn't understand the simplicity in his way of life. But George had a peace about him that was evident, and even though they couldn't understand him, they respected him. Carl too was affected by his serenity and struck up a conversation with the old gentleman. He seemed to have a deep sincerity about him.

"How long you been working here?"

"Oh, let's see now, I reckon it's been about 38 years now."

"I bet you've seen a lot of patients come and go, huh?"

"Yes suh, and I've pushed them all up and down these halls. I been working here so long I don't know if I could ever retire. I been here since Elvis was first a patient up on the 14th floor at Baptist Central. He used to ask them to send George out to get some cookin' like his mamma's. They'd come around an say, 'Elvis wants you to get him some supper George.' I'd go on down to Front Street and git him a mess of mash 'taters with gravy, black-eyed peas, greens and corn bread. He liked a little greasy fried chicken too, down from the Arcade Restaurant where he'd go with his buddies in the middle of the night. Every time, I bring him a whole box full of food and he's always asking me to set down an eat with him."

"You ate with Elvis?" Carl asked, astonished.

"Yes suh, I'd talk to him every time he come up to the hospital. We was friends. He always tellin' me about Hollywood and the movie stars and all about makin' that music of his. Sometime when I'm in his room, he start singin' gospel songs and get me to join in. Me and Elvis. Lawdy, you wouldn't believe some of the things we done. Naw suh. You just wouldn't believe 'em even if ol' George told you nothin' but the truth." George spoke as if reciting lines from a play. Clearly, he had told this story many times.

The patient elevator opened and George pushed Carl into the shiny metal box without a strain. George was nearly 70, but he was still strong and healthy. Pushing gurneys and lifting patients all day had been somewhat hard on his back, but he had kept fit and trim. He loved his job and he had been a comfort to many anxious patients throughout the years.

As George delivered Carl to the X-ray holding area, he looked into Carl's face a moment and said real quietly, "You be prayin' now like that little miss waitin' for you back there in that room, and the Lord, he'll take care of you like he's done ol' George."

"Thanks, George," Carl said appreciatively.

"I know the Lord real good, and he's gonna make things all right." George touched Carl's head and turned away.

⊿⊿   ⊿⊿   ⊿⊿

"Dr. Bell, Dr. Johnson is on the phone for you, sir," the receptionist blared over the speaker phone.

"Put him through," Dr. Bell instructed.

"Jack, that arteriogram on Wheat in 3241 shows a well-circumscribed renal cell. I went ahead and did a tumor survey and so far I don't see any metastasis. It looks pretty good for a radical nephrectomy."

"In that case, I'd like to get Greson to come in on this one, if you don't mind."

"Good idea. Meanwhile I'll get my office to schedule surgery for Thursday," the surgeon said.

"You don't think we're too late on this one do you?" Bell asked, feeling somewhat at fault for the delay.

"I don't know for sure, but it looks good so far."

"I hope you're right. I'll get with the patient and call Greson."

⊿⊿   ⊿⊿   ⊿⊿

"Dr. Greson? Ms. Stein is on line one, and you have a consultation at Baptist Hospital East, room 3241 — a Carl Wheat from Dr. Bell." Although young, Kim was extremely organized and Greson depended upon her heavily.

"Got it, put Ms. Stein through."

"Dr. Greson? Diane Stein. I'm calling to update you on the Hinkley case. We need to schedule the completion of your deposition. I think Kelly will finally review the hospital records with you."

"What? Not again!" Greson was becoming indignant. "How long is this going to drag on?" The frustration was evident in his voice and Diane spoke quietly in order to calm his nerves.

"Well, usually the depositions can be finished in one day. Unfortunately, Kelly often uses depositions to aggravate. He'll schedule and depose all the way to court to get your emotions worked up. It's best to comply with his wishes and not give him any indication that he's affecting your nerves."

"Can't we do something?" Greson asked, though he already knew the answer.

"We could ask the judge to limit the area of inquiry during the deposition. However, it is unlikely that the judge would set any limitations. Kelly would argue that his questions are relevant and necessary to his case."

"Damn lawyers. This system stinks." Greson stood and began to pace around his desk as he talked.

"I'm sorry. There's not much we can do at this point. Kelly will try to get you irritated so that you will say something to hurt yourself. Maybe this time it will be another lawyer from his office," she added, attempting to console the angry doctor.

"Well, I can see how he gets his way. I've already lost three or four days work, not to mention God knows how many nights of sleep over this thing. It's really getting to be a hassle."

"For now, let's go ahead and cooperate with this deposition. If he requests another one, I'll file a motion for a protective order."

"Okay, okay. Whatever you think Ms. Stein," Greson relinquished.

"I'll call your secretary to give her some available dates."

Dr. Greson looked on his calendar and noticed that he and Linda were going out of town for the weekend to a conference in Nashville. He relished the thought of a few days out of town, away from this nightmare, away from the children, just the two of them. A little time to relax and forget all this. "Just what the doctor ordered," he said to himself and grinned for the first time in weeks.

CHAPTER THIRTEEN

Agent Simon unfolded his badge over the secretary's desk. "This the office of Mr. Philip Wilson, Miss?" he asked. "I'd like to speak with Mr. Wilson if I could, please. Official Bureau business."

"I'll see if he's in. Will you please wait, sir?" the startled secretary requested, picking up the phone and buzzing Wilson in his office.

"Mr. Wilson, there's a Mr. Simon here to see you, sir," the secretary said into the phone "He says he has official business."

Wilson didn't understand what she meant. "What kind of official business? What does he want?"

"I don't know sir, he's from the FBI. He didn't say specifically what business he meant."

Wilson went tense when he heard FBI. A kaleidoscope of thoughts raced through his mind: Congressional hearings, trials, press mobs, lawyers and jail terms. He pictured a courtroom scene with the judge pounding the guilty gavel.

"Mr. Wilson," the secretary repeated. "What shall I tell him, sir?"

"I'll be right out," Wilson managed.

He carefully replaced the telephone receiver, handling it as if it were made of nitroglycerine. His breathing was quick and shallow. The ends of his fingers began to tingle. He felt like he might not survive the next moment. He reached for his briefcase and fumbled with a plastic prescription bottle, finally popping the damn thing open and scattering purple pills all over his desk. As he swallowed, he wondered if the agent was there to arrest him. Would he use handcuffs? Would he draw a gun? His heart was pounding so hard his ears rang. He could hear every small sound in the room and along the causeway outside. Everything seemed so loud.

Wilson reached for the door, gripped the brass handle tightly and squeezed. Slowly he pulled the door toward him, trying to see the waiting area through the small opening. He could see his secretary's desk. Her shoes were off and she was twitching her feet. He opened the door a bit further until a man in a dark suit and sunglasses standing with his arms folded came into view. He was glaring directly at the opening door. To Wilson, he looked like Darth Vader. He knew he had to muster the courage to walk confidently out into the reception area so as not to create suspicion. It took all his courage to swing the door completely open and approach the dark figure.

"Hi, I'm Philip Wilson," he choked, with his hand extended.

"Sir, I'm agent Charles Simon with the Bureau," the agent stated matter-of-factly, displaying his badge without extending a handshake. Wilson's panic increased instantly to terror.

"I must speak to you in private, sir," the agent reported as he nodded toward the door.

"Come into my office, Agent Simon. No calls please," Wilson managed to say steadily to his secretary.

He guided the agent into his office and stood by the door, gesturing the man in with his arm. "Have a seat," he invited.

"I prefer to stand, sir," the agent stated firmly as if it were a sign of weakness to sit.

"Okay. Now what can I do for the FBI?"

"Sir, I was sent to inform you that the Bureau is investigating a member of your senior staff — Ms. Janet Kesner. We have reason to believe that she and an accomplice may be using Department of Interior documents to conceal certain illegal activities. Our investigation might require your cooperation. We have a lead in Tampa, Florida, that may shed some light on the situation, but we need someone on the inside to help us with surveillance to prove the connection. Of course, this is all extremely confidential, sir, and I am not at liberty to disclose any more details at this time. We ask that you speak to no one regarding this matter, including your superior. The director has asked me to thank you in advance for your understanding and cooperation. I've been instructed to report to you when we have the suspect near arrest. You can call me at any time if you see anything suspicious." The agent handed Wilson a card with his name and a telephone number printed on it. The sight of the words Federal Bureau of Investigation gave him cold chills.

"Now sir, if you don't mind, that is all I have to report, and I will be leaving. Glad to meet you, sir." The agent had recited the whole briefing as if from a manuscript. He turned and withdrew from the room quietly.

Wilson nodded an affirmative and watched him leave. As the door closed behind Agent Charles Simon, Wilson almost collapsed. He sat motionless for about five minutes. Then, suddenly, a small grin spread across his face. Just as suddenly, it was replaced by a look of terror. He wasn't sure what the FBI was up to. Was there really an operation like the one described or was the FBI trying to get him to make a move and expose his secret? Wilson tried to imagine every possible angle. Were they on to him about the LDC thing, or was he just paranoid? He remained in his office until 10:30 that night. Philip Wilson was formulating a plan.

△△   △△   △△

"Mr. Wheat, I'm Dr. Greson."

"Oh, come in. Another doctor?" Carl responded. Becky sat up in her chair when she heard his voice, and Dr. Greson looked at Becky and smiled even before he recognized her. He knew her, but he couldn't recall her name. Becky stood up and walked directly toward the doctor. She extended her hand with a smile. "I'm Becky Summers, you took care of my late husband, Jim Summers."

"Oh, yes, yes. I thought you looked familiar. It's been about a year now hasn't it?"

"Yes," Becky responded.

"And how are those boys of yours, Ms. Summers?"

"They're doing just fine," Becky assured. She couldn't believe he was standing there. It was like she was reliving a nightmare. "Why are you here Dr. Greson? I mean … is Carl?" Becky began.

"Oh, is Mr Wheat your ah …?" Greson started off awkwardly. "Um, are you here with him as …?" Awkwardly again.

"Well, Carl is a very good frie, …" Becky stumbled and then added, "my boyfriend." She smiled weakly at Carl as she said this. She wasn't sure they had officially made that arrangement.

Everyone was a little clumsy and uncomfortable. "How tragic that Becky might have to go through another medical ordeal with someone she loves," he thought.

"Well, I'm here because Dr. Bell asked me to help out," he said in explanation, trying to recover his bedside manner. "He and Dr. Johnson have consulted me on Carl's

— 115 —

case, and I want to talk to you about some things that we've found." Dr. Greson sat on the edge of the bed. "Carl, your X-rays show a growth on the right kidney that is probably a tumor, but we can't be certain without surgery."

"Surgery! What do you mean?" Carl raised up in the bed.

"Well Carl, if it is a tumor, then it could be a cancerous tumor. The sooner we get in there and remove it, the better our chances of catching any cancer before it spreads. Surgery is our best option. Dr. Johnson has scheduled you for Thursday. I'm sorry, I thought he had already told you about this."

"No!" Carl shot back.

Greson was caught somewhat off guard by the whole situation. "Overall, Carl, I think you have a good chance of coming out of the surgery a much healthier man," he said awkwardly. "If the tumor is benign, it is still probably the cause of your recurring pain, and if it is not, then the sooner it is removed, the better."

Carl was dumfounded. His lips mouthed "Thursday?" without making a sound. He looked into the eyes of his new doctor — an oncologist. He had never needed one of those before. He looked deeper into Greson's eyes to see if there was more. He was left speechless and numb from the news. He had a million questions, but he wasn't ready for any of the answers. Carl was thinking, "Someone must have made a mistake."

"Do you have any questions, Carl?" Greson offered.

"No, not now Doc. I'll just think about it awhile. I appreciate you're helping," Carl said in a monotone voice. "I'm kinda all shook up right now."

"I understand. I'll come back early tomorrow, and we can talk some more. Ah, nice to see you again, Becky." Greson left the room. He thought Dr. Bell had told Carl about the tumor and surgery. He was certainly not expecting to deliver the blow himself. He hated to have to tell people the bad news, and even though it was a big part of his job, he had never gotten used to it.

Becky was crying when Carl turned to see her face. They reached for each other the moment their eyes met. Becky wrapped her arms around Carl's neck as she melted into the small hospital bed with him. Their eyes welled up with tears. She loved him so much. "Not again. Not again," she thought to herself. They held each other and cried for 20 minutes. Sometimes Becky would comfort Carl, and sometimes he comforted her. After a whole box of tissues, they looked searchingly at one another. As soon as their eyes met, the tears welled up again. Between sobs and words of encouragement, Becky and Carl had fallen deeply into love — the kind of love that transcends all problems, even cancer. Becky knew this kind of love, and now she would teach Carl. She was stronger and wiser than most women twice her age.

That night Becky began to wonder if she could make it. For a tired moment she even thought of backing out of her relationship with Carl. Then she remembered how much she loved him. "Nothing happens by accident," she consoled herself. She must stay with Carl because she loved him. It was apparent to her that she had more to learn. Becky believed that you are where you are for a reason — that God put things in a person's life in order to teach them what they need to know so they can fulfill His divine plan. As tired as she was, she couldn't fall asleep until she had made up her mind that she was committed to staying with Carl, no matter what. She wouldn't realize until later how this decision changed the course of her life.

⚐ ⚐ ⚐

Marion Kelly called his partner Bill Pritchard, a well-known criminal defense lawyer in the firm. Bill was also known for his involvement in numerous ethical violations. He had always managed to slip through reprimand without much consequence. Damage control was one of Pritchard's better assets. The call lasted only a few moments, but during that call Kelly was given the answer he needed.

Pritchard was currently defending a client, Stumpy Johnson, for transportation of firearms across state lines and grand theft, auto. Stumpy was clearly guilty of these charges and more, but chances were he would soon be a free man because of a technicality. The arrangement made between Kelly and Pritchard, however, would soon change Stumpy's fate.

Stumpy was a 28-year-old male with a criminal record as long as his arm. He had been arrested about 30 times and was currently an inmate at the Memphis Correctional facility downtown. Pritchard agreed to accommodate Kelly by losing Stumpy's case. Then, after the judge sentenced Stumpy to Carlson Prison, it would be easy to persuade him to ferret out the information needed by the warden in exchange for his freedom. Prison officials would arrange all the details. "What are partners for?" Kelly chuckled to himself when the deal was set. He was pleased that he had solved the problem for the warden so quickly and efficiently.

Stumpy had been arrested two months earlier. He had built a nice little business for providing any car a customer wanted from his Third Street used car lot. A client could request a certain make, model, and color and Stumpy promised delivery within six weeks. If a person wanted a green Eddie Bauer Explorer, Stumpy's boys would find a new, low mileage model and steal it. The auto would then go to Stumpy's warehouse where the doors, radio, wheels and battery were removed and stored. The mechanics took special care not to damage the vehicle.

After 30 days, the auto insurance company would consider the car unrecoverable and pay the owner. A week later, Stumpy's crew would place the auto back on the street where they watched until the police recovered it and took it to the impoundment lot. After the recovery, the insurance company would auction the stolen vehicle and Stumpy was always there to place his bid and get the auto delivered into his hands with a clean, legal title. The car would be returned to Stumpy's warehouse where his boys replaced the missing parts and delivered it to the customer as good as new. Stumpy ran a cash-only business and made a clean profit of about $10,000 per auto. Multiply this by 20 or 30 times a month and you figured Stumpy wasn't doing too badly at all.

An observant, undercover ATF agent became suspicious of Stumpy's continuous presence at the auctions. Eventually, a surveillance team of ATF and FBI agents followed one of Stumpy's shipments of stolen firearms from Arkansas to his Memphis warehouse and exposed the operation. On the night of the arrest, Agent Sam Baker was sent to see a federal judge for a warrant to raid the warehouse. Meanwhile, at the warehouse, things had started to deteriorate, and the team decided to go in before the warrant was issued. They were afraid the suspects would leave the warehouse and blow the whole operation. The agents moved in and successfully apprehended the principles involved in Stumpy's operation, including Stumpy himself, and an alarming arsenal of firearms.

Pritchard had planned to use the fact that the warrant was not actually in hand when the raid took place to get Stumpy off, but Kelly convinced him to let it go and get Stumpy a new address at Carlson. Suddenly, the Fourth Amendment no longer existed for Mr. Pritchard or for Stumpy either.

CHAPTER FOURTEEN

Carl rolled over toward Becky and grabbed the railing of his hospital bed as the nurse rubbed a small area on his buttock with cool alcohol. Immediately he felt the sharp prick, the sting and the deep pressure of the injection. Carl winced. He was no more fond of injections than anyone else. The drugs — Demerol, Phenergan and Robinal — had been mixed into one syringe and delivered deep into the muscle in preparation for Carl's surgery. The combination of narcotic, antinausea and drying agents reduced anxiety so effectively that it had been nicknamed the "Don't Give a Care Shot."

Surgery was scheduled for 7:30 a.m., and Becky had been holding Carl's hand since 6:00 that morning. She had been in such a rush to get to the hospital that she'd stopped by McDonald's and brought her breakfast with her. She felt a little guilty when she noticed Carl eyeing her every bite. "Boy, that coffee smells so good I can taste it," he said, trying to keep up the small-talk and avoid any tearful scenes. Carl was scared, but he knew Becky was scared, too. At least he would be asleep through the whole thing. Poor Becky would be a nervous wreck.

Gradually, Carl forgot his concerns; he focused his mind on the rich aroma of the coffee once again. The narcotic effect had started to take over and he was beginning to sense a feeling of "well being." He became talkative and brave.

"I'm ready for this show to start."

"I know."

"When I get outta here, I'm gonna take those boys camping and fishing."

"That'll be nice, Carl."

"What color are you painting your fingernails?"

"You're silly, I'm not painting my nails. That medicine has you goofy. Just lay back and relax, they'll be here soon."

Just as Carl started to drift off, the door opened slowly.

"Mornin'," the old gentleman called out.

"Is that you George?" Carl sat up, hardly able to see straight.

"Yes, suh, it's me. You knew I'd be here to take you off to surgery," George said with his customary cheerfulness.

"I wouldn't go if it weren't you, George, takin' me," Carl slurred.

"We're gonna getcha to slide over on this here stretcher real easy like." George motioned with his hand to Becky to help keep Carl from falling. Between the two of them, they got him situated on the gurney and covered with the thin sheet. Becky put both hands on Carl's face and held it close to hers as she squeezed out a kiss.

"I'll be praying for you, baby, and I'll be here when you wake up. I love you, Carl." The tears streamed down Becky's face. Carl smiled. He was seeing two of her.

"It's s'okay, I'm gonna be all right, but I don't know which one of you to kiss."

"Not me!" George proclaimed, misunderstanding.

George wheeled Carl down the hall on an almost identical route to the one he had taken days before to X-ray. "George, you know Dr. Johnson?" Carl inquired.

"Yes suh, I know him." George rambled on down the hallway.

"Is he a good surgeon?" Carl asked, knowing there was nothing he could do now.

"Yes suh, he's the best. I've been takin' his patients back and forth for years, and they all say he's real good. Some of these docs don't take time with the patients, but Doc Johnson, he's real careful and good to his patients. Yes suh, he's all right."

"That makes me feel better, George," Carl spoke through the fog.

"Yes suh, he'll take good care of ya. The Lord lookin' down on you, too. Don't you worry, Mr. Wheat, I know the Lord, and he told me you gonna make it through this here surgery. I talk to him every day, every day of my life, yes suh, every day."

George delivered Carl to the holding area where 14 other patients were lined up on gurneys awaiting surgery. The nurses were hurriedly completing the paperwork and preoperative checklists on all of them. The surgery plans were like a pilot's preflight inventory: patient I.D. bracelet verified, permit signed, history and physical completed, lab returned and reviewed — not much different than: mixture rich, mags checked, flaps at 10.

Dr. Miller, the anesthesiologist, reviewed Carl's chart and asked him another round of redundant questions about medication, last food eaten, allergies and illnesses. Carl wondered to himself how many times he would have to repeat the story. When all systems were go, Dr. Miller and the circulating nurse wheeled Carl into operating room four.

"Let's move over to the operating table, Mr. Wheat, and be careful not to roll off, the table is narrow. I'm Cindy, and I'll be one of the nurses here during your operation."

As Carl moved over to the icy operating table, reality

made its way through the narcotic fog. Carl was starting to get scared. The anesthesiologist attached the blood pressure cuff to one arm and started an IV in the other. He also attached EKG pads to Carl's chest and placed a red-lighted monitor on his finger. Carl studied the OR lights to keep his mind off his anxiety. He saw Dr. Miller inject something into his IV. Moments later he felt a wave of heat pass through his body, and a cloud of sedation blanketed his fears.

"Mr. Wheat, it's Dr. Johnson. I wanted to let you see I'm here before they put you to sleep. When you wake up, you'll be in recovery and your stomach will be pretty sore. Let the nurses know if you hurt so they can give you a shot for pain. Don't wait, okay?" Carl attempted a nod.

"Mr. Wheat, take a deep breath of this oxygen for me," Dr. Miller instructed as he reviewed the monitors. "I'm going to give you medicine to put you to sleep. Now just relax and breathe the oxygen."

Carl did as he was instructed. The air was cold in his nostrils. He could feel it traveling down into his lungs. As the anesthesiologist injected the Diprivan, Carl tasted something funny and then felt a dark, overpowering wave of oblivion. Carl's reflexes were tested, and Dr. Miller inserted an endotracheal tube to assist his breathing. His eyes were taped shut and his elbows padded. Cindy washed Carl's stomach with betadine, a germicide, and shaved off the curly hairs.

"May I begin the operation, Doctor?" Dr. Johnson asked Dr. Miller.

"The patient is paralyzed and ready, Doctor."

The knife paused one-half inch above the skin of the abdomen. The pause was for the surgeon to meditate and focus on the serious undertaking upon which he was about to embark. The skin gave way under the number 10 Bard-Parker blade and Carl began to bleed.

"Hold this."

"Here, sir?" the scrub assistant questioned.

"Ah-ha. Retract the colon."

"Yes sir."

"Hold this back while I expose the retropertioneum."

"This way?"

"Yes."

Both scrub assistant and nurse were in a complete mind meld with the surgeon. After thousands of hours in surgery and hundreds of operations, the skilled team was able to forecast the needs of the surgeon and his particular instruments. They did this without conscious knowledge, like figure skating partners making complex moves together without gesture or sign.

"Here's the renal artery. Be careful with that retractor, it looks fragile."

"Yes sir."

"Hold this back. I'm going to dissect the tumor away from the aorta. Get more light in here."

"Is that better?" the scrub nurse asked.

"Oh shit! suction!"

"What's the matter?" Miller said poking his head over the curtain.

"The renal artery has ruptured. I can't see a thing. Damnit, more suction!"

"More suction, sir. Get me another suction bucket."

"Are you able to see it?"

"No! Hell, I can't see anything but blood."

"Get me two units of whole blood, stat."

"I'm not able to see where the renal comes out. There's too much blood. Hold that."

"His pressure is dropping."

"Hold this. Now, damnit!"

"Nurse get me more fluids. A liter of anything." Miller motioned frantically for her to hurry.

"I'll have to clamp the aorta."

"Well you better do something, 'cause his pressure is in his boots now," Miller shot back.

The renal artery is capable of pumping two to three liters per minute, and in only a short while, there's nothing left to pump. "His blood pressure has dropped seriously, and his pulse is 150. How are you coming?" Miller worried.

"I can't see a thing. Get me a large vascular clamp. Now! I'm going to clamp the aorta at the diaphragm as soon as I can find it. Give me a vascular clamp." The surgeon located the entry of the aorta into the abdominal area and placed a large vascular clamp across the entire artery. This would stop all blood flow from the diaphragm down and give him time to suction and locate the pumping renal artery. He could only clamp the aorta for a brief while or risk serious consequences.

"I've got it! It's clamped," Johnson said as he looked up, blood soaked from his mask to the edge of the operating table. "More suction."

"Doctor, we have a problem, I think his blood volume is too low already. He's got no pressure, and he's beginning to have heart irregularities," Miller reported.

"I've done all I can here."

"Well, start CPR, 'cause we ain't got nothin' now."

"Code Blue. Get those crash carts in here now!" The room exploded with the entry of 10 additional personnel and four different crash carts. Carl lay completely unaware of the people around him. He drifted deeper into an unknown darkness.

Marc studied the scene through binoculars. He was careful not to allow any reflections off the lenses. They would have to move quickly after the shot. The Viet Cong would swarm in all directions like bees from an overturned hive.

Carl raised his Styer SSG, covered with cloth and canvas also to prevent reflection. He removed the lens cover from the Schmitt and Bender scope. He made himself a nest and got comfortable. Below them, the Marines could see soldiers running right and left, responding to the Red Major's orders.

"Distance: 210 yards. Windage: cross wind two knots. Elevation: 60-foot drop," Marc whispered. Carl placed a red-tipped .308 round into the breech and closed the bolt smoothly. Through the scope he could see the back of the Red Major's head as he barked orders from his vehicle. Payback time! The crosshairs came to rest on the nape of the major's neck. Carl drew a moderate breath and exhaled completely. His finger began to exert slow, even pressure on the trigger. The shot rang out. Carl saw the back of the major's head explode, and a great shower of blood and brains slide down the inside of the Jeep's windshield.

"Let's go, let's go!" Marc whispered hoarsely as he pulled at Carl's arm.

They quickly made off along the south side of the ridge as planned. When they were over the crest, they stood and began a careful trot through the dense jungle. Suddenly, Carl's boot caught on something that wouldn't give, and he and his rifle took off through the air. As he landed, a red-hot, burning pain hit him hard in the stomach. The pain grew, and Carl felt himself passing out. He looked along the trail, and there he saw George standing and smiling at him.

"George?" Carl called out in confusion.

"Yes suh, I'm here with you now, don't you worry."

"Where am I, George? What are you doing here?"

"Don't you worry none Mr. Carl. Ol' George, he'll lead you outta here. This here isn't where you belong now."

"Where am I George?" Carl shouted in his confusion.

"Shh … it's okay now, Mr. Wheat. You're in the recovery room. Just settle down," nurse Cindy's voice broke through the fog. "Everything is all right. Do you have any pain?"

Carl stared blankly at the faces that stood before him, trying to figure out who they were and where he was. He couldn't focus, and his throat was sore. He tried to say something, but his mouth felt like he could spit cotton. He had a tight sensation in his stomach, but it didn't hurt. Carl still didn't understand who these people were or what the nurse was talking about.

"I was in Vietnam," he thought. "What? Ah … and George … George, where are you?" Carl faded back into sleep.

CHAPTER FIFTEEN

The jury returned with a solemn look. Stumpy stood sluggishly next to Counselor Pritchard. The judge asked, "Have you reached a verdict?"

"We have, your honor." When the verdict was announced, Stumpy had been found guilty on all counts. He looked at his lawyer with disdain. The judge addressed the defendant sternly. "Mr. Johnson, the jury has found you guilty on all counts. You have repeatedly engaged in unlawful activities that have caused intentional harm to the citizens of this city. I only wish the law would allow me to deal you the hand you deserve, but I am constrained to a sentence that, in my opinion, is completely inadequate. I reluctantly sentence you to seven years incarceration, without parole, at Carlson Federal Penitentiary. Your term there will begin immediately. Case closed." The judge banged his gavel down hard in disgust.

Pritchard turned to Stumpy. "I'll visit you tomorrow before the transfer to Carlson. I have a friend down there who may be able to help you," he lied. "Let me get in touch with him and see what we can work out. Don't worry, it won't be that bad."

"It ain't you doin' time," Stumpy sneered. "I thought you was supposed to get me off on some technical thing.

I don't believe this," he grumbled, knowing there wasn't a damn thing he could do about it now.

⟁   ⟁   ⟁

The next day, Kelly and Pritchard met on the front steps outside the jailhouse before their visit with Stumpy. They exchanged the usual small talk, then got down to business.

"You think we should give him the information?" Kelly asked.

"No, let's just reel him in first."

"Right."

The two dark-suited attorneys entered the main doorway and passed through security. Pritchard knew the path well to the lawyer's small, time-worn interview room where the two waited in silence for Stumpy to arrive. Shortly, the door swung open at the hands of a tall deputy jailer and Stumpy moped in and sat down.

"Stumpy, this is Marion Kelly; he's a partner of mine," Pritchard said as he made the introductions. "We've been in touch with some people down at Carlson, and they're willing to work out a deal for you. If you take their deal, they've agreed to arrange for your escape from Carlson without really trying to catch you. They'll make it seem like you slipped through their fingers. And there will be a car and $5,000 waiting for you outside."

"Now the lawyer's providin' Stumpy Johnson with cars. That's a good one. Okay, let's hear the deal." Stumpy wasn't going to pass up a chance to get out quick, even if the pay was lousy.

"I'm afraid you're going to have to agree to do the job before we give you any details. Well, Stumpy, whaddya say? You agree to accept the deal?"

"It depends on the job, man."

"You didn't hear the man, Stumpy," Kelly interjected,

quickly rising. "You'll have to accept the terms as they are stated or you get no further information."

Kelly towered over Stumpy, who sat slumped in his chair staring up at him. Stumpy glanced at Pritchard and grinned. "Make it $25,000 and it's a deal." His stale breath blew across the table into Pritchard's face. Pritchard looked at Kelly. Kelly nodded in agreement. "Okay, we'll make it $25,000. Do we have a deal, Stumpy?"

"And a late-model fast car. No, wait, make it a dark-colored RX7." Stumpy figured he might as well go for the works since these guys seemed willing to cough it up. "I want a fast getaway, man."

Kelly took a sharp breath to keep from punching Stumpy, gained control and said, "Sure, Stumpy, a dark RX7, now listen carefully. Here's the deal. There's a guy in Carlson by the name of Jack Kempner. He's in for attempted murder of a federal official, and he's been running off his mouth to the U.S Attorney's office for a plea bargain. We're not sure what he's selling to the Feds, but we have a good idea. And certain individuals at the prison might be embarrassed by some of his statements. They don't want any trouble. You'll be in the same cell with Kempner. Your job is to find out what he's up to and report back to me. I'll come down there and visit once a week to see what you've learned. When we have the information that we need, then we'll make plans for your escape."

"How do I know you gonna do like you say, man. I mean, how can you arrange my escape?"

"Let's just say that the warden and I are very close associates, Stumpy. Trust me."

"Warden! You got a deal with the warden? He's in this? Man, I'm lovin' this. Got 'da warden worried 'bout this shit. Maybe I should ask for more money." Stumpy cocked his head back as he spoke.

"Look, dipshit, my patience is about to run thin with

you. You take this offer or your ass is going to rot in Carlson. Got it?" Kelly boomed.

"Okay, okay, dude, I'm cool. I'll do the job."

Kelly looked at the two men in front of him with contempt then walked out of the room.

"Stumpy, you gotta be more cooperative if you want to get out of this mess," Pritchard lectured.

"I don't like that bastard."

"Look, all you have to do is go in there and get a little information outta Kempner, then we'll get you out."

"You mean I gotta see that, what's his name? ..."

"Kelly."

"Yeah, Kelly down at the prison, too?"

"He's working with the warden."

"I don't like that bastard."

Pritchard said, "Nobody does."

⚎   ⚎   ⚎

Several days had passed since Carl's successful surgery, and he was back in a regular hospital room with Becky at his side. The boys had brought a large banner made from butcher's paper that read, "Let's Go Fishing Soon, Love Stephen and Jay." Becky taped the banner on the wall below the television. The boys had been so solemn since the surgery, but now that Carl was feeling better, their moods had shifted by degrees.

"Hey Carl, what do ya get when you cross 10 male deer and 10 female pigs?" Stephen asked bright eyed.

"I don't know, buddy, what do ya get?"

"Hundred sows and bucks."

Carl laughed out loud. "This is the first time I've been able to laugh without holding that pillow on my stomach."

"I'm glad you're feeling better, Carl," Becky said softly.

"I can't wait to get you home with me. I'll take care of

— 131 —

you till you are all well." She nuzzled her head against his playfully.

Dr. Johnson had been by earlier, as well as Dr. Bell and Dr. Greson. They all agreed that if Carl continued to recover at his present pace, he could go home in four or five days. According to the test results, it looked like they had gotten all the cancer for now. Dr. Greson wanted Carl to see him every month for six months, and then, if all went well, every three months thereafter. "You should be back to your normal self in about two months," Greson had said, grasping Carl by the hand. Becky and Carl celebrated the good news with French vanilla ice cream and a kiss. The glow had returned to Becky's face.

⟁   ⟁   ⟁

Paul and Linda Greson had planned a trip to Nashville for the weekend. Paul wanted to attend a conference on bone marrow transplants, and Linda wanted time to relax without the kids. Paul closed the office early on Friday, turned his calls over to a colleague and headed home, glad the week was over. Linda had packed two small bags that were waiting by the door when Paul arrived. After 15 years of marriage, she had learned to avoid the "packing fights" that plague married couples by getting everything completely ready before Paul knew what was happening. That suited him just fine.

The trip was not a long one, but the cab ride to the airport and the short plane ride gave Paul and Linda a chance to sit quietly holding hands, anticipating their first weekend alone together in a long time. They had been a couple for so long that it wasn't always necessary for one person to talk in order for the other to know what he or she was thinking. That aspect of their marriage was a comfort to them both.

Once in Nashville, Paul hailed a Yellow Cab. Much to

his astonishment he saw that the driver was a "blue hair," and he hesitated a moment before getting in. The old lady's name was Matty, and as soon as she pulled up to the curb, she immediately instructed Paul and Linda to heave their luggage into the trunk and get in. They climbed into the back seat, looking at one another in amusement. The trip was already starting to be fun. "How long have you been a cabby?" Paul asked as she lurched from the curb.

"Thirty-two years, and my name's Matty, case you're interested."

"Well, Matty, I'll bet you've driven a lot of famous people here in Nashville. Tell me, who was the most famous one?"

"Oh, I've given 'em all a ride, but those so-called famous folk are just like you and me. I drove 'em when they didn't have no money. Shoot, even after they get famous and uppity, they still don't have cab fare half the time." She cackled loudly.

The old lady drove surprisingly well, despite her initial lurch from the curb. She was 72 years old and claimed to have been the first woman cab driver in Nashville.

Linda couldn't quit laughing at the antics of the matron and decided that she could well have been the first any-kind-of cab driver in Nashville.

"I bet you've gotten into a lot of mischief," Paul probed laughingly.

"No, I haven't," Matty snapped.

"How about dancin'? I bet you shake a leg and cut a rug every chance you get."

"Now don't you let Preacher John hear you talkin' about Sister Matty that way."

"Oh, I see, you're Baptist."

"No sir, I'm Pentecostal." Matty smiled into the rearview mirror. "What you folks call a Holy Roller." Matty laughed again.

"Really," Paul continued, "I bet you can really roll."

"No sir, I don't roll anymore." Matty paused, then fumbled with the two-way radio.

"Why did you stop rollin', Matty?" Linda asked elbowing Paul in the ribs and stifling her laughter.

"I got too durn old!" exclaimed Matty. "I can get down, but I can't get back up. I usually spend the whole service prayin' for them that are rollin' so's they got the strength to get up again." Matty chuckled.

"Now, I know where the expression, 'Help, I've fallen and I can't get up' came from." Paul grinned at Matty in the rearview mirror.

"Yeah, probably. You know, we Pentecostal folks have been on TV for snake handlin', but I don't handle snakes. No sir, I don't want nothin' to do with no snakes."

Matty was still reciting a short history of Holy Rollerdom when they arrived at the hotel. She let Paul and Linda out, telling them they had to get their own luggage. They stood watching and laughing as she screeched away from the curb.

After Paul and Linda had settled into their hotel room they ordered room service. Once finished, they laid back on the bed with the TV turned low.

"It's nice to be here alone for a change, darling."

"Yeah. I'm glad not to have that beeper."

"I bet you are."

"You know, Linda, this lawsuit thing has really ruined my practice for me. I would rather die than work the rest of my life to send the Hinkleys a check every month."

"What do you mean?"

"You know, I told you. The insurance doesn't cover the full amount they are suing for. If the jury awards them all of it, we'll have to sell the house and I'll go to work for that son-of-a-bitch, Kelly and those Hinkleys."

"Don't worry about that. It'll work out okay."

"I wish I had the guts to strangle that bastard. He's the cause of all this. If it weren't for people like him, people like the Hinkleys couldn't do this kind of nonsense."

"Yeah, and if you did strangle him you'd end up in prison. That would be great, now wouldn't it?"

"Sometimes I think it would be worth it."

"You don't mean that, Paul."

"But, I do."

⏢   ⏢   ⏢

Two officers, one tall and one fat, stood by the entrance to the main cell block awaiting the arrival of their new charge, Stumpy. Neither of the officers had much tolerance for the criminals they transported. More than once their charges had shown up with an extra bruise or two after they had been in these fellows' care. As soon as the fat one saw Stumpy coming down the corridor, he was reminded of the time when another prisoner had cut his face with a dirty knife. The wound had become grossly infected. The scar still snaked across his forehead from eyebrow to eyebrow. He already hated Stumpy on first sight.

As the cell block electronic doors were opened by the attendant, Stumpy came forward like he was out for a ride in the park. The two officers stared at him coldly. Both despised his proud airs. As soon as he cleared the doors, they wheeled him around to slap on the handcuffs.

"He's all yours," the attendant joked.

"Yeah, we got him," the fat one said and belched.

"Come on you," the tall one commanded with a shove.

The officers marched Stumpy outside towards the back of a windowless van.

"Hey, I gotta take a leak, man."

The complaint was ignored.

"Hey, I gotta piss."

The two men unlocked the handcuffs, pushed Stumpy through the open van doors and then slammed the doors shut behind him. The next sound Stumpy heard was the click of the lock. It was a sound he would soon get to know all too well.

The van started moving, and the officers sat silent in the front seat. Stumpy slumped over a bare bench seat in the back of the van bouncing around with every pot hole. Each bounce reminded him of his overfilled bladder. After about 10 minutes Stumpy couldn't stand the mounting pressure.

"Hey you creeps, I gotta pee. Now!" he shouted through the wire partition. The officers remained quiet, but the fat one did turn and leer at Stumpy through the grating.

"Hey, I'm gonna tell my lawyer as soon as I get to a phone."

At the next intersection the driver suddenly slammed the brakes to the floor, flinging Stumpy and his full bladder forward against the bulkhead and onto the floor. He rose in a rage.

"You bastards, let me pee. I got rights you know. I'll tell my lawyer to have you brought up on charges of brutality," Stumpy hollered. "If you don't let me out then I'm gonna pee right here." No response.

"Okay, assholes, don't say I didn't warn you."

A stream of urine splattered against the wire mesh partition. As the sound and odor of urine reached the cabin, the van was wheeled abruptly off the highway and stopped quickly on an obscure gravel road, throwing Stumpy forward onto the floor. The officers stepped from the van without uttering a word. Stumpy rose from the floor, wet with his own urine. He could hear the door lock twisting. As the door swung open, the two officers entered the van with a grunt. "I been waitin' to do this," the tall one sneered as he drew back his fist and punched Stumpy square in the nose. Blood erupted and mixed with the urine. Stumpy had only a few body fluids remaining to provide a complete sample.

He covered his face as fists, kicks, punches, pain and blood engulfed him. When the officers had sufficiently released their pent-up anger, they paused.

"Whew, I'm plum tuckered out," the fat one said later, as he leaned back in his seat in the front of the van.

"Yeah, me too."

"I remember when I could beat the hell outta somebody twice as long without gettin' tired."

"Yeah, those were the days."

"We're getting too old to do our job. Maybe I'll cut back and lose a few pounds."

"Yeah."

Stumpy was delivered to Carlson Prison — swollen, bleeding and complaining.

"Hey, they done beat the crap outta me man. You gotta do something. Them two. They knocked my teeth loose," Stumpy said, struggling to break free with both arms.

"Settle down or I'm gonna club you myself," the official returned and looked at Stumpy quizzically.

"Officers, do you hear what this man has said about you?" he asked.

"He should be so lucky," the fat one said. "We were near an intersection on 61 when this pickup ran a stop sign. It was all I could do to avoid an accident. We told him back in Memphis to stay put, but naw, he was up yappin' and pacin'. When I braked, he fell against the wire. Damn shame, innit? Cost the taxpayers all that money jus' to bandage that pretty face of his."

"Yeah," the jailer agreed. "Damn shame."

CHAPTER SIXTEEN

Jo Ann pushed the sugar bowl tightly against the napkin dispenser and aligned the salt-and-pepper shakers squarely in front of them. The cafe had been emptied by the 3:00 sun burning through the west plate-glass window.

Someone had said earlier that his front porch thermometer read 101. The old wall-banger air conditioner groaned and dripped as hard as it could, but the heat from the noon rush had made the cafe impossibly hot. Jo Ann wiped off the worn countertop and turned to look at her reflection in the shiny, metal towel dispenser.

"Whew, it's hot," she said to herself, offering the dispenser a smile full of crooked teeth and brushing back her red hair. She moved closer to check her eye makeup. "Yep, just as I suspected. It's done got so hot my mascara's a'runnin'. A girl can't be glamorous in this kinda weather." She was alone in the cafe; the cook had gone out. She fumbled through her purse, gathering a handful of tiny compacts, pencils and brushes. Peering into the dispenser, she strained to repair the damage. Its wavy reflection did her a favor. She almost looked pretty.

The old cafe door screeched open slowly. Jo Ann saw the reflected figure of a man dressed in black. "He's either a preacher or Johnny Cash," she thought to herself.

Completing her reconstruction, she turned to greet him.

"Howdy, there. What can I git for you on this hot afternoon?"

"Afternoon, ma'am. How 'bout a Pepsi with lots of ice." The man in black spoke with a clear deep voice. He seated himself on the round, vinyl counter stool, propping his chin up by his elbows.

"Here ya go," said Jo Ann. "Need a little something to eat with that Pepsi?"

"No. This'll do."

Jo Ann began wiping out glasses and the dark stranger sat silent, sipping.

"Shore is hot out there, ain't it?" Jo Ann offered from the far end of the counter.

The stranger looked at her and nodded.

"I ain't never seen you 'round here. You new in town or just passin' through?"

"Just passin' through."

"What brings you to Byhalia?"

"I come to see one of my brethren down at the county jail. He got drunk and got himself locked up. His wife asked me to help."

"They gonna let him out?"

"Well, the sheriff said he could go if his wife posted bond, but otherwise he's got to stay till the judge comes on Thursday."

"I hate them jails."

"Sounds like you know somethin' bout 'em."

"I ... I got a boyfriend in over at Carlson. I go visit him once or twice a week. He shouldn't oughta be in there. He didn't do nothin' he wasn't supposta. ... "

"Then why's he in Carlson?"

"Well, Preacher — you are a preacher, ain'tcha?"

He nodded.

"They say he tried to kill a man — well he did really, but

that man deserved to die. There ain't no justice in this world, Preacher. Lettin' men like my Jack go to jail and that old pervert goin' to therapy. There ain't no justice at all."

Jo Ann fell silent. She looked through the plate-glass window across the dusty street, and further still. Her thoughts took her back to something very painful. Her face changed. She turned to the preacher. Looking him in the eye, she spoke from her heart. "Jack Kempner has been my boyfriend for almost eight years. I think I know him pretty good. His wife left him one night 10 years ago with two kids, a boy and a girl, without so much as a thank you very much. It ain't been easy for him. But Jack, he's a honest man, Preacher. He's been doin' the best he can to raise those kids and work that farm all day. He don't have any help. Anyway, I got to know him and we sorta took to one another, you know? And one night we went to the movies and when we come home, Jack's uncle was ..." she stumbled, " ... he was messin' with one of the kids."

"You mean he was doing somethin' to his girl?"

"No. He was messin' with ... he was doin' it to the boy. Jack beat him up pretty bad, Preacher, and both he and his uncle ended up in jail. After it was all said and done, they let Jack out. But he couldn't git it out of his mind, and he got madder and madder. I mean, his boy had to go to the hospital. Well, one day Jack takes his shotgun up to the jail and starts shootin'. He missed the old coot, but he hit a federal judge by accident, not bad though. They arrested Jack and sent him to prison. His uncle got out in a week, and all they did was send him to a shrink. It ain't right, Preacher."

"Now, Sister, the Lord will see that justice is done. Man cannot judge like the Lord will. He knows what was in the heart of a man, and He'll see justice done."

"Yeah? Well now his kids ain't got nothin' left but a prisoner daddy. First their mama runs off and now this.

They up there livin' with foster parents now. I see 'em once in a while. But I think it's gonna be all right. I think Jack's gonna be gettin' out soon."

"How's that?"

"Well, don't tell nobody, but he's got somethin' goin' with them folks down in Jackson that'll get him out if he's lucky."

"Whatd'ya mean?"

"I ain't supposed to be talkin' 'bout this to nobody, but seein' as you're a preacher and all ... see Jack seen somethin' goin' on down at the prison where they counterfeit money orders. He calls it the Post Office."

"Post Office?"

"Yeah, that's what they call it. I got the names of the ones sendin' in the money orders. Jack said to keep it till he gets them people to keep up the bargain and transfer him outta there."

"Do other people know 'bout this deal, like his family?"

"No. He ain't got no family. Besides, he ain't tellin' nobody nothin' till they get him outta that prison. He ain't stupid and I sure ain't talkin'."

"I hope he gets out soon, for the kids' sake." The man sipped the last of his soft drink and stood. "I'd like to stay and talk, but I must be gettin' back to my flock. How much do I owe ya?"

"Oh shucks, Preacher, nothin' for that Pepsi, but I would sure appreciate a prayer or two for Jack."

"You got it."

The heat was still oppressive when the man stepped into the bright, summer sun.

"I don't know how they can wear that black get-up this time a year," said Jo Ann, turning to the comfort of the groaning wall-banger.

△△   △△   △△

Summer was drawing to a close, and the boys would soon be returning to school. It had been six weeks since Carl's surgery, and he was feeling great. He had spent a lot of time with Jay and Stephen during his recovery, regularly losing to the two of them playing SEGA games.

The clock rang out at 5:30 a.m.

"Hey. Stop it." Jay wriggled as Carl delivered a proper tickling.

"Wake up sleepy-head, it's time to go fishin'."

Jay grabbed his blue jeans, pushing his small feet through. When dressed, he and Carl attacked the sleeping brother.

"Apple Jacks anyone?" Carl made breakfast.

In no time they were tooling along in the Suburban over the Arkansas bridge headed for Horseshoe Lake, fishing gear packed neatly in the back. A white Styrofoam ice chest squeaked and screeched with each motion. Inside were cupcakes, potato chips, root beer, Cokes and candy bars. Mosquito repellent, called "Arkansas perfume" by Carl, was secured behind the seat.

Carl had fished at Horseshoe Lake for many years and knew the best holes. The fish weren't big, but there were plenty of them, and they bit often. They drove up to the Midway dock and paid the $3 fishing fee. "Be careful about that ..." Carl shouted hopelessly to the running boys. They had reached the end of the pier that jutted out into the lake before he could gather his gear.

The sky was bright and the breeze cool. As the sun climbed higher in the morning sky, the corks bobbed and the fish were reeled in. The boys jumped and hollered, getting a bite every few minutes. There couldn't have been a better day for fishing. Carl surveyed the world around him and looked at the boys rebaiting their hooks with excitement. "Thank you, Lord, for giving me my life back a second time. It sure is wonderful to be alive again," Carl said to the sky. The beauty of the moment made gooseflesh rise on his arms.

⚖   ⚖   ⚖

Kelly had visited Stumpy at Carlson Prison twice in the past two weeks, and that irritated him. He found the ride from Memphis south to the prison boring and tedious, and he despised being surrounded by what he called the "bumpkins and yokels" down in Mississippi. This was Kelly's third visit, and he could only tolerate Stumpy for a grand total of five minutes. Stumpy was about to ask for some cigarettes when Kelly stood up and walked out. He snarled over his shoulder that he would be back in a week, and Stumpy better have gotten some information by then. As Kelly left the visitation room, Stumpy's voice came through the screen, "You arrogant son-of-a-bitch." Kelly never turned around.

He drove from the prison site to the administrative offices. The countryside was parched and dry in the late summer sun and badly needed some cool autumn weather. Kelly pulled up to the gate and telephoned the warden for authorization to enter. He sauntered into the office, offered an indignant look to the secretary and walked right past her.

"You can't go in there!" She said with her hands on her hips.

He entered the warden's office as she protested in anger. Kelly loved to ignore women who attempted to exercise control over him; he always found the effect it had on them amusing.

"Harry, I've been to see Stumpy," Kelly reported, lowering himself into a chair. "He hasn't gotten squat from Kempner yet. I'm beginning to wonder if he's really trying."

"Well, if it means anything, those lawyers from the U.S. Attorney's office haven't been back since last month.

They may be waitin' on somethin'," the warden replied, "but he's been talkin' to that woman of his every few days."

"Stumpy's supposed to be finding out this stuff. I'm going to give him one more week, and if he isn't getting anywhere by then, I think it's time to give him a better incentive. Maybe your boys could think up a few ways to get him motivated."

"You think Stumpy's the problem, or is Kempner just not talkin'?" Harry scratched his beard. "I've got somebody checkin' out his woman now."

"Maybe it is Kempner, but we can't rough him up at the moment. We can rough up Stumpy."

As far as Kelly was concerned, his business was over. He glad-handed the warden with his right hand, receiving an envelope full of cash with the other. He tucked the envelope inside his jacket, turned and left the office, not even bothering to close the door. As he passed the secretary, she stared at him coldly, hoping for a chance to give him the "what for," but Kelly never acknowledged her existence.

Meanwhile, back in his cell, Stumpy found Kempner propped up on a pillow, chewing on a wooden match and deep in thought. He didn't seem to notice the screeching sound of the closing cell door or the appearance of his cell mate. Stumpy stood in the middle of the small cubicle looking at Kempner and waiting for him to speak. Kempner remained silent.

"What you thinkin' 'bout, Jack?" Stumpy asked, walking over to his cot.

"I want outta here, that's what I'm thinkin' about. That's what I think about every day, all day long, dipshit. I thought I'd be outta here by now. But instead, here I sit, lookin' at you."

"How you plannin' to get out."

"Why do you keep askin' me that? What's it to you?"

"I don't know, something to talk about I guess. If it

works for you, it may work for me. I'd like to get outta here myself. You gonna break out?"

Jack Kempner sat up and looked at Stumpy. He remained expressionless for almost a minute. He wondered if he should tell him. "What the hell," he rationalized. "You know there's a thing goin' on 'round here that's gonna get some people in trouble. You've probably heard by now about the Post Office. Them lawyers want me to provide them with information, and they say they'll get me outta here if I testify."

"What Post Office? I don't know nothin' 'bout no Post Office."

"Some of the boys at the far end of block D get $10 money orders sent in to them by the loads. They take 'em and doctor 'em up for $100 money orders. Then they mail 'em back and get half the cash for their trouble. The cash ends up buyin' drugs, booze and cigarettes from the guards. Them people down in Jackson got wind of it and want me to give them the names and details. They tell me it's mail fraud and counterfeiting. Seems like a bunch of people could get in a lot of trouble. In return, they're gonna get me out."

"What have you told them?" Stumpy asked as he shuffled his feet.

"I ain't told 'em nothin' yet. They haven't made good on their promise to transfer me outta here. I'm not tellin' anything until I get outta here. I'd be strung up dead, suicide-like, if I stayed here."

"Man, you better be careful. How you gonna be sure those boys in the Post Office ain't gonna find out what you up to and come in here and cut you?"

"I got that all figured out. I wrote the names down all neat and tidy and got it out of here and into some safe hands. If anything happens to me, my partner on the outside will turn them all in."

"Yeah. I guess you pretty smart. I guess you got it all worked out. Unless somebody on the outside already know about yo' man out there and cut him too."

Kempner fell silent. He hadn't thought about that. He stuck the match back in his mouth and leaned back on his pillow.

Stumpy climbed into his bunk and began to think. He would like to see Kelly sooner than next week. The quicker he got out of there, the better he'd like it.

CHAPTER SEVENTEEN

"It's finally getting interesting," Kelly said to Jackson as they sat alone in the hallway. Hollywood Productions had sent a clutch of high-dollar LA lawyers to Memphis. This was their first meeting, and Kelly couldn't wait to match wits with the Hollywood pros.

"As you know, Mr. Kelly," one of the out-of-town attorneys began as they all adjusted their chairs in unison, "Hollywood Productions does not wish to argue this matter unnecessarily." The darkly tanned man spoke with a crisp voice. Kelly checked out his loose-fitting Armani suit. "But I must tell you, we are determined to go to court if necessary."

"Don't think for a minute that you've got a solid case," another Angeleno piped in.

"Well, fellahs, for not being worried, they sure sent a lot of you to Memphis." Kelly stood and slowly walked the length of the conference room. "My client has every right to share in the profits of your movie. By all accounts, she should have been the star. Now I'm not saying," he paused, drawing a breath, "that you boys don't have a point to make, but let's look at it clearly, shall we? My client, Karen Hinkley — young, beautiful, a promising career — gets treated by this incompetent doctor and, through no fault of her own, loses her hair. Then Hollywood Productions decides that the contract they entered into isn't valid without her hair. The contract, gentleman, that Hollywood Productions executives signed, said nothing about the condition of my client's hair."

"You know damn well they couldn't use a bald actress. For God's sake, she didn't even have any eyebrows!" a short, balding lawyer injected.

"And who are you?" Kelly asked quickly, putting him on the defensive.

"Wesley Martin," the man said, puffing himself up like a rooster.

"Well, Mr. Martin, I can think of a few — let's see, Sinead O'Connor and the lieutenant on that Star Trek thing, VEJA or something, and I believe …"

"You've made your point, Kelly, but this was a sequel to *Pretty Woman*, for crying out loud!" Martin shouted back, clearly indignant.

"Mr. Kelly," the attorney in charge said as he motioned for Martin to sit, "Hollywood Productions is not without its sympathies for your client, but we do not intend to write her a fat check."

"We can let the people of Tennessee decide on that, my good fellow, since the contract is legally in this jurisdiction," Kelly followed, undaunted.

"You haven't got a relevant precedent," said a fat attorney, wiping sweat from his forehead.

"Is that so?" Kelly shot back.

"We'll kick your Southern ass all the way across the Midwest if we have to," a sixth lawyer chimed in.

"Now gentlemen, I see it differently. I mean, a young beautiful girl with cancer, cheated by the bad ol' corporate executives at Hollywood Productions." Kelly shook his head and clicked his tongue as if he were telling a child "no-no." "I think the jury might even be convinced to increase the award, if I read public sympathy right. And gentleman, I usually do. Especially Southern public sentiment. Let's see," Kelly held up his hands, making an imaginary banner headline, "Beautiful Young Actress Cheated By Movie Mogul On Death Bed."

"She's not dying, and you know it," the tan one said coolly.

"Now gentleman, you know that we're all dying," Kelly grinned, including them all with a sweeping motion of his arm.

The lawyers turned to one another in a huddle. Whispers erupted like a tire puncture. The short one looked back at Kelly. "We'll cut a check for $500 thousand and forget about all this," he said in a generous voice.

"Now tell me, do I look senile or are you all just that stupid?" Kelly leaned over the table on his finger tips.

"I suppose $1 million would insult you, too," Martin spoke with intentional sarcasm.

"The suit was filed for the terms of the original contract, and that's what we'll take. Let's see, by my calculations, that makes the check somewhere in the neighborhood of $7 million, give or take a couple hundred thousand." Kelly glared at the tan faces. "That, of course, does not include the punitive damages, which I expect to be at least double that amount."

"Well, Mr. Kelly, we'll need to give this matter further consideration," the overweight one said, walking around the table to confront him. "But don't think I can't kick your ass any day of the week," he wheezed, stepping closer as turrets of hot air blew from his fat nostrils.

"Why, I'll take that as a challenge, sir," Kelly said as he stared straight back. "I'm looking forward to it."

◬   ◬   ◬

Carl kept his scheduled appointment with Dr. Greson at 9:30 Monday morning. It had been six weeks and he had learned his lesson about skipping appointments.

After he signed in, Kim, the receptionist, asked him to fill out the usual three pages of questions on insurance information and next of kin. In addition to the customary paperwork, a living will had been inserted. Carl read it through carefully, pausing when he came to the section that asked him if he wanted to be attached to any life-support machines or have heroic measures taken in the event of terminal illness. Even though Carl was better now, he had been in the grips of death twice. He concluded that it would be a good idea to sign, but it gave him an eerie feeling.

Carl returned the forms to Kim and started back to his seat. Suddenly, he became aware of the other patients around him. He had been so busy with the forms that he hadn't noticed them. When he turned to sit down, he saw the true face of cancer. Several patients sat with their loved ones. One man stared blankly at the floor, holding a wooden cane in his left hand. His face was expressionless and his eyes were hollow. When he was called by the nurse, his eyes turned sadly upward. He rose slowly and deliberately, and it was clear that when he walked, he was in pain. His elderly wife silently supported his arm as he took a few short steps at a time, paused to rest, and resumed his arduous journey to the hallway door.

In the corner, by the television, a woman sat in a wheelchair in a green and purple muu-muu. She also wore a matching green tube that delivered oxygen to her nose. The tubing circled around her ears and came together at her Adam's apple. It reminded Carl of the felt cowboy hats he wore as a child that fastened under his chin with a slip cord. The green and purple lady had swollen, red eyes, and she panted and puffed, pursing her lips to force just enough air through her lungs to keep her a light shade of blue.

She too had a hollow appearance. Carl thought to himself, "How can these doctors and nurses deal with this all day without going nutty?" Perhaps they couldn't.

Carl's name was called and he followed the nurse into the examining room. It wasn't long before Dr. Greson appeared in the door. He greeted Carl warmly, but he seemed tired. "Well, Mr. Wheat, how have you been since you got out of the hospital?"

"Call me Carl, Doc, and I've been fine."

"Splendid. I'll get your lab reports off my desk. See you in a minute."

As Dr. Greson turned to leave, his lab coat caught on the latch of the door, jerking him back into the room. He looked at Carl and they both broke into laughter. Greson realized that it was the first time that morning he hadn't been solemn. Greson hated days when he was tired before noon, but they seemed to be getting more frequent. He looked at the pile of papers and files on his desk. A week's worth of patients, and he needed to review all of them. He never seemed to catch up. He sunk down in his chair and thought with a sigh about his recent weekend in Nashville with Linda. "I've got to get away more often," he said aloud, closing his eyes for a quick moment's rest before heading back to the examination room.

"Well, Carl, it looks like your lab is fine. How is your appetite and bowel function?"

"Back up to speed, Doc."

"Good. Do you have any new problems or symptoms you think I need to know about?"

"No. In fact, I feel like going back to work. My boss said if you will give me a note, I can start back next week."

"If you feel up to it, I think it would be great for you. I'll want to see you every three months for a follow-up and be sure to call me if you have problems in the meantime. Don't take any medications without calling me first. There are medications that could damage your functioning kidney, and we don't want that to happen." Greson could hear himself reciting these instructions like a tired robot. He had always prided himself on his close relationships with his patients, and he realized he hadn't even been looking at Carl.

Attempting to get back in his old form, he patted Carl on the shoulder and said, "You seem to have a nice tan. Where did you get so much sun?"

"Oh, I've been fishing a few times."

"Fishing? I like to fish myself, but it seems I'm so busy lately I never get around to it. Where do you go?"

"Oh, anywhere's all right with me, but most of the time I go to Horseshoe because it's so close. I took the boys over there a couple of weeks ago, and we must of caught 40 crappie in less than three hours. Man, they were biting as fast as you could put a hook in. The boys had a ball. I had more fun watching them pull 'em in than fishing."

"I took care of Jim, you know," Greson said, hesitantly.

"Yeah, Becky told me you treated him real good. She said you did all you could do and more for him. She said you took good care of her and the boys too, and she didn't know what she would have done if it weren't for you and your staff. That girl's had a tough time, Doc."

"I know, Carl. Jim died real slow and had a lot of problems in the last year or so. She was there with him all the time, attending to his every need, but she never neglected the boys. She would bring them here to the office with Jim, and give them peanut butter and jelly sandwiches to eat while they waited for their daddy to have chemo. She's a real special lady. I'm glad she's got somebody like you, Carl. She deserves to have a happy life."

"I know she's special. I just hope I can make her happy."

"What's she doing these days?" Greson wondered.

"She's been working for a law firm downtown for about

10 months now. She don't like it much, but she has to have a check and insurance to cover her and the boys. I guess I shouldn't be telling you this, but she works for Marion Kelly."

At the sound of Kelly's name, Greson went rigid. He tried to compose himself and keep from saying anything nasty about Kelly, but inside he felt all the anger welling up again. He was visibly upset.

Carl knew immediately that he had made a mistake by mentioning Kelly. "I'm sorry, but Becky told me all about that mess. She thinks the world of you, and I know she doesn't like Kelly one bit." He was fumbling all over himself.

"You got any kids, Doc?" he said, trying to change the subject to something lighter.

"You bet," responded Greson, glad to have a chance to talk about something else. "I've got two girls and a boy."

"Hey, me and the boys are planning to go back and check out those crappie this weekend. Why don't you and your kids come along?"

"You know, Carl, that might be a good idea. It would give me some time with the kids and give my wife the day to herself. You've got a deal."

⚖   ⚖   ⚖

It was nearly 6:00 p.m., and the office was empty. Becky was going through a file cabinet in the small corner library. For the last hour she had been looking for a file that was supposed to be placed under "Escrow Accounts." She was so engrossed in her task that she didn't notice Marion Kelly watching her from behind. Kelly was on his way out the door when he walked past the library and saw Becky bending over the file cabinet. He couldn't resist stopping and having another little go at the Widow Summers.

Kelly leaned against the door frame taking in the sight before him. In an attempt to reach some papers that had fallen behind the file cabinet, Becky had managed to get herself in a most unladylike position. Her skirt, hiked up from the stretching, exposed not only the dark part of her panty hose but the white lace panties underneath them. Kelly stood quietly, smirking to himself. When he had committed the scene to memory, he cleared his throat.

"Oh gosh!" Becky gasped, trying unsuccessfully to straighten up. "You scared me."

"Working late, Ms. Summers? My, what a dedicated secretary you are."

"I promised Mr. Jackson I would have him a file by tomorrow, but I can't seem to find it," Becky said nervously, attempting desperately to reposition herself.

Kelly moved in her direction and squatted down to her level as he came near. Becky was half on her knees now, and off balance. She put her right arm back to brace herself and reached for the library table with her left. Kelly moved in uncomfortably close. He leered at her and placed his hand on her thigh. He started stroking her leg, feeling the roughness of her stockings. Becky couldn't get her balance and was unable to move away from him. If she tried to get up, she would have to get closer.

"Back off, buster," Becky said through clenched teeth.

"What? Are you going to kick me again, huh?" Kelly laughed. "You have nice legs. How about me feeling how smooth they are without those stockings."

"Look, mister, I'm going to scream at the top of my lungs at the count of three. One ... two ..."

Kelly grinned and stood up, holding his hands out in front of him. "Hey, I was just trying to help you up, Becky. Don't get all worked up. That is," he added snidely, "unless you're ready to do something about it."

Becky glared at him, and he turned and disappeared

through the doorway. She found her balance and sat on her knees, listening to Kelly retreat down the hall. Then she got up and closed the door. Sitting at the table, she put her head in her hands and breathed deeply, trying to compose herself. "I won't cry, I won't cry," she muttered over and over again.

CHAPTER EIGHTEEN

Two attorneys appeared before the desk outside the warden's office. "Can I help you?" the secretary asked, somewhat surprised by the unexpected visit.

"We want to see ..." She reached for the phone without taking her eyes from the two handsomely dressed men and rang the warden's intercom. The warden appeared at the door to welcome the strangers before his secretary had replaced the receiver.

Harry shook their hands and introduced himself before inviting them into his office. He acted like a politician about to receive a labor endorsement. Ushered inside, the lawyers each sat down, crossed their legs and set down their ubiquitous briefcases. "Now gentlemen, how can I be of assistance," Harry opened, locking his fingers together as if in prayer.

"We are here representing the U.S Attorney's office, Fifth Judicial Circuit," said the tall, black attorney with a Northern accent. "I have with me a court order from the U.S. Attorney to have one of your inmates transferred to the Mobile Correctional Facility." He leaned forward to offer Harry the document. Harry stood.

"Jack Kempner, hmm? Jack's a good inmate. I can handle this right away, of course, but what's the interest in

Kempner at the U.S. Attorney's office?"

"The office has not authorized us to discuss the particulars of this request, Warden, but he does send his deep appreciation to you for taking care of this matter expeditiously," the shorter one informed.

Harry sensed he was not going to pump any information out of these two and decided brown-nosing might be more effective. "What ever I can do for the U.S. Attorney, just let me know. I'm always available when he needs me."

The two offered a follow-up handshake and departed solemnly. The first attorney turned as he passed through the doorway, looking back at Harry. "I suppose the transfer process will begin immediately?"

"Get my staff right on it," Harry said as he nodded affirmatively.

Before the white, late-model government car had pulled out of the parking area, Harry was on the phone to Memphis trying to locate Kelly. While he waited, he ordered his secretary to gather his boys together to discuss the situation. "Oh, and get Luther in here, too."

⚊⚊   ⚊⚊   ⚊⚊

Three FDIC Inspectors waited in the bank foyer for an executive to escort them. They had come to audit the banking securities, loan and escrow accounts as a matter of routine. The Commerce Bank of Memphis was not the top bank in town, but it had designs to be. Secretly, the bank's board had allowed several influential and privileged members of the community to enjoy certain leniencies. As a matter of routine, the auditors unpacked their briefcases, secured a work area and set to work. One auditor was assigned to review the activities of all the existing escrow accounts that had exceeded a balance of $100,000 or had been notified of insufficient funds since the last inspection.

These included 620 accounts. The auditor adjusted his glasses and started his review of the first account on the list. He, like most bank auditors, was a humorless and obsessive man.

As the day wore on, the pile of accounts singled out for more thorough review steadily grew. One of these accounts was titled: Marion Kelly, Esq., Escrow Account. At the end of the day, the auditor requested that the banking staff supply him with complete details of this and several other accounts. He intended to start fresh in the morning with the files he thought looked suspicious.

△△　　　　　△△　　　　　△△

"Man, It must be six or seven years since I've been to the rifle range," Greson said as he drove his Land Cruiser along Walnut Grove Road.

"I come out here every few weeks or so if I can. It gets real crowded around deer season of course, but I don't come out here then," Carl replied.

"What did you bring to shoot today. I saw you had several long guns."

"I've got a Ruger .22 that I like to plink with. And I brought a Winchester .270 and my old Marine rifle, a Styer SSG. It's not the one I had in 'Nam, but it's the same model. I qualified with that SSG."

"That's right, you told me you were a sniper. That must have been a wild job."

"You bet it was. It took me a while to get used to watching men's heads blow off through a scope and knowing it was me that did it. But I eventually managed."

"How many? I mean, did you kill … sorry, it's none of my business, but …"

"I'm not proud of it, Doc, but I tell you, I must of killed about 45 men. It's okay though. I did what my country told me to do. I made my peace with God about it a long time ago. You know, the Bible is full of wars and killings that God told the men to do. I don't guess He's totally opposed to it, or he'd put a stop to it."

"Yeah, I suppose so." For some reason, Greson felt extremely uncomfortable with the conversation. "Could you teach me how to shoot that good, Carl?"

"I'd love to, Doc. Nothin' to it, just hold her tight, don't breathe and pull the trigger through real gentle-like. That's the key, pulling through gently."

"You make it sound easy, Carl."

"Well, the Marines trained me real good and I can teach you some tricks that'll improve your shooting 100 percent. Why, when I get through with you, you'll be able to blind a gnat at 100 yards." Carl grinned.

The targets, shaped like men, were positioned at various distances from the shooting cages. Unlike Carl, Paul Greson was not accustomed to the shooting range. Several times he caught himself drawing a bead on the black silhouette of a man and imagining that it was Marion Kelly.

They headed home as the long day was coming to a close. Carl's thoughts returned to the conversation of that morning.

"The first time I had to kill a man was the worst, but I didn't have a choice. It was the strangest feeling to be standing there wanting to see a man die." He paused. Greson could see his face in the dim light. He could see that even now the experience disturbed him.

"Me and two buddies, Dave and Jerry, were out on perimeter watch one night. Those guys were like brothers to me. We were told that the VC were on the move in that area, but we'd been out there for 15 hours with nothing. It was about 3:00 in the morning and we were tired of being crunched down in that hole. It had rained the day before and the mud was sticking to our boots like glue. My feet felt like they weighed a ton. We talked about getting out for a minute to stretch, take a pee and get some of the mud off. Jerry and Dave were all for it, but I wasn't so sure." Carl paused and fell silent.

"Go on."

"Well, we decided to get out for five minutes. We climbed out and started stretching and groaning, you know, like you do when you've been cramped up. I kinda walked around a bit. When I came back to the hole, I couldn't find either one of them. I called out quiet-like, but no answer. I was afraid to make too much noise. Then I heard screams from out in front of the perimeter. It sounded horrible. I was scared, and I screamed out. Then all hell broke loose. Bullets started whizzing all around me. I returned fire and just started running; I think I killed a couple. When I came to a clearing ..." Carl choked up. Greson reached out to comfort him, placing his hand on Carl's shoulder.

"When I got there, Jerry was already dead, lying there with his throat cut. Dave was being held by two Viet Cong. One had a knife at his chest, and the other was holding him by the neck. His head was down and he was crying out my name. 'Carl, help me,' I can still hear him say it. I was operating on pure adrenalin. I opened fire over their heads with an M-60. When they threw Dave down, I lowered the barrel and cut them to pieces. Man, there wasn't anything left of one of them. When I got to Dave he rolled over and said, 'Thanks, buddy.' At first, I thought he was all right, but then I saw a knife in his chest. I held him and called for a medic for five or ten minutes. By that time the mortar rounds had started falling, and there was no sign of a medic anywhere. Dave died in my arms. I loved that guy like a brother," Carl said, shaking his head, fighting back tears. Greson gripped his shoulder.

They sat quietly, lost in thought for a few moments. Then Greson said, "You did all you could, Carl. That was a very brave thing you did."

"Yeah, but it wasn't enough. If I could do it over again, I'd do more. I tell you, it's easy to kill a man who's got your buddy by the throat. It's easy as pie."

⟁   ⟁   ⟁

Kelly returned Harry's call by mid-afternoon. Harry was worked up about the visit from the U.S. Attorney's office. He pressed Kelly to do something fast. Harry knew he couldn't stall the court order for more than a few days. If something didn't break, they would have to take their chances and handle the situation.

Kelly canceled two afternoon depositions, one of which was scheduled to begin in his office in 10 minutes. The court reporter, opposing attorney and witnesses had all arrived and were waiting in the reception area. Kelly sent Becky in to deliver the news. She tried to break it to them gently, but one man had come all the way from Kansas. As she explained that they would have to reschedule, she could feel the daggers in their eyes.

As Kelly drove through the farmlands down Highway 61 to Carlson, the warden called Jack Kempner into his office. He wanted one more chance to sweet-talk Kempner into telling him what he knew before informing him about his pending transfer. "Sit down, Jack." Harry hollered out the door to his secretary, "Get Jack here a cup of coffee."

"Black's fine," said Jack.

"Heard from the Feds, Jack?"

"Warden, I told you. I can't really talk about that."

"I know Jack, I thought there might be something we could help you with. Well, at least I got that little outdoor work detail we talked about earlier cleared. You can start in the mornin'."

Jack really didn't care one way or another about the

outdoor work detail, but he supposed that any change in routine would be welcome, even if it was almost 102 degrees in the shade. He was so frustrated waiting for the Feds to move him, he was going nuts.

Jack thanked the warden for his trouble, took a few sips of the coffee and returned to his cell.

When Jack had gone, Harry sent for Luther. The warden told Luther to be prepared to take the necessary steps at any time. "But don't do anything until I say so," Harry warned. Luther was known for jumping the gun when given a job. He liked his work so much, he sometimes got impatient.

CHAPTER NINETEEN

Kelly faced Stumpy across the corroded, steel screen in the dingy visitation area. Stumpy was eager to tell Kelly the news from Kempner and speed on his way to freedom in his new car. The all-too-familiar, eight-by-ten cell was not agreeing with Stumpy. He leaned into the wire screen and whispered, "Man, I got what you wantin'. Kempner done told me what he up to."

Kelly leaned in closer. He could smell Stumpy's rancid breath. "You better hope this is the last time I've got to come down here, asshole. I'm sick of looking at your ugly face. Now, what do you know?"

Stumpy motioned Kelly closer with a crooked finger. Reluctantly, preparing himself for the noxious odor, Kelly turned his ear to the informant. "I know who he done told about this on the outside."

"Who is it?"

"His girlfriend. I think Jo Ann's her name. She's got a list or sumpin' with the names."

"All right, Stumpy. Fine. You just sit tight while I check out your story. I'll be back in a few days to get you out." Kelly turned to leave.

"Listen man," Stumpy said, banging on the screen to get Kelly's attention, "you promised me. I don't want you to forget. And, hey," he shouted as Kelly kept on walking, "I need some clothes."

Before Kelly left the grounds he met with Harry Fields. Five minutes after Kelly entered the warden's office, Luther appeared in the doorway and was motioned inside.

△△   △△   △△

The door to her old Ford moaned when opened. Jo Ann had long ago given up on having a decent car. She lived down a dirt and gravel road that would be hard on any vehicle. In the winter, the mud would get so bad that sometimes she would have to get a neighbor to pull her out with a tractor. In the summer, the dust would powder up and form great billowing clouds of grime and grit. The air conditioner hadn't worked in years, and she had to shut the windows because of the dust.

Jo Ann rounded the curve leading to her trailer, parked alongside a cotton field. Her nearest neighbor was two miles away. She had lived there for six or seven years and never even gave a second thought to coming home late at night by herself. She unlatched the door and entered the stale, poorly ventilated room. Opening the refrigerator, she took out her last bottle of beer and twisted the top off with a dish rag. "Damn, I forgot to pick up some more beer. Well, too bad, I'm not going back out there now. It's too late." Jo Ann talked to herself a lot. She'd lived alone for so long she didn't think anything about it.

She pulled off her shoes, plopped down on the couch, propped her feet on the coffee table and took a sip of her beer. She was wiggling her toes and admiring her coral-pink nail polish when she heard a knock at the door.

"Who in the world could that be?" Jo Ann said to the blank TV screen. She pulled back the curtains and opened the door. "Preacher!"

ᐃᐃ   ᐃᐃ   ᐃᐃ

Becky couldn't wait to get off work. She and Carl were going out dancing for the first time since his operation. In happier times, Becky had been known to dance all night. But that was a long time ago, and she was looking forward to staying out till almost morning.

When Carl got home from work, he fed and walked his dog, then rushed off to shower. He was singing Beatles' tunes at the top of his lungs. He hadn't felt this way about anyone since high school.

The evening started off with a perfect sunset. Carl and Becky walked along the bluffs high above the Mississippi River, holding hands and watching the big, orange ball sink into the rice fields of Arkansas. The two lovers, silhouetted against the crimson sky, held each other and spoke of nothing sad. As the night fell and the mosquitoes came out in force, they walked up the bluff to a riverside nightclub.

Before long, Becky and Carl were ordering their second bottle of wine. Somehow, the subject turned to her work, and eventually they began to talk about Kelly. The wine had made Becky careless. She seemed oblivious to the effect her words had on Carl.

"I never told my mother about that night at The Peabody, 'cause I knew it would upset her and she would worry."

"Why didn't you tell me?"

"I didn't know you then."

"Why are you just now telling me?"

"I don't know."

"What else happened?"

"Well, there was a time when I was in the library and got myself caught up under the table by the file cabinets. He came over and started rubbing my legs. I told him, 'back off mister' and he left me alone."

"Why didn't you tell your bosses or somebody about that?"

"Well, I did after the time he went in the women's bathroom and grabbed me under my blouse."

"What!"

"Uh huh. Pour me another glass, honey."

"Becky!" Carl stood at their dinner table. "What's wrong with you letting him do stuff like that. And you never told me."

"Sit down Carl, people are looking at us."

"I don't give a damn what people are doing."

"Sit down, Carl. It was nothing."

Carl sat back down tensely. "Tell me about the bathroom thing."

"It was nothing to worry about. I talked to Mary and she had me talk to the office manager. He told me he would have a word with him about it."

"I want to know what happened."

"If you must. It was late one afternoon, most everyone had gone home. I went into the ladies room and over my shoulder, just before pushing the door open, I saw Mr. Kelly looking at me. I went in and used the bathroom and when I came out of the stall, there he stood."

"Inside the ladies room?"

"Yep. He walked up to me real close. I was shocked he'd do something like that. He said he wanted to date me or something and put his hand inside my blouse. He grabbed at me and I slapped him."

As Becky spoke the last line she smiled as if she knew Kelly had been properly punished and Carl would be satisfied. Carl was not satisfied.

"That son-of-a-bitch," Carl stood again, this time knocking over his chair.

"Carl, what's the matter with you?"

"What's the matter? You don't get it. Man, what's the

matter with you, Becky? What did you do with Kelly? Have you been sleeping with him?"

"Carl! Quiet! And sit down. Stop making a spectacle of yourself."

"No, I won't. You are the one making a spectacle of yourself. I won't have a girl of mine being felt up by her boss."

"Carl!"

"I need some air. Here, you pay the bill." Carl threw money down on the table and stormed out, leaving Becky seated at the center of the dining drama.

After about an hour, and a walk outside, Carl was less volatile. Becky realized she had made a mistake, and it took most of their night out to put things right. Eventually, she convinced Carl to dance with her, which lightened him up considerably. They drank one or two more beers and went home. There was a definite space between them in the bed.

The next morning, Carl's first words to Becky were, "I want you to tell me about this thing with Kelly."

Becky, barely awake and somewhat suffering from the previous evening's excesses, sat up rubbing her eyes. "Carl, not now. I'm not awake."

"Well, I am. I've been awake all night, as a matter of fact. I can't get over the fact that you let Kelly do those things and didn't tell me."

"Carl. I can't, really. I need some coffee and a shower. Can we wait on this a while? Please."

Carl sat up in bed with his arms folded across his chest and said nothing. He had not been this angry in years. By the time they went to her mom's to pick up the boys, Becky was worn out and confused. She and Carl did not speak much the rest of the morning. When he decided to go to his house about noon, Becky could see he had changed.

Linda Greson stayed in bed longer than usual. It was Sunday morning and she could hear the children playing in their rooms. It sounded like the clash of dolls and toy soldiers. When her eyes opened fully, she shut them again while choreographing a long, full body stretch. It felt so good. She looked over for her husband and saw that his side of the bed was empty. The covers were turned back, leaving only a ghostly impression on the white sheets.

Linda rose, put on her housecoat, and started toward the kitchen. As she passed the hallway window, she noticed Paul's hunched-over back in the rose garden. He was wearing a blue denim shirt and faded jeans. A half bucket of orange, yellow, red and white blooms sat next to him on the ground.

Linda poured herself a cup of fresh coffee. As she made her way through the back porch and down the steps to join Paul, she could smell the sweet fragrance of honeysuckle. She walked along the pathway by the side of the house and came upon Paul slowly, reaching out and touching him on the shoulder."

"Good morning sweetheart. Enjoying the roses?" she asked, tousling his hair.

Paul turned to her and looked up. His eyes were red and swollen from crying.

"Paul! what's the matter?"

Paul wrapped his arms around her legs and rested his face against her knees. He began to sob.

"It's okay," Linda said lovingly, stroking his hair.

She stooped down to hug him and Paul continued to cry. The two sat with their arms around each other alone in the garden, their hearts joined together in pain.

"Linda, I don't know what to do anymore," Paul sighed with his face half buried in his wife's shoulder. "I just can't understand why these people want to hurt me." He sat back and looked into her eyes. "I mean, I don't even want to see patients anymore. I don't want to wonder if they are going to make up some story and rake me over the coals. I do everything I can to do a good job, but I can't perform miracles."

"Paul, look at me and hear what I have to say. You are not an ordinary person. You are a gifted, dedicated and capable healer. You give all you know how to and do the very best you can. You are the target of a money-making scam and nothing more. What those people think of you does not matter. They are not important. Their purpose in life is to cause intentional harm. Unfortunately, the world is full of people like that. I love you, sweetheart and I'll stand by your side no matter what happens." Linda lifted his face like she would if he were one of her children. A tear slid down her cheek.

Paul wiped his nose and eyes and turned to his rose garden. "Looks like the black spot is about to take over again. I don't understand it, I spray every two weeks with two different fungicides and it still comes back."

"We still have some marvelous roses, anyway. Let me help you cut a few more and we'll go fill up the house with them. I just love it when we have them everywhere!"

The morning silence was shattered by the sound of the two younger children, Jenny and Leland, bursting onto the scene. "Mom, Dad, Mom, Dad, Mom ... look what Leland's got," Jenny broadcast with her tiny voice. Leland held out his hand with a proud smile. Inside his tiny palm lay a dead mouse.

△△   △△   △△

Kempner saw Luther for the first time when he was boarding the prison van to go out on the work crew. He'd heard about Luther, a local yokel who supervised work crews on the highway. Luther was striking in appearance, tall and broad-shouldered with a belly that drooped over his dingy blue jeans and a cold, blinkless stare. Luther chewed tobacco continuously — he was usually seen with a streak of brown spittle at the corner of his mouth. Shaving was not one of his priorities, nor was bathing. When on watch over a crew, he maintained a minuteman stance, holding a lever-action 30-30 Winchester. Rumor had it he could shoot the head off a match at 50 yards. He could spit his chew with precision, too, and that's how he communicated.

Jack Kempner rocked and jostled back and forth with the other inmates in the back of the prison van. He could tell they were travelling down a dirt and gravel road. Eventually, the van tilted to the side and stopped. Their destination was a rural, wooden bridge that needed repairing. As the van doors opened, the lackluster, orange-clad workers ambled into the morning sunlight one by one. Each paused at the rear of the vehicle and surveyed the new work site before moving on. The rural Mississippi gravel road wound through several thickets, turned south along a soybean field, crossed the wooden bridge, and continued into rolling cattle farms. The cedar bridge spanned a steep bank and a muddy, stagnant, snake-infested stream. The pylons of the bridge had not been changed from the day they were set in place 20 years ago. The struts, however, were loose and in need of replacement. The crew started their task by cutting and pulling down huge vines of poison ivy.

"Hey, this is poison ivy," one orange-shirted inmate complained.

"Shut-up," Luther spoke and motioned him back to work with the barrel of his rifle.

"Ain't no use complainin' 'cause it don't do no good," another inmate told the first. They returned to their labor wearing the face of oppression. Jack Kempner worked quietly and steadily, wishing the warden hadn't been so generous with his "favors." The work was hard, and his nerves were frayed. Every time he looked up, he saw Luther looking straight at him with an eerie detachment.

CHAPTER TWENTY

Two of the FDIC auditors conferred for several hours. Before they left that day, they requested the Commerce Bank of Memphis CEO to provide them with copies of several accounts. The account over which they showed the most concern was that of Marion Kelly.

△△   △△   △△

Jack Kempner had not been outside the prison gates in more than two years. It had also been a long while since he'd done any manual labor. The combination of 102-degree heat, high humidity and hard work had brought Kempner to near collapse by 11:00 a.m. None of the crew cared to work too hard, but with Luther surveying them, they didn't dare stop until he gave them the sign.

Luther motioned at the crew with his rifle and spit on the ground. That was the signal for a rest and a water break. The small, orange army headed wearily toward an old Ford truck. On the flatbed there were four red water coolers; the inmates slowly and wearily lined up in front of them. As each man got his turn, he took long swills of water from a communal aluminum cup. Several put their mouths underneath the spigot and held the release button until they were full. Most splashed water over their sweaty heads as well. Little was said by the tired, sullen crew.

After the water break, the inmates separated into small groups and sprawled out on the ground in shady spots. Kempner sat by himself against the stump of a fallen tree. He didn't know any of these men well and he was not interested in socializing anyway. Suddenly, Luther appeared, startling him. They were not within earshot of the others.

"Wanna see a big snake?" Luther asked, looking down at Kempner and spitting. Kempner pretended to be interested. Luther motioned with his head and his gun toward the ditch bank. Kempner turned and walked along a pathway worn into the bank by locals who fished around the bridge's pylons. He could hear Luther treading along behind him. Luther gave him the creeps.

Kempner arrived at the edge of the brown stream and stood with his hands in his pockets. Luther stopped just behind him. Kempner looked around, not seeing any snakes. He turned to Luther. "Where's the snake?" Luther nodded his head without speaking, then propelled a bullet of dark brown tobacco spit toward the water. Kempner understood the instructions and turned to look in the direction indicated by the brown stream of spittle, keeping one eye on Luther.

Luther nodded toward the water again, motioning Kempner's full attention toward the water. Straining to discern if a stick oscillating with the current was possibly a snake, Kempner leaned forward.

"Where is it? I don't see no big snake. That's a stick in ..."

At that moment, a thick, brown, canvas feed sack enveloped his head in one fell swoop. Kempner started twisting and struggling to free himself from his captor, then he suddenly froze in panic.

Inside the sack a cool object with a rancid smell bumped against Jack's face. It seemed to Kempner that things were moving in slow motion. There was a sting, then a burning and then a horrible pain came across his face below his left eye. Kempner fell to his knees and let out a blood-curdling scream. A second strike, and the searing pain throbbed underneath his right ear. Again Kempner screamed in agony. Suddenly the sack was removed, and the loud percussion of Luther's 30/30 made Kempner's ears ring deaf.

The inmate, stunned on his knees, deaf and in horrible pain, saw the body of a large cottonmouth snake curl upon itself and roll. Its head had been blown off. The yellow belly of the snake, writhing, shone in the midday sun. The remaining crew and guards came running toward the sound of the gunfire. One at a time they froze in place as they spotted the sight of Jack Kempner on the ground. Jack had not moved. He looked up the bank's incline to see a dozen or so men looking down at him with horror. His eyes were swelling shut, and his head felt the size of a basketball. One of the guards came over to help him up.

"My God, what's done happen to you?"

"He needs to get to a doctor, fast."

Kempner came off his knees unsteadily without speaking. He felt very strange. The fangs of the cottonmouth had first struck Kempner below the left eye, pumping five cc's of venom into his face. The second strike, below the left ear, pierced deep into his neck muscle, depositing an additional three cc's of poison. The venom was quickly absorbed and began breaking down red blood cells in Kempner's vessels. As the process spread to his brain, it caused the tissue to swell within 30 seconds. No power on this earth could have saved Jack Kempner. He was dead before the crew could get him on the flatbed Ford.

"He was leaning over to pick somethin' up when that bad-ass snake just came outta nowhere. I killed him, but not in time," Luther told the inmates. He spit underneath the flatbed and shook his head at the sight of Kempner's face. It was swollen to the size of a watermelon, blue-black in color.

In an office in Nashville on the third floor of the Federal Building, the state bank inspector arrived at 9:00 a.m. sharp to find a fax from Memphis lying on his desk.

The report, filed by FDIC auditors, was regarding several accounts at the Commerce Bank of Memphis. During their investigation, the auditors had found more than one instance of impropriety involving escrow accounts and unsecured loans. It appeared that several laws had been violated.

By 2:00 that afternoon, the offices of the Federal Banking Commission in Washington were involved in the investigation.

Before the end of the workday, a clandestine call from Washington was placed to the Commerce Bank of Memphis. The call was received by the bank's chairman of the board, Richard Goldstein. He sat in silence as the voice relayed vital information. The call took 10 minutes. During that time, Goldstein spoke only one full sentence. He hung up and immediately placed a call to the Gold Coin Casino in Tunica. Victor Jennison answered his private line.

"Look, Victor, we've got some big trouble up here. I just got a call from the Federal Banking Commission in Washington, and it looks like the Feds are going to be investigating some of our files. This was not an official call, mind you. My friend up there didn't know all the details, but he did hear something about the escrow accounts of Marion Kelly mentioned."

"Damn. We don't need any problems right now. If Kelly gets nailed, he may disclose our LDC plan to the Feds. They may even trace his work into the casino accounts."

"I believe you're right, Victor. I think I'm gonna take a vacation starting next week. I don't want the press running around here sticking microphones in my face. You'll have to see to Kelly."

Victor hung up, paused a minute, and placed a call to Vegas. By the end of the conversation, a meeting had been set up in Memphis for the next day.

⚠️ ⚠️ ⚠️

Jimmy Kempner looked over the dash of his foster parents' car. He had never seen so many people at Aunty Jo's. As their car pulled up the gravel drive, the ambulance crew could be seen carrying a stretcher through the narrow doorway. The unmistakable shape of a body lay beneath the sheet, the face completely covered. That body had at one time restrained the soul of Jo Ann from flight. The Preacher had released it and her trailer had been thoroughly ransacked.

CHAPTER TWENTY-ONE

Carl placed a call to his friend and physician Paul Greson. Since their trip to the shooting range two weeks ago, Carl had begun experiencing daily headaches. He first thought the pain was due to his high-powered rifle, but as time passed he knew this was not the case.

"Hello, Carl. What's up?"

"Sorry to bother you, but I still got this headache I told you about and it seems to be getting worse. This morning I noticed I had trouble seeing the TV straight and my left arm feels kind of numb."

"I want you to come in the office today. Can you do that?"

"Sure, I'll be there this afternoon."

Carl reported in by the end of the day and met Dr. Greson in the examination room. After some innocuous small-talk, they finally turned to Carl's problem.

"So, what's the matter? What's this about headaches?" Greson asked, looking concerned.

"Doc," Carl still called him, "I've had this headache since we went to the firing range. I thought it was from the recoil of my rifle, but it hasn't gone away in two weeks. It's over the left side of my eye and it makes me nauseated."

The doctor performed a cursory neurologic exam and

checked Carl's eyes with the ophthalmoscope. Carl could see his blood vessels reflected in the tiny device. Greson had to get very close to Carl in order to do the exam. Even though they had become friends, it made Carl uncomfortable to be face-to-face.

Greson stood back and drew a long breath. "Carl, I don't see a thing wrong, but I think we should get a CAT scan just to be sure. Have you been under any extra stress here lately?"

"Naw, Doc, things have been going pretty well lately. Well, Becky and I did have a little spat, our first, about her working for that jerk Kelly."

"Don't get me started," Greson moaned, leaning back against the exam table.

"Well, I got outta hand really. She told me about him grabbing her in the bathroom at work and trying to rape her in a hotel and, well, I lost it. I said some things I shouldn't have. I'm kind of a jealous type anyway."

"I wish I could ring his neck for you myself."

"I want her to get another job, but she says she can take care of herself."

"You know, he takes every opportunity he can to harass people. I stay awake at night thinking about those depositions and what might happen in court. He grilled me about my family and everything else, none of which had anything to do with this case. I wish somebody would put him out of our misery."

"There's assholes like him everywhere."

"Now that's the truth. Well, we've wasted enough time on him. Let's get you off to the diagnostic center and have these tests run."

It seemed that all he did anymore was get tested. At the center, he was again herded into a gown and placed inside another machine. The CAT scanner was a large, round object with a hole in its middle — the gantry, as it was called. It was there that Carl placed his head under the crosshairs of a laser marker. He was instructed to breathe, not breathe, for more than 30 minutes. When the ordeal was over and the nurse told him he could crawl out of the machine, Carl felt like an emancipated crab.

△△   △△   △△

Within five days of the FDIC examination, federal authorities opened an investigation of possible criminal violations. In addition, the Tennessee Board of Professional Responsibility began a preliminary investigation into the activities of Marion Kelly. The Tennessee Supreme Court required all banks to report overdrafts in lawyer's escrow accounts. The Commerce Bank of Memphis had failed to report 17 overdrafts in connection with the Kelly account. The banking authorities were not pleased. In less than a week, "no comment" was spewing from numerous offices as various news agencies questioned them about the account. Kelly had made himself big news lately, and everyone wanted to know if he was in trouble. They also wanted to know how the latest developments affected the Hollywood and malpractice suits.

Marion Kelly dodged the questions of various members of his office. Several of the senior partners had been seen speaking in low voices. A quiet damage-control survey was conducted by a secret committee of the firm. These kinds of allegations might be damaging to the firm's client relations. There was, of course, a quiet, "good-ole-boy" way of handling such matters.

△△   △△   △△

Marion Kelly awoke at 5:30 a.m. He started his usual routine of dressing and warming up for his morning run through Overton Park. Today, Kelly was somewhat distracted by the recent turn of events concerning the escrow accounts. He had gone over the records several times, and the only other person who could access the escrow accounts was Richard Jackson. He remembered seeing him with the files in his briefcase. Kelly was convinced that Jackson had misappropriated funds from the account, leaving it subject to investigation.

Kelly ran along a thicket that bordered the golf course. He had reached his target heart rate five minutes ago and had 25 minutes to go. The park was usually quiet at this hour, and most of the people he encountered were "regulars." This morning, however, out of the corner of his eye, Kelly thought he saw someone with a black bag. He passed it off.

△△   △△   △△

The reporter shoved the microphone in Kelly's face as he entered his office building.

"Mr. Kelly, Cheryl Thompson with Action News Five. What does your firm have to say about the grand jury investigation?"

Kelly, caught off guard, paused and composed himself. "My firm stands behind me on this matter. We are confident that the grand jury will find no evidence of wrongdoing, and that this matter will be cleared up in a few days."

"What about the escrow accounts, Mr. Kelly?"

"I'm no banker," Kelly smiled into the camera, "but I think there has been some accounting error. I know the Commerce Bank is sorting those accounts out as we speak. It will all be cleared up soon."

"Mr. Kelly, what is the latest development in the Hinkley case."

"Of course, you know I cannot speak directly on this

issue, as we are about to go to court. I will say, however, that the counsel for Hollywood Productions has made conciliatory offers. My client does not wish to pursue any unnecessary litigation, but she expects ample compensation for her unjust losses."

"Mr. Kelly, back to the escrow accounts."

"I'm sorry, but I must attend a meeting." As Kelly turned to the elevators he could hear the reporter speaking to the camera, closing her piece. "I handled that pretty well," Kelly thought as the doors closed.

"It's tough being famous," Jackson said to Kelly.

Kelly turned to him; they were alone. "What did you do with those escrow accounts?"

"What do you mean? I have done nothing."

Kelly backed Jackson up in the corner. "I'll kick your butt out of the 22nd-story window if I find out you got me in this mess."

Before Jackson could answer, the door opened. They relaxed their grips on each other. As Kelly exited the elevator, one of the senior partners pushed the daily paper in Kelly's face and walked off. On the front page was an article circled in red. "Memphis Lawyer Charged with Professional Violations."

CHAPTER TWENTY-TWO

When Stumpy reached the prison van, he glanced around, only to be drawn like a compass needle to the cold stare of Luther. Stumpy hesitated and then climbed on board. The ride was as expected — bumpy, hot and boring. When they reached the work site, one of the old crew looked up at Stumpy and said, "Know what happened to the last new guy?" and grinned.

Stumpy picked up his shovel along with the rest of the crew and went to work digging out road culverts. By lunch break, he was worn out and wringing wet. By the time the afternoon sun had fallen lower and the temperature leveled off, Stumpy had given up thinking about his escape.

On the last water break of the day, he found himself in the back of the cooler line. Luther came up behind him and motioned with his head while spitting in the direction of the levy. Stumpy moved toward the levy with Luther following closely. Looking back, Stumpy could see that the other inmates had not noticed his departure. Nervously, he topped the crest and fell below the line of sight. Nobody could see him if anything funny happened. Stumpy was waiting for Luther to club him in the head with that 30-30 at any moment. Luther had not uttered a word.

Stumpy had just about decided to take a chance and run

for it when he saw a dark-blue Mazda parked in a clearing. He turned to look at Luther, who was right behind him. Luther spat toward the Mazda. "He could probably hit it if he wanted to," Stumpy thought. The car was about 50 yards away.

In the driver's seat was a change of clothes — blue jeans, green T-shirt and size 11 shoes. Stumpy wasted no time peeling off the orange prison clothes. Luther looked on with detachment.

"Hey man, you got any idea where they put the money?" Stumpy asked. Luther just leaned to one side and spat around Stumpy into the open window of the car. Stumpy saw the filthy tobacco spittle running down the side of a dark-red bag. He opened the bag, avoiding the spittle. The money was there. He felt a great sense of relief. "They wouldn't have gone to all this trouble if they were planning to kill me. Man, I'm home free now," Stumpy thought.

He climbed into the driver's seat and started the engine. "So long, Lurch," he called out the window as he sped away down the gravel road, watching the rearview mirror as Luther's silhouette became consumed by dust. Stumpy began laughing out loud. "Whew, hot-damn!" he shouted. He felt like he had just fallen in love, and he had — with freedom.

As he coursed along the gravel road with his arm out the window, he felt a sharp sting on the left side of his neck. Jerking around, he saw a big, red wasp. Stumpy hated wasps. He swerved the car and shoved his foot on the brakes. The peddle collapsed to the floor. The brakes were out.

Luckily, he was traveling only 25 mph. The road ahead was loose gravel and curvy. A Kudzu-covered ravine fell to both sides and dropped about 60 feet. "So, that's it. Those bastards wanted to kill me after all. That Kelly is such a son-of-a-bitch," Stumpy spoke to himself. Then he laughed. He had fouled up their plans. He felt better knowing they had tried and he could rest easy now.

Seconds later, a dust trail appeared in his rearview mirror. As the trail grew closer, Stumpy could make out a blue and white Chevrolet pickup truck. He sat in the car, waiting to see what the truck was going to do. It approached at normal speed, but as it drew closer, it slowed and stopped several car lengths back. The Mazda was still running. The truck doors opened and two redneck white boys appeared with sawed-off shotguns. Stumpy was no rocket scientist, but he knew when to run. Ahead of him lay a curvy, gravel road and he had no brakes. Behind, double-Bubba with four barrels. No additional information was needed for his computations. The chase was on.

⚐⚐   ⚐⚐   ⚐⚐

Carl had fallen asleep on the sofa at Becky's house watching *Star Trek*, his favorite show. He drifted and bounced through scenes until his mind again fixed on the mission of the Red Major. Carl could smell the jungle with its thick, acrid odor and dense humidity and heat. Carl knew he was dreaming this time. Or was he? Marc was by his side on the ridge. The major was in the passenger's side of the open-topped vehicle. Carl drew a breath and exhaled. His finger applied slow, even pressure to the trigger. The shot rang out, and the back of the Red Major's head exploded. Carl kept his place this time in spite of Marc's tugging at his sleeve. He wanted to savor the moment of his kill. Carl had felt joy. He liked it. He wanted to do it again.

Carl kept brushing Marc away as he tugged on his sleeve. "Come on, man, we gotta get outta here!" Marc exclaimed.

"Go away, leave me alone," Carl responded.

"No suh, you gotta go." Carl recognized that voice. It wasn't Marc, it was George.

"George, George," Carl called out.

"No, Carl, wake up." Becky was shaking the sleeve of his shirt.

"What?" Carl sat up.

"Are you having that dream again, Carl?" Becky asked. Carl nodded. This time he had not wanted to wake up.

⚊   ⚊   ⚊

Dr. Greson sat in his desk chair and reviewed the previous day's X-ray reports. Most were routine, until the report of Carl Wheat appeared. The CAT scan indicated the presence of a tumor on the right mid-brain area extending into the brain stem. The tumor was the size of a walnut. Dr. Greson let the report fall onto his desk and cupped his hands over his forehead. As he rubbed his eyes, he let out a shout that frightened his office staff.

"Damn!" He pounded the desktop. "Why does it always happen to the nice guys?" the doctor questioned God.

The impact of Carl's report took a while to settle in. First, the doctor considered how and when to tell Carl the bad news. Then, he began to consider the best method of treating the problem. From the report, it appeared that the tumor had invaded several brain stem centers. That ruled out surgery. The tumor had also caused considerable swelling of the surrounding brain tissue and pushed much of it to the opposite side. Should he tell Carl before or after he had formulated a plan of treatment? Greson recognized, for the first time, that Carl was more than a patient — he had become a close friend.

Dr. Greson placed calls to his neurosurgery colleague and the radiation therapist. Both consultants arrived at the same conclusion: The tumor was not operable and would probably respond poorly to chemotherapy or radiation. Greson felt yet another wave of despair strike his core. Science had again failed to provide the answers he needed.

◿◺   ◿◺   ◿◺

Becky heard shouting coming from Kelly's office through the closed door. He and Jackson had been meeting for more than two hours, but in the last 20 minutes the noise level inside the room had risen several decibels. Accusations and blame ping-ponged around the hallway outside Kelly's door. The imbroglio continued to escalate until Kelly could be heard plainly. "It's all your fault!" he yelled. "You did this, you asshole."

"Look, Kelly, I don't have to take this kind of crap from you. You're in a bind and you just want somebody to blame," Jackson retorted. "Admit it. You just screwed up this time."

Several times during the argument, office workers who were headed for Kelly's office turned around and went the other way, shaking their heads and whispering to one another. Everyone in the office was starting to feel the heat.

In one great commotion, Jackson threw open Kelly's office door with a thud and marched out. He turned after a few steps and suggested that Kelly go forth and multiply, in so many words. Kelly stood, walked to his door and pushed it shut. His phone line remained busy for the next several hours.

A reporter from the *Memphis Daily* hovered around Becky's desk for about an hour after the fireworks. He had hoped to interview Mr. Kelly, but was turned back by a senior partner who had gotten wind of his presence. "This firm," he said, "is not in the business of discussing such matters with the newspaper." The reporter retreated, but he didn't seem the type to give up altogether.

It was late in the afternoon when Kelly's door finally opened and the irate attorney stormed out. He was scheduled to meet with Victor Jennison at 5:00 p.m. The day before, Victor had attended a meeting at The Peabody where the subject of Marion Kelly had taken top billing. The "concerns" so gathered had reviewed the problem extensively. They had concluded that Kelly would have to be silenced.

⚊⚊   ⚊⚊   ⚊⚊

Stumpy took the opportunity to spin his wheels in the loose gravel, hurling a barrage of road fodder into the faces of the oncoming Bubbas. He didn't wait to see if they raised to fire. He was mostly concerned with navigating the winding road without ending up in the ravine. Stumpy used the transmission to control his speed. He saw the blue and white pickup moving up behind him and closing in. Carefully, he increased his speed by moving into second gear.

As he rounded the first set of turns, he noticed that the truck had gained on him considerably. The Bubba on the passenger side was leaning out the window, pointing the sawed-off shotgun in his direction. Stumpy heard the weapon discharge. No hit. The other barrel followed the first with the same result. Stumpy increased his speed, even though he could feel the back wheels lose traction on the turns. The pickup continued to close. Several shotgun blasts struck the rear window, smattering it into a million pieces. As the glass fell away, Stumpy gained an undesired improvement in rearward view. The next blast could easily blow off the back of his head.

Deciding he better take his chances with the ravine, Stumpy shoved the car into third and pushed the peddle to the floor. The Mazda soon out-paced the pickup. The pursuing forces redoubled their efforts, and both Bubbas began blasting away at Stumpy's car from their side windows. That was their mistake. The complication of reloading the shotgun and driving must have been overwhelming for the Bubba in charge, because the next thing Stumpy saw was the chassis of the Chevy as the truck overturned and crashed down into the ravine. Stumpy geared down and drew a sigh of relief for the second time that afternoon. He had spoiled two attempts on his life in the same hour.

Slowly, now, he drove his way down to a small-town gas station, where he stole a new Jeep Cherokee in 40 seconds. As he pulled out of town behind the wheel of his new vehicle, he felt confident and in charge. "I'll teach that Kelly to double-cross me. I got a little message to deliver him about ole Stumpy. He ain't as smart as he thinks he is." Stumpy headed towards Memphis with the money and a cause.

CHAPTER TWENTY-THREE

"Hello?"

"Marion, this is Wilson."

"Well, hello. I was just about to call you. How is Washington?"

"Fine. The LDC application went through last week."

"That's really good news, my man. I'm proud of you for seeing everything put right."

"That's what I'm calling about. I'm coming to Memphis and we need to talk."

"Why sure. What's this about?"

"I'm not going to do this anymore, Marion. My nerves are shot. I had the FBI and the internal audit people breathing down my neck. I can't take it any longer. I'm not doing any more of your deals."

"Don't get to hasty, Philip. Relax. Didn't that little gift I brought help settle your nerves?"

"No. As a matter of fact I want you to take it back."

"Take it back! Are you daft or what? Take that money and go to the Bahamas for a long vacation. Live it up a little, Wilson. That's your problem. All you do is mope around Washington and take pills. Didn't your psychiatrist ever tell you to take a vacation?"

"I'm going to. I'm coming down to my grandmother's

farm this week. I want to see you when I get there. I'm bringing the money, Marion."

"You will do no such thing. I'll tell you ... hello? That bastard hung up on me."

Kelly dialed Tunica as he looked out his office window. He propped his legs up on his desk and tapped his chin with a pen while waiting for Victor to get to the phone.

"Victor? Kelly."

"Yeah."

"The LDC plan went through last week. I just heard from Washington."

"Good. Good. Everyone will be glad to hear it. Listen what's all this mess I read about you in the papers?"

"It's nothing, Victor. Just a little banking error, that's all. It'll get cleared up in a few weeks."

"You make it sound awfully simple. Why are they considering a grand jury investigation if it's just a simple matter?"

"That's routine, Victor, don't worry."

"Well, we do worry. My people are concerned. You are our man on the LDC deal and we can't afford to have anything go wrong, especially now."

"Why would anything go wrong?"

"When a big-shot attorney like you starts getting himself in the papers and TV, well it makes it open season. The press loves this stuff. Usually somebody will talk. I think we need to have a meeting. What about next Sunday, a week from now, out at the lake house. It'll be nice and quiet there and we can discuss a few things."

"Like what, Victor?" Kelly said, becoming suspicious.

"Maybe you should take some time off or lay low for a while."

"No way, Victor. I'm in my prime. I'm not going to cower over a few bad press reports."

"About that meeting."

"Okay, but I would like to meet at the Barnstormer bar, Sunday at 2:00 p.m."

"The Barnstormer?"

"Yeah, that's where we met after my Washington trip. I have to be at the airport anyway and it'll be quiet enough there," Kelly lied.

"That won't do, Marion."

"It'll do all right and I have to go. See you Sunday at 2:00 p.m."

Kelly had become suspicious about Victor's conversation and his invitation to the lake house. Jennison was beginning to sound like he may have an unwelcome agenda for Kelly. Kelly planned the meeting at the Barnstormer because of the airport security checks. Kelly at least knew they couldn't carry any weapons to the meeting. Being clever was the reason Kelly had gotten where he was.

By the time Kelly hung up the phone with Victor, Philip Wilson had taken 10 more Xanax and packed for his trip to Memphis. He planned to drive because he was afraid to take the money on board a plane. Victor had scolded several subordinates over his current misery with Kelly, and he'd developed a good case of heartburn from a greasy Polish sausage.

⚖⚖   ⚖⚖   ⚖⚖

Becky left work early. She had plans that night for a special evening alone with Carl. Even though she wasn't a gourmet cook, she had a few dishes down to a very tasty experience. Tonight, she planned linguini pasta with pesto sauce, fresh spinach salad, garlic bread from a nearby French pastry shop, red wine and a bouquet of flowers.

Long, late-summer, early fall shadows fell across the lawn at the back of Becky's house. Her porch was made of tongue-and-groove planks that were painted blue.

The bead-board ceiling supported several hanging ferns and a large, old ceiling fan, which made a slow arc and created a gentle breeze. In the middle of her porch sat a roomy wicker slider with too many pillows for comfort. The small back garden was lushly planted with flowers and magnolia trees.

Becky and Carl sat in the wicker love seat holding hands and watching the shadows alter the landscape. The early evening air was cool and fragrant from the smell of her late-blooming flowers. It was so quiet and peaceful.

"Becky," Carl said as he turned toward her, "I love you."

"I love you," she mouthed without speaking.

"I'm not really hungry, are you?"

"Yes, I'm starved, but not for food. I want you."

They fell into a long, tender embrace and kissed. Within a few minutes their passion overcame them. Like Handsel and Gretel's bread crumbs, their clothing made a pathway to the bedroom.

The sun's last beams, fading through Becky's window, created shadows reaching from the blinds to outline slender fingers across their naked bodies. They lay motionless on the white sheets, holding each other and thinking. Carl ran his hands through Becky's hair, and she traced circles across his shoulder with her fingers.

"Carl?" Becky asked looking through the blinds. "Do you think we could ever be married?" As she spoke the "heavy" word she turned to look in his eyes.

"I've thought about it," Carl replied without hesitation.

"Do you think you would have a problem taking on the responsibility of the boys?" Becky asked with trepidation.

"No, I couldn't ask for better children, but I might want to have some of my own some day," Carl added.

"That's okay with me," Becky replied in a soft, loving voice.

They hugged and kissed, rubbed and caressed, and then

made love again. The long, fading rays of the summer sun brushed across the lover's bodies, over the bed and onto the dresser, at last resting and then disappearing into the wall. While evening gave way to darkness, several crickets orchestrated a sunset symphony outside the window as the two lovers lay asleep in each others' arms. It was a perfect evening. Dinner sat lonely and forgotten on the table.

△△   △△   △△

"Hell no! I won't have any part of it. I know Kelly's causing lots of trouble, but that's going too far." The fat lawyer pounded the oak table with his fist.

The meeting of the 12 senior partners had been arranged on a Monday night to avoid suspicion. They had gathered to discuss the problem of Marion Kelly. A possible grand jury investigation, overdrawn accounts and ethics violations were the main concerns. Some members wanted to expel Kelly, but according to the firm's partnership agreement, this would be difficult. Others wanted to solve matters by sending him on a leave of absence. This idea was bantered about for some time and finally discarded. At the meeting's conclusion, the firm was unable to implement any significant damage-control measures. A small committee of three was appointed to continue discussions.

△△   △△   △△

On a service road just off I-40 near the West Virginia state line, an 18-Wheeler swerved toward the shoulder with its air breaks throbbing, tires smoking, and gravel flying in a cloud of roadside dust. Out of control, the big truck jack-knifed and overturned. The force of so many tons slammed the driver against the door, the inertia crushing his head through the window, and caused a great strain on his cervical vertebra. The trucker lay bloody, semiconscious and critically injured. He didn't move when the first police officer arrived; he was paralyzed from the neck down. The impact of his head against the window, countered with the motion of his body, had irreparably damaged the third cervical vertebra. The pressure caused the body of the bone to collapse, sending its fragmented destruction back against the fragile spinal cord. The cord was bruised, compressed and severed. The trucker would never raise his arms again to hold his wife. He would never again walk across the park with his little girl. A moment in time had changed everything he had known.

The dark-blue sedan, driven by Philip Wilson, did not stop until it reached a truck stop 10 miles down the road from the accident. When he opened the car door to get out, Wilson's knees almost buckled from panic. He had run a red light in front of the 18-wheeler. The skill of the trucker was all that had saved Wilson's neck, but only in exchange for his own.

Inside the cafe, Wilson ordered breakfast and washed down 12 Xanax with a cup of coffee. He kept telling himself that there was no stoplight, and that the trucker was at fault. He hoped the driver couldn't describe him to the police. His thoughts kept going to his grandmother's farm and the hope that he might be able to get his head straight there and figure out a way to get the money back to Kelly. What if the police stopped him before he got there? They wouldn't understand the $1 million in cash that lay beneath the spare tire in his car.

Wilson cursed himself for driving all this distance as he tried to drink his coffee. His hand was shaking and coffee was spilling everywhere. He wasn't fond of driving so far, but he had become more afraid of flying in recent months. His last flight had nearly produced a full-blown panic attack, in spite of a handful of tranquilizers. He was also worried that someone might want to see what was inside his briefcase. "What if they could tell it was money in that blasted X- ray machine?" he thought. Wilson gave up trying to drink the coffee, paid his bill and left.

He decided to stay over in a motel along the interstate, somewhere in West Virginia. Sleep came quickly after a half-pint of vodka.

CHAPTER TWENTY-FOUR

Dr. Greson's hands were shaking with rage. On his desk lay a letter from Lifetime Insurance requesting a detailed explanation of his malpractice suit. Until the review board could decide on the matter, he was suspended from filing claims with the company. "We are not suggesting that you stop treating patients," the letter stated, "but you will not be paid for any services rendered until the matter has been reviewed." Dr. Greson wadded the letter into a tight ball and hurled it across the room.

"Looks like about 32 patients from that carrier, Doctor," the office manager spoke.

"And all of them are active?"

"Yes."

"How much are we treating them for?"

"I've done a quick calculation and it looks like about 18 are on chemo, which is roughly $12,000 per week."

"What can we do?" Greson asked.

"Not much. Stop treating them or eat the expenses. You know the patients don't have that kind of money."

Greson canceled the rest of the day, needing some time to get a grip on his feelings. He called it a "mental health day." In the parking garage he cranked up his Acura. As soon as he was out of sight of the hospital, he floored the accelerator and squealed the tires. He drove until he found himself lost on a Mississippi back road. In his anger and frustration, he never noticed passing a black Mercedes. Inside was Marion Kelly, the architect of his woes.

ΔΔ   ΔΔ   ΔΔ

Kelly pulled up to the prison office area and parked under the shade of a lone oak. Shade, this time of year, was at a premium, and there were already several cars nestled up to the tree as if some magnetic substance attracted them. Kelly pushed his way through the warden's door, ignoring the secretary as usual. They were meeting about the botched release of Stumpy. The warden wanted to issue an APB on him, but Kelly was concerned that Stumpy might get loose-lipped and cause trouble.

"Well, hell, we can't just let a prisoner escape without doing somethin'. I mean, we gotta at least inform the county sheriff's department," Harry complained. "What if we send some of your boys out to find him?"

"I've been thinkin' about that, but we'll still have to tell the sheriff."

Outside, a white Ford sedan pulled off alongside a soybean field. The two occupants had been tracking Kelly's movements for days. A report of the day's activities would soon be sent Federal Delivery to Washington. As they waited in the sultry, mid-afternoon heat, a skillful company of field mosquitoes found its way through an open rear window. Their mission: to torture and exsanguinate the surveillance team.

Field mosquitoes are large, Bible-black creatures with white-striped legs and ruthless intent. Cleverly, they began to attack along the ankle line. The saliva they inject produces intense itching and burning that can last for hours. The two occupants were soon engrossed in swatting and scratching in a whirlwind of misery. They were so distracted that they never noticed Kelly drive away. The only thing that could compound their misery was the castigation by their boss when he learned that they had lost Kelly.

△△   △△   △△

"Miami Control, this is Delta, Mike niner niner four, L-1011, inbound from Guarulhos International, Brazil, do you copy?"

"Delta, Mike, niner-niner-four, this is Miami control, *squawk*, two-niner-one-zero."

"Roger, two-niner-one-zero."

"State your intentions Delta, Mike, niner-niner-four."

"Niner-niner-four is inbound for Miami International, one zero eight miles south, requesting vector."

The crew of the L-1011 prepared their passengers for landing at Miami International. On board was Catrina Dias. After passing through customs, she boarded a second flight to Memphis. She was scheduled to meet Alverto Sanches in the Memphis airport. The meeting was pre-arranged for the baggage claim area. It was 1:00 a.m. and the airport was virtually empty.

Catrina opened the men's room door off a side hallway next to the baggage claim area. She scanned the room. It smelled of urine and cleaner. Sanches was waiting in the last stall. She approached him.

"You're in the wrong bathroom, Miss."

"No, you are in the wrong bathroom."

"I thought you weren't coming. They told me you'd be here by 10:00 p.m."

"What can I say? Customs delayed us."

"Here's your baggage." Sanches reached out with a briefcase. Catrina took it and placed it on the floor.

She opened the latch, thumbed through the cash and inspected the handgun — a Walther PPKS. She attached the screw-on silencer, inserted a full clip and cycled the receiver. She stood, pointed the pistol at Sanches and placed a nine-millimeter hole in the center of his forehead. Sanches fell limp against the tile wall and slithered between the plumbing. Catrina replaced the pistol inside the brief-case and calmly walked out.

Catrina Dias was a native Brazilian. At the age of 19 she had fallen in love with a Sicilian. She met Piero Baroni at the feast of Nossa Senhora Da Chiropta. Piero's family had sent him to Sao Paulo to get him out of trouble with the La Costa Nostra in Sicily. Piero moved to Bexiga, an all-Italian neighborhood, and promptly joined the criminal elements.

After meeting Piero, Catrina became a woman obsessed. She was in a state of both infatuation and psychosis. She learned quickly of love, betrayal, hate, vengeance, violence, guns and jealousy. She devoted herself to him, body and soul. She made love to him, cradled him, worshipped him, fought with him and killed for him. Every move he made, Catrina was there — the fights, the killings, the ruthless-ness, the deals, the money and, of course, the passion. In time, Catrina became a clever, capable and merciless assas-sin.

Catrina was a slender, dark-complected beauty with long, curly hair. Her 28-year-old figure was extremely fit from four hours of daily exercise. Her work required that she be strong, and Catrina was continually honing her skills. After Piero's murder, she became devoid of emotions. She looked eagerly for an opportunity to kill. These days it was the only time she felt anything. Catrina was a lioness.

The dossier she had studied was that of a Memphis attorney. She had memorized his schedule, hangouts, acquaintances, girlfriends and habits. She had reviewed the video sent to her often enough to see him with her eyes closed. She knew she was the best, and that's why they had chosen her for the job.

⟁⟁   ⟁⟁   ⟁⟁

Greson called Carl at work. Carl was surprised to hear from him. He was afraid there was bad news from his test, but his fears were soon relieved when Greson asked him to go fishing the next morning, just the two of them.

As daylight broke, they were on their way across the Arkansas bridge, headed for Horseshoe. Paul seemed rather quiet to Carl. "Maybe it's too early in the morning for Doc," he thought. They arrived at the boating dock and unpacked their gear. Carl lumbered up the pathway to the bait shop. The old codger who ran the store had lived there 52 years.

"Mornin," the old man gummed out his words.

"Mornin," Carl replied, smiling.

"They're bitin' like crazy the past few days. 'Em boys down at the gas station told me they caught 82 yesterdee. I ain't never seen nothin' like it."

Carl looked at Paul and grinned.

"They bitin' crickets real good, ye wanna mess of 'em?" The old codger held up a handful.

"Yep," Carl agreed.

When the fishing started, it was apparent the old geezer was right. The fish were biting one right after another. The morning seemed to fly by. The two fisherman barely had enough time to manage their catch, let alone chat. As the morning sun climbed to 10:30, the fish quieted down. Carl and Paul had gotten hungry and agreed to go the bait shop and have a sandwich. The old man kept bologna, cheese, bread, mustard, tomatoes, pickles, sardines and crackers, along with assorted cold drinks for the fishermen.

The two looked on as the old man wrapped the sandwiches in white butcher paper. The cheese and bologna were sliced so thick, they looked like layers of plywood.

Carl looked over at Paul as if to say, "I hope he washed his hands clean of crickets before he made my sandwich." The two hungry fisherman took their sandwiches and a couple of Pepsi Colas down the trail to a tired, old, majestic oak, found a grassy spot, settled in and unwrapped the paper. Carl took the first big bite.

"How is it?" Paul inquired.

"Not bad," Carl managed around his mouthful.

"Man, we sure tore them up this mornin'. I bet your boss won't believe it when you tell him."

"I guess we oughta take a picture."

"Good idea. I've got a camera in the car. We can get the old man to take it for us when we get them all laid out."

"Okay," Carl agreed. "Say, you never told me about the test I had the other day." Carl looked at Greson. The doctor seemed to be avoiding eye contact.

"Yeah, I was going to tell you and I got all caught up in fishing."

Carl sensed a diversion. "Is there something wrong?"

Paul looked at Carl, then away. He fumbled with the tab on the Pepsi can, remaining quiet and collecting his thoughts. He had been telling patients the bad news for 12 years, but it had never gotten any easier. This time, the words he would have to speak were choking him.

"The cancer's back, Carl. I wanted to tell you sooner, but I, well, I just couldn't." Paul spoke toward the ground. Looking up at Carl, he said, "It's spread to your brain, Carl, and there's nothing we can do about it."

"What do you mean?" Carl shot back.

"I mean, Carl, it's in a part of your brain that can't be operated on. The only thing I know of is radiation treatments, which we can start right away. With any luck, the tumor will shrink some."

"You mean there's still a chance to kill it?"

"No, but it'll slow it down."

"How long have I got, Paul?" It was the first time Carl had called the doctor by his first name. His eyes were forlorn and tearful.

"Maybe three months." Paul said the words as clearly and strongly as his feelings would allow. He saw Carl's face change. His shoulders seemed weighted down by tons of pressure.

"Carl," Paul spoke softly, looking into the sad eyes, "you're my friend, my dear friend, and I'll be there with you the whole time."

Carl leaned forward and the two men embraced under the comfort and shade of the tired, old oak. They never got the old man to take their picture. Paul always regretted that.

CHAPTER TWENTY-FIVE

Kelly began his usual run along the thicket next to the Overton Park golf course, except this time it was late afternoon. When Kelly felt stress he sometimes worked out with weights in the morning and then ran late in the afternoon. He was thinking about getting some help from Jennison with his trouble. It seemed that every week the investigations broadened and the allegations multiplied. His attention was distracted from his misery when out of the corner of his eye he saw another jogger along an intersecting course.

The jogger was tall, slender, muscular and female. She ran with seeming comfort and grace — her movements fluid and precise. Her course placed her directly in front of Kelly, about 10 yards ahead. Kelly admired her shapely figure. He picked up his pace to come alongside her. The closer he got, the more beautiful she became. He moved up until he could see the side of her face. She was dark, mysterious and smooth-skinned.

"Hey," Kelly managed while panting.

The lady jogger looked over her shoulder at Kelly and broke a minor smile, acknowledging his presence. Kelly kept up his pace. He had been intrigued by her eyes when she looked over.

"I've never seen you — are you new around here?" Kelly puffed.

She looked toward him again and then picked up her pace. Kelly increased his to keep up. She ran faster until she was in a full sprint. Kelly was getting tired and when he realized he couldn't maintain this level of speed, began to drop back slowly. The shapely figure distanced herself and disappeared. Kelly felt a strange sensation watching her fade away. It was the same feeling he used to get when his mother turned away from him as a child. But Kelly had conveniently forgotten all that through the years. The strange sensation he felt was never consciously identified as rejection.

ᐃᐃ   ᐃᐃ   ᐃᐃ

Becky closed the door to Carl's hospital room. Dr. Greson had admitted him for his radiation treatments and nausea.

"Can I get you anything?"

"No. I'm okay. I'm too sick to my stomach to eat anything."

Dr. Greson entered the room. "How's my favorite patient today?"

"Okay," Carl responded. "I need to ask you some questions."

"Sure, Carl. What's on your mind?"

"As I understand it, I got this tumor in the middle of my brain. It is mashing on some nerve or other that keeps making my arm hurt and go numb. This radiation treatment I'm getting is gonna make the tumor lay off and not mash on it so bad, right?"

"Pretty much, that's the plan, Carl. The tumor is in a deep part and it is causing swelling. The radiation will hopefully reduce some of that swelling."

"Doc, how long will I be able to use this arm?"

"I don't know, Carl. I hope this treatment will help that problem," Greson guessed.

"I need to get out of here. I have some things I need to do. When will you let me go?"

"In a few days you will have completed the first treatment and the IV medications I ordered. So you can plan on being out soon."

"Becky and I want to get married. We decided last night. We thought of doing it today, here."

"Congratulations!" Greson spoke awkwardly. "I think that's wonderful." Secretly, he was not so sure.

"Can the hospital chaplain do that?" Becky asked.

"I don't see why not. I'll be happy to call him for you. He's a real nice guy."

"Thanks," Carl offered.

ᐃᐃ   ᐃᐃ   ᐃᐃ

Stumpy drove the stolen Jeep to North Memphis. He had friends that were still in the business and he had to dump the Jeep.

"Whoa! Wha'cha doin' here, man? I thought you be in prison," the black youth barked.

"Not so loud," Stumpy scolded and looked around nervously. "I busted out. Where's Rastaman?"

"He's in the office." the youth motioned with a greasy car part.

Stumpy walked across the dirty concrete floor. The chop shop, littered with metal fragments, mud, spent welding rods and bolts, was dark and grimy. Around him was the occasional spark of a welder, the clank of a fallen wrench and distorted rap music from an old radio. Stumpy entered the door of an office constructed inside the warehouse like a plywood shelter. When the door opened, smoke tornadoes formed in its wake.

"Stumpy, my mahn." Rastaman grinned. "Haven't seen you in some time. Have a toke of de splif mahn." He handed him a joint the size of a small pocket flashlight.

"No. I need to do some business. I got a Jeep out here and I want a clean car."

"Why you bring dat ting to me, mahn?" Rastaman leaned back in the crater-marked, seed-burned chair.

"I don't have a shop anymore. I got busted, remember?"

"Oh yeah, I comin' wit' you now, mahn. Extreme, very extreme." Rastaman rolled his red eyes at his fat companion across the room. "What can de Rastaman do to relieve your struggle?" he crooned, pushing back his dreadlocks.

"I need a fast car, a gun and somewhere to stay for a few days."

"Sounds like you be lookin' for a demon, brother," he paused. "When you find 'dis demon, what you gonna do?" Rastaman was clearly amused.

"I'm gonna tear out his heart." Stumpy clenched his fist in front of his snarled face.

Rastaman picked up a brown straw figurine and danced it before him. "Sounds like you be needin' some voodoo magic. Yes, mahn. Voodoo Magic, mahn." Rastaman let out a long, sinister laugh and twisted the head off the figure.

⚐⚐   ⚐⚐   ⚐⚐

The room had two bouquets of flowers, one from Greson's office and the other from the floor nurses. The chaplain, dressed in his usual black and white, was rusty at weddings. As a matter of fact, he hadn't done one in eight years. Becky had dressed in an ankle-length, flapper-style dress. She wore her mother's old pearls and a pair of cameo earrings she had purchased the day before. Carl had managed, with some help, to squeeze into his Marine dress uniform. The nurses had snaked the IV through the sleeves with exceptional skill. Carl and Becky had decided to use Becky's old wedding rings to save money.

Becky had persuaded the chaplain to make the service short and simple. The boys were absent; Becky had decided it would be too confusing for them. In the hallway outside the hospital room, a cluster of nurses and attendants looked on. Weddings were uncommon in cancer units.

The chaplain stood underneath the hanging TV. The bed had been shoved to one corner. Becky stood by the window at Carl's side. He had his arm wrapped around the IV pump. The nurses hoped it wouldn't beep during the ceremony.

"Beloved," he opened, "we gather here today to celebrate the consecration of a holy marriage. This courageous man and woman stand now before God Almighty and dedicate themselves to a life of love and respect." The priest paused for a moment and looked around. "Do you, Carl Wheat, take this woman, Becky, to be your lawfully-wedded wife?"

"I do, sir," Carl replied, feeling military in his uniform.

"And Becky Summers, do you take this man, Carl, to be your lawfully-wedded husband?"

Becky looked up at Carl with tears in her eyes. "I do."

"Please exchange your rings."

Becky took Carl's hand and placed Jim's ring on his little finger, the only one it would fit. She had to help Carl place hers. They looked at one another, both tearful and silent. The world felt suspended in time, like the morning at the pool when they first made love.

"By the power vested in me by the State of Tennessee," the chaplain interrupted, "I pronounce you husband and wife." He nodded his head. "You may kiss the bride."

Becky reached up and took Carl's face in her hands. They kissed with meaning. The small gathering outside the room erupted into cheers, trying to be as merry as possible under the strange circumstances. Several other patients and on-lookers had joined in while Greson stood in the corner. Tears fell freely from his cheeks.

When the cheering faded, the nurses rolled in a wedding cake on a small tray table. Paper plates were passed and everyone extended their congratulations to the newlyweds as if a darker day did not loom before them. Dr. Greson stayed the longest. He was amazed at the courage he witnessed in his patients. A wedding on a cancer ward signified a special human spirit.

"What?" Greson asked, turning to the head nurse who was pulling on his arm.

She motioned with her head, "Come on, Doctor, you've got work to do."

"What do you mean?" Greson seemed surprised.

"Wake up," she scolded. "They're newlyweds. Get it? It's their honeymoon!"

The nurses made a banner they taped across the closed doorway to Carl's room that said, "Just Married."

Becky helped Carl out of his uniform. "Husband, you look ever so handsome," she whispered, making Carl proud. Once she had him mostly undressed and in bed, Becky began to slowly undress herself. She was afraid that Carl might feel obligated to make love even if he didn't feel up to it.

"Sugar, I just want to lie in the bed and hold you. I know you don't feel well, so don't worry about me. I will be very happy just to hold you tight."

"Yeah, I'm sorry. I think that'll be real nice. I'm too much man for you anyway." Carl managed a wink.

Carl watched his new bride undressing, admiring her beauty and feeling nervous.

"Carl, I talked to the nurses. No one will be bothering us unless we press the call button. I don't have to stay long if you feel bad." She wanted to protect Carl's feelings.

They lay together with Becky holding Carl close and Carl stroking her hair. They did make love. Softly, gently, lovingly and for the last time.

CHAPTER TWENTY-SIX

On his usual jogging route, Kelly rounded the golf course and ran near the Brooks Museum of Art. Up ahead, he saw "that girl" jogger headed for the small sitting area off the front steps of the museum. He altered his course to intercept her. As he approached, she was stretching her hamstrings on a park bench.

"Hi," Kelly spoke, somewhat out of breath.

She looked up at him and smiled.

"I've seen you out here several times lately. You're a good runner."

"I try to keep in shape," she replied coolly.

"My name is Marion Kelly," he offered with an extended hand.

"I'm Catrina, Catrina Dias." She shook his hand.

"Where are you from?"

"Brazil."

"Do you live in Memphis now?"

"No, I'm here on business."

"You run every day?"

"Every day."

"You look very fit," Kelly said. Catrina only rubbed her shin.

"Would you like to have lunch today?"

"I'm sorry, Mr. Kelly, but I have business to attend to today. Perhaps another time." She flexed her leg muscles. "I must be going now. Nice to meet you." Catrina turned and began to jog, leaving Kelly on the park bench to watch her bouncing figure diminish around the edge of the golf course.

Kelly thought about her beauty. He wanted her. He sat fantasizing about her until his thoughts drifted to the recent allegations regarding the escrow accounts. He needed a way out of this one.

△△   △△   △△

"Good morning Carl. How are you feeling today?" Dr. Greson asked.

"Outside of trying to eat this hospital food, pretty good."

"I see you've been to radiation treatment already today. How's that going?"

"I don't mind it, Doc. I'm a little sick to my stomach, but that's all."

"I'll give you something for that," Greson said, writing in the chart. He turned and sat on Carl's bed. "How are you really doing, buddy?"

"I'm okay, really. I feel bad for Becky. She shouldn't have to go through this again. I thought of being mean to her and making her leave me alone, but I wouldn't know how."

"She's a tough girl, Carl, she can take care of herself."

"Yeah, but it isn't fair."

"What is fair in this world, Carl? Certainly nothing in my business. It seems to me that the jerks of this world never get sick. You know the saying, 'Only the good die young.'"

"I've lived longer than I was supposed to anyway. I mean, I should have died in Vietnam. Hey! I've got a joke you'd like. A girl down in X-ray told me."

"Sure."

"What do you do if you're in the room with Adolf Hitler, Benito Mussolini and a lawyer, and your gun only has two bullets?"

"Shoot yourself?" Greson laughed.

"No, you shoot the lawyer twice."

Carl and Greson laughed and for a moment forgot the painful reality. Then Greson looked solemnly at Carl. "I really consider you a kindred spirit, Carl. I mean, for not knowing you any longer than I have, I feel very close to you."

"Me too. I'm sorry I'm gonna wimp out on you."

"Let's not think of that now."

"I don't have long, do I?"

Greson looked deep into Carl's eyes. He reached out and gave Carl a hug before starting to speak. They held tight for several minutes. There were tears, but no other words.

⏶⏶   ⏶⏶   ⏶⏶

Stumpy reached his sister-in-law's house unnoticed. Rastaman had set him up with cash, a new set of fast wheels and a Mac 10 submachine gun.

"Lawdy, whatchew doin' here?"

"Quiet, I ain't got time to explain a lot. I want to stay in your attic for a few days, then I'll be outta here."

"Whatchew doin' outta prison? Lawd help me. He done gone and busted out. Ain't ye?"

Stumpy didn't reply, but pushed on into the house with his in-law behind him. She followed him into the kitchen where he invaded the refrigerator, taking out everything he could see. Two children in diapers looked on from the kitchen door. Sister-in-law drew back a rollin' pin and struck Stumpy flat across the back of his head.

"You listen to me. I ain't gonna have none of yo' messin' around at this house. Do you hear me?"

Stumpy only groaned and rolled on the floor holding his head.

"What'd yah do that fo'?"

"I wanted to get your attention. I got children here and dere no-good daddy ain't been back in two weeks. I ain't got time for no trouble 'round here. You mess with me and I'll lay you in the ground. You got that?"

"Yeah, I got it. I'll just get me sumpin' to eat and go on up in the attic. I won't be comin' down and messn' witchew."

Stumpy's appetite had diminished somewhat. He took several pieces of fried chicken, a wad of clothing and lumbered up the pull-down stairs to the attic. His sister- in-law watched his every step.

CHAPTER TWENTY-SEVEN

This was Kelly's element — the operating suite of the judicial system. The courtroom was packed to capacity and a throng of onlookers and reporters lined the hallway outside. This was slated to be a highly publicized case. For Judge Gillmore, however, it was just another day. Gillmore had sat on the bench for 18 years. He didn't care much for theatrics.

"All rise," the bailiff announced.

Kelly stood with his clients. Diane Stein and Dr. Greson were already standing. Greson was ready to get this thing over with, and Diane was ready to have a go at Kelly.

The Honorable Judge Gillmore entered. He was followed by his faithful companion, Watson — an aging Jack Russell terrier that had attended every hearing since 1978. Watson took his position alongside the judge and the courtroom was seated. On objections, rumor had it that the dog bit the judge once for sustained and twice for overruled. However, no one had thoroughly investigated this theory.

"Division 10 of Circuit Court is now in session, the Honorable Judge Milton Gillmore presiding. The case: Hinkley vs. Greson."

The gavel pounded. Kelly opened, parading around in his expensive suit, "Ladies and gentleman of the jury, I will prove that my client, Ms. Karen Louise Hinkley, was harmed by the negligence and intentional actions of Dr. Paul Greson. Further, I will prove she lost a promising and lucrative career as a result of his malpractice. It's not all about money, ladies and gentlemen, but we will prove that Ms. Hinkley would have made millions had she been able to continue her career as a famous movie star."

Kelly spent the next 30 minutes setting the stage for the testimony about to be heard by the jury.

Ms. Stein followed after a brief pause and a review of her notes. She stood, wearing a cream-colored silk suit, and turned to the jury. "I am Diane Stein and I represent Dr. Paul Greson. I am here to defend the good doctor against slanderous and money-grubbing accusations being made by the plaintiff. I will demonstrate to the jury that Dr. Greson performed his duties as a medical doctor with skill and care. Further, I will show that he saved the life of the one who now is screaming injustice. Ladies and gentlemen, Dr. Greson does not concern himself with photo opportunities, but he did concern himself with saving the life of a 23-year-old patient, and he did that with excellence in his field." Diane gave a preview of the medical aspects of the case and described to the jury how Dr. Greson had saved Karen Hinkley's life.

During opening statements, neither side had scored any points with the waiting jury.

"The plaintiffs may call their first witness," the judge opened.

"Your Honor, we would like to call Mr. Jeff Ranks, editor of *Fabulous Look Magazine*," Kelly said.

As the drama began to unfold, Kelly was laying the groundwork for proving Karen Hinkley's damaged fame and potential fortune.

"Yes, Ms. Hinkley would likely have been one of the most famous stars, had her career continued on its original course," Ranks spoke.

"And what do you think changed the course of her career, Mr. Ranks?"

"Her hair loss, of course."

Ms. Stein did not cross-examine.

"This court is in recess until 2:00 p.m.," the judge declared.

⚖   ⚖   ⚖

Stumpy crawled out of his sister-in-law's dusty attic by lowering the ceiling ladder. He stretched and checked each way for her. Stumpy did not want another encounter. The house was quiet when he opened the refrigerator door and removed the better remains of a ham.

Out the door and around back, Stumpy climbed into his new vehicle and drove to the Old Time Billiard Parlor. Once inside he was greeted by the usual crowd with few remarks. No one had even mentioned his reappearance.

Stumpy stood, leaning against a pool table, chewing on a match stick and watching a dull game of pool. The old TV above the counter caught his attention.

"Today, the long awaited trial of Karen Hinkley began in Memphis. There has been much publicity surrounding the case of Ms. Hinkley, a Memphis model, and her physician, Dr. Paul Greson. Her lawyer, Marion Kelly, said today he expects the jury to return a quick verdict in favor of his clients. Mr. Kelly himself has been under close public scrutiny regarding alleged banking violations. No matter what the outcome of the trial, this reporter thinks it will be interesting to say the least."

Stumpy let the match droop from his mouth as he watched the film in the background. Marion Kelly was pictured on the courthouse steps speaking into a microphone and smiling widely. Stumpy felt his anger building as he saw more of Kelly's face.

Stumpy collected his thoughts and looked around the pool hall as if someone might have overheard his mental plot. Out back he checked the Mac-10 the Rastaman gave him. Two clips full. He didn't have time to test fire the weapon. He would have to rely on Rastaman's word that it worked.

By 1:40 p.m., Stumpy had parked and started toward the courthouse. He was not thinking. Stumpy was walking straight up the steps when it hit him. "Man, what the hell am I doin'? I just busted out of prison and here I am walkin' right up ... man, what's done got into you?" he said to himself. Stumpy did a 180-degree turn, got back in his car and drove away. His anger for Kelly had been replaced by his fear of prison. Stumpy was still shaking his head when he drove up to the Rastaman's shop and parked. "I gotta find me another way to get to that bastard."

⚖   ⚖   ⚖

After the lunch recess, the courtroom filled again to capacity with plantiffs, defendants and onlookers. When the judge called the court back to order, he settled into his chair and allowed the sleepy narcotic of a full stomach to overtake him.

Since it was Friday afternoon and only the first day of testimony, Kelly did not want to cover much of the technical, medical or legal details he would rely on next week. Juries had notoriously short memories. Today, he planned only to gain sympathy for Karen's lost career and the stress she suffered as a result.

"We call Dr. Dick Withers, your Honor."

"Do you solemnly swear ..."

"Now, Dr. Withers, what is your field of practice?"

"I'm a clinical psychologist."

"And, in the course of your practice, did you have the opportunity to treat my client, Ms. Karen Hinkley?"

"I did."

"Now, Doctor, what did Ms. Hinkley see you for? What was her problem?"

"She was suffering from post traumatic stress disorder."

"That's a big name, Doctor. What do you mean by that in layman's language?"

"She developed a state of prolonged shock, like an anxiety disorder, after the loss of her hair."

"How did this affect Ms. Hinkley?"

"She was unable to go outside, read a newspaper, watch television or do anything for that matter."

"Why is that?"

"She was afraid she would see something frightening or something that reminded her of her lost career."

"In your opinion, is this a permanent or temporary condition?"

"Oh, it's permanent."

"No further questions."

"Ms. Stein, you may cross-examine the witness," the judge motioned.

"Thank you, your Honor." Diane stood and placed her hands on the table then leaned forward over her notes. She raised her head and turned on a serious look.

"Dr. Withers, what is the most common disorder you see in your practice?"

"Well, I'd say it is post traumatic stress disorder."

"Is this the most frequent diagnosis you give to your patients, Doctor?"

"Yes, they're under stress and need help."

"Isn't it true that your patients file a large number of Social Security disability claims?"

"I wouldn't say a large number."

"I have here a summary from the U.S. Department of

Human Services indicating that you have approved 241 such applications for disability by your patients this year. Is that true?"

"Well, I guess."

"And all of these people have post traumatic stress disorder?"

"Well, most of them."

"No, Dr. Withers, all of them. I have here, for the court's examination, a summary of other psychologists in this area. The most disability claims in Memphis were filed by Dr. Withers." Diane turned, shaking the reports toward the jury. "The other psychologists combined filed a total of eight. Eight, ladies and gentlemen." Diane looked back at the doctor. "Now, Doctor, you tell me all these people are under such great stress that the State of Tennessee has to take care of them? Are you also telling me that Ms. Hinkley should be considered disabled because she is nervous. She is 24 years old and too nervous to even go grocery shopping?" Diane spoke clearly, punctuating the absurdity of it all for the sake of the jury.

"Well, Counselor, that's current theory."

"Beep, beep, beep ..." Greson's pager sounded. He quickly covered it with his hand. Watson turned an ear, trying to locate the disturbance, then placed his head back down between his front paws. The proceedings continued.

"How many times have you testified on behalf of patients to try to prove an injury in the past year, Doctor?"

"I don't keep count."

"Isn't it true that you have a reputation in the lawyers' back rooms as 'ole-you-pay-it, and he'll-say-it?'"

"Objection, your Honor." Kelly rose as the courtroom let out a murmur.

"Sustained."

"Isn't it true, Dr. Withers, that you are widely used by plaintiffs' attorneys for testimony?"

"I do some legal work."

"Isn't it true that you have testified in court over 60 times this year already?" Diane paused, looking from the doctor to the jury. "No further questions, your Honor."

Greson smiled as he whispered into Diane's ear after she returned to her seat, "Well done, Counselor."

The judge looked down at Watson. The dog appeared to be weary of the case.

"This court is recessed until 10:00 Monday morning," he announced, pounding the gavel.

The courtroom rose, mumbling and milling about. A crowd had gathered outside, waiting for Kelly and his clients to exit. Cameras and videos whirred, and reporters surged to field their questions as the entourage exited.

Greson answered his page on his cellular phone. It was the hospital. Carl was ill. He turned to Linda, waiting closely at his side. "I've got to go, it's Carl."

Linda knew he would be gone for a while.

Outside, the reporters thrashed out the questions.

"Mr. Kelly, how do you feel about the opening day of your trial?"

"I think the good people of Tennessee will see things our way in the end. The defense is, of course, going to try to discredit our witness. That's their usual tactic."

"Mr. Kelly, what about the grand jury investigation?"

"This is not the forum to discuss that matter. Please confine your questions to the Hinkley case, ladies and gentleman."

"Ms. Hinkley, are you relieved the case has started?"

"Yes. I want to see that monster pay."

△△   △△   △△

Philip Wilson awoke very late with an oversized headache. He had stayed at his grandmother's farm for a week after arriving in Memphis. He managed to eat something, but only after swallowing a handful of pills.

Today, he would see Kelly. It was Friday.

Wilson managed to make it into town without incident, but as he was parking, he dented the fender of both the car in front and the one behind before coming to a stop. His car was half on the curb in the parallel slot. He fumbled with the door.

Once in the elevator, he took several more pills and punched Kelly's floor. The receptionist in Kelly's office had stepped away from her desk, so Wilson wandered down the hallway, stopping at the first occupied cubicle. "I want to see Kelly," he blurted into Becky's face, startling her.

"Mr. Kelly is in court today, sir," Becky said to the strange man.

"I want to see him."

"Mr. Kelly has had this court date posted on his calendar for several months. Maybe you made a mistake with your appointment date."

"I want to see him now," Wilson slurred.

"Can I ask what this is in relation to, sir?"

"None of your business," Wilson spit back.

"If you'll have a seat in the library, I'll see when he might return." Becky pointed toward the corner room.

Wilson entered the small, legal library and seated himself at the oval table in the middle. Becky peeked around the corner to see if he was all right and then went to find Mary.

"I've been told that Mr. Kelly will probably return to the office after court today," Becky reported back to Wilson around the door facing. "If you want to, you can wait here. I'll let you know when he arrives."

Wilson nodded.

"Can I get you anything, sir, like a cup of coffee?"

"Coffee would be nice."

Becky returned with the coffee and placed it on the

table in front of Wilson. His eyes were half closed. He held a briefcase under his folded arms, over which his head bobbed as if he were falling asleep. Becky looked at him curiously and decided he was pretty drugged up.

"Is there anything else, sir?"

"How long?"

"Well, it's almost 5:00 p.m. now," Becky said, checking her watch, "and it's the first day of the Hinkley case. I would expect court to be recessed by now. He should be here any minute."

Wilson nodded. "Okay."

Becky returned to her usual transcriptions and filing as the office gradually emptied on Friday afternoon.

It was 10 minutes till 6:00 and Kelly still had not shown. Becky tried his car phone and home number several times. Just as she was standing to tell the mystery visitor that Kelly was probably not coming back, she heard a loud crash.

"Oh my God. Sir ... Sir!" Becky dropped her files. Wilson had fallen to the floor into a pool of his own vomit. Becky tried unsuccessfully to wake him.

"911."

"Yes, this is Becky Summers. I'm in the Kline Office Building, 22nd floor, and a man has passed out. He looks bad. I need an ambulance."

The ambulance crew followed the standard protocol — checking pupils, getting vital signs, starting IV, giving glucose. Without avail. They questioned Becky, but all she could tell them was that he seemed drugged. One of the paramedics said he could smell alcohol.

By the time the confusion was over, it was nearly 7:00 p.m. Becky was straightening up her cubicle some before going home when she noticed Wilson's briefcase. In the confusion, it had been set aside in the library. She placed it in Marion Kelly's office behind the door, switched off the light and headed out.

CHAPTER TWENTY-EIGHT

Catrina allowed herself to be lured into Kelly's lair. This time, Kelly ran in the afternoon and met the mysterious, dark-haired Brazilian near the playing fields. She was much more cordial. Kelly was surprised when she accepted his invitation to cross the park to his house for drinks.

Thirsty and sweaty from running, they approached the back of Kelly's house through the hedges from the roadway. The late-fall evening began draping its platinum hue over the treetops as leaves crunched beneath their feet. Catrina watched behind her. The weather had turned cold.

"Do you always carry that fanny pouch with you?" Kelly questioned, pointing to Catrina's black waist belt.

"Yes, it has my essentials. A girl never knows what she might need," Catrina responded with a sexy wink, entering the kitchen doorway.

"I see, well how about something to drink? What would you like?" Kelly turned to the refrigerator.

"I only drink water. Thanks."

"We could get in the Jacuzzi, but I guess you don't have a suit," Kelly said jokingly.

"So. Why do I need a suit?" Catrina replied quickly. "Where is it?"

Kelly hastened his drink-making frenzy with the

promise of a more interesting proposition. He pointed her through the hallway to the solarium, where a large Jacuzzi was surrounded by ferns and flowering plants.

"Fabulous! This will do very nicely," Catrina said.

"There's a bathroom just over there if you need one," Kelly motioned.

"No. I don't," she spoke softly and flipped on the Jacuzzi. As the water bubbled, Catrina cast a sensuous look toward Kelly. Slowly, she unclipped her waist belt and let it fall. Sitting on the edge of the tub, she unfastened her shoes.

Kelly tried to conceal his excitement. "The hunt is over. Now for the kill," he thought.

"Turn around," Catrina said coyly, making a whirlybird motion with her finger.

Kelly complied.

"Okay, come on in," Catrina invited after sinking into the tub.

Kelly, not so modest, disrobed before her. When completely naked, he walked slowly to the side of the tub, displaying his manhood. Catrina appeared uninterested. Once submerged, they made small-talk and began exploring each other's bodies with their feet. Kelly was ready, but didn't want to seem too eager. Catrina had played hard to get, and he wanted to keep up a cool appearance. His attempts to conceal his lust were, however, betrayed by his body.

"Where's the bedroom?" Catrina asked out of nowhere.

"Up the stairs, to the right."

With her eyes locked on his, Catrina stepped out of the Jacuzzi, picked up her things and headed for the stairs. Over her shoulder, she invited Kelly to follow with a wink. Kelly felt the urge of millions of years of natural selection flowing through him. He studied her shape as she navigated out the doorway. He needed no further encouragement. Restraint was no longer an option.

For the first time in a long while, Catrina really wanted someone. She didn't know why. "Maybe it's like the cat playing with the mouse before the kill," she thought. The energy of her passion overtook her.

Catrina folded herself neatly on his bed, throwing back the covers in eager anticipation. Kelly stood at the bedside, admiring her. His towel fell to the floor. Quick and to the point, the two lovers began their merge with eager intention. Deep moans and utterances emerged from the bedroom as their desires took over. The bed moved in syncopation. Their physically fit bodies rose and twisted, devoured by wanting. Secretly, neither wanted to be the first to climax; they were competitive lovers. Moments later, overruled by their passions, they lost interest in such games; yet neither was easily satisfied.

After what seemed like hours, they released each other and fell back on separate corners of the bed. Both lay motionless and spent. Looking into the quiet, dim light, they held the same thoughts in their minds. What was it? In heated passion, they had both been moved by a deep, unfamiliar feeling — a feeling neither had experienced in many years. Tired and sleepy now, they remained retracted into their own spaces.

Kelly awoke at his usual 5:30 a.m. He turned to admire the dark, beautiful figure that graced his bed. For reasons unknown, he felt an overwhelming desire to kiss her. Leaning over, he delivered a gentle kiss on her forehead.

Dressed in his usual jogging attire, he bent forward over the bathroom basin to splash his face. He felt unusually tired this morning. "Probably from the additional work-out last night," he thought. He splashed his face again, the cold water shocking him back to life.

He stood. His gaze was fixed in the mirror. "Catrina, you're dressed." He started to turn to her, then saw the unmistakable dark object in her hand that could only be a gun.

Kelly flinched, grabbing for Catrina's arm.

The gun discharged. Ricochet.

The mirror shattered. Thousands of pieces of glass rained over the bathtub.

Kelly body-slammed Catrina against the doorway, and in one motion she fell as the gun spun across the smooth, tile floor of the bathroom.

They struggled to reach it.

Kelly fell.

Catrina grabbed the gun and leveled it at Kelly, still on the floor.

Her look was cold. Kelly ducked as she fired a shot. It sank deeply into his shoulder.

Catrina tried to raise up, slightly losing her balance. A second shot splintered the door-facing above his head.

Kelly bolted down the stairs and through the back doorway with Catrina in close pursuit, pain gnawing at his shoulder. He ran through the hedges and across the street to the park. It was barely light.

Kelly could hear Catrina behind him. He ran faster, his cold muscles groaning beneath their adrenalin taskmaster. Branches of low-lying bushes slapped his face as he entered the forested area. His cheeks stung as if assaulted by bees.

Kelly heard the subdued thud of a suppressed gun shot. A small branch fell just over his head. He was fatiguing, but Catrina was closing in and he had to keep moving. Up ahead lay a concrete drainage ditch that bisected the park, 10-feet deep and 20-feet wide. He could barely see his way in the darkness beneath the trees.

Jumping into the drainage culvert, he landed unsteadily on his injured shoulder at the bottom. Blood surged from the wound. Out of breath, he forced himself up. He ran, the splashing water beneath his feet betraying his position.

Catrina jumped into the culvert with one controlled

bound and landed squarely. Listening in the darkness of the forest, she could hear him huffing and stumbling down the concrete corridor. She followed in the dim light. He ran for half a mile before coming to an enclosure. He grasped a large tree vine that dipped into the culvert. Pulling himself up, his shoulder, weakened and tired, failed him. He fell backwards into the shallow water.

Catrina appeared. Kelly rose to confront her, out of breath and cornered.

"Who sent you?"

"Somebody who wants you dead," Catrina spoke coldly.

"I ... I," he gasped and clenched his shoulder. "I was beginning to like you. I might have known you were just like me. That's why you're different from the others."

"This is no time for repentance of your ways, Marion. It's too late for that. Maybe I am different, or maybe I'm just like you. We both have learned how to use people to suit our own purpose."

"You felt nothing last night?" Kelly asked, cutting to the point.

Catrina hesitated, looking at him. "No."

"Are you going to just leave my body here? I'll be eaten by animals," wailed Kelly, suddenly taking an interest in his short future.

"From what I've heard, you were never concerned about where you left *your* victims' bodies. Maybe this is your cosmic payback. Really," Catrina raised her gun, "I don't give a damn."

Catrina moved closer in the dim light. The sky was beginning to brighten a little, but the culvert remained dark. She wanted to see Kelly's eyes when she killed him. That was her victory. She would win after all. As she stepped forward, a rusty piece of barbed wire snagged her foot and toppled her. The gun fell into the dark, shallow water.

Kelly, partially recovered now, mustered his strength, drew himself out of the culvert by the vine and headed toward the zoo entrance, hoping to find refuge. He pushed back the low branches with his good arm as he ran. A seven-foot, chain-link fence spread out in both directions. He would soon be caged in. He altered his direction, forcing his way through the underbrush.

Catrina appeared close behind. Her shot missed by inches. The muffled sound of the suppressed bullet brought new energy to his step. Kelly ran another half-mile.

Gasping.

Pain.

Fatigue.

The sky had still not fully lightened. Kelly made his way to the south entrance of the zoo where there were numerous concrete animal statues. He leaned against a large lion, catching his breath. The sting of his shoulder was eclipsed by the sting of bullet-chipped concrete ricocheting off his face.

"Damn."

Kelly ran.

Catrina was still in steady pursuit. She was closing. Kelly found himself in a fenced corner. He grabbed the low branch of a magnolia tree and scaled halfway up, forcing his injured shoulder to support him. Climbing out on a limb, he jumped over the fence and into the exhibition area. Wild animals were of no concern to Kelly at this point. He was in Cat Country, the new, open-air residence for the big cats.

Catrina slammed against the chain-link fence, agitated by her failure. She scaled the fence with little trouble. Betrayed by his own blood, Kelly was tracked like a wounded animal. The bright-red drops, barely visible in the early light, led Catrina to the carnivore area. "How appropriate," she thought, "a lion and a lioness."

She stalked carefully, skillfully.

Kelly was nowhere in sight.

The blood trail continued. Gravel beneath her feet diminished her stealth. One by one, the zoo creatures began their morning bellowing. Lions cleared their throats. Elephants trumpeted. Fowl began staking their territory. The wild noises made Catrina feel as though she were on an African safari.

Catrina approached a newly completed concrete exhibit. Blood stains pointed the way inside. She could hear Kelly's labored breathing resonating within its walls. Slowly, she maneuvered her position. There he stood. In a corner. Beaten.

"I can't run any more, just kill me."

"Oh, I will kill you, you can be sure of that. Maybe I did get too personal with you and let it dull my edge. I'll know better next time." Catrina now smiled. "But for now, Mister, this hunt is over."

Five feet away she leveled the gun at Kelly's head, looked him squarely in the eyes and ...

△△   △△   △△

Carl had positioned himself along a low ridge. He held his rifle steady against the ground. Checking his scope and placing a gold-tipped .308 round into the breech, he cleared his mind of all thoughts. Now, focused and ready, he waited.

At last, he appeared. Carl adjusted himself again. His finger reached for the set trigger. Through the scope he could see the back of his head. The crosshairs came to rest just above the base of his skull. Carl drew a moderate breath and exhaled completely. His finger, exerting slow, even pressure on the trigger, moved with precision. The shot erupted into the morning silence. Dogs began barking. Carl raised to see that his target's head had exploded. He was relieved.

CHAPTER TWENTY-NINE

Becky was worried. She called Dr. Greson. She wanted to talk. They met in the hospital cafeteria for coffee. Greson, both physician and friend, was also deeply troubled. He had hoped that Carl would respond positively to the radiation. He hadn't.

"What's going to happen?" Becky queried.

"I don't know, Becky. I'll ask one of the neuro boys to help. Maybe we could use steroids to shrink the tumor some."

"But it's not going to help for long, is it?"

"No." Paul looked down and rolled his fingers in remorse.

They sat quietly for a while, wandering in their own private sorrows. The silence was interrupted by a call for Dr. Greson over the intercom. He turned to the wall phone behind them and dialed.

"Dr. Greson here," he said, listening intently. "When?" he asked, looking over at Becky. Becky sensed trouble. "I'll come right up." Greson replaced the phone and turned to Becky. "Carl's not in his room."

"Where is he then?"

"I thought you might know."

"I haven't seen him since I left last night about 11:00."

"Let's go."

Dr. Greson and Becky rode the elevator to the eleventh floor, both puzzled by Carl's absence. They rushed down the hallway, turned the corner and entered Carl's room. Carl sat propped up by several pillows, watching the morning news. The TV, hung on the wall, had captured Carl's full attention.

"They said you were gone," Greson said strongly to Carl.

The floor nurse appeared in the doorway behind them. "I checked again right after I called you, and there he was. I'm sorry Doctor, but the 6:00 a.m. shift couldn't find him."

"Where have you been?" Becky questioned.

"I just took a walk downstairs. This room is too confining for me," Carl said shrugging, as if to ask, "What's the big deal?"

"We were worried about you, Mr. Wheat," the nurse spoke. "Next time, please let us know when you plan to leave the floor."

The tension over, Dr. Greson and Becky sat down at Carl's bedside. Becky leaned over and kissed him on the lips.

"Good morning, husband," she smiled.

Carl smiled back, "Hey lover."

"Give me a hug." Becky reached both arms around his neck.

Carl responded with one arm around her and a light squeeze.

"That's all I get?" Becky stood back. Then, suddenly frightened, she looked at Greson. "Carl, what's the matter?"

"I can't move my left arm."

Greson examined Carl's arm. "When did this happen?"

"This morning. It just quit working. It quit hurting, too." Carl grinned weakly. "That's a good thing. It went numb all of a sudden and now it just lies there."

"What does this mean?" Becky asked the doctor.

Before Greson could collect himself to answer, a TV newscaster caught everyone's attention. "This just in; two mysterious deaths have been reported today by Memphis police. Just hours ago, the body of a man identified as Marion Kelly was found at his home in Midtown Memphis. Detectives at the scene say he was fatally shot. Mr. Kelly, a well-known Memphis attorney from the Bensen Keller Gregory & Kelly law firm, was under federal investigation for banking violations and faced possible criminal charges. The firm could not be reached for comment. We'll have more on that story at noon."

"In other news, mysterious circumstances surround the discovery of the body of a young woman at the Memphis Zoological Gardens and Aquarium this morning. Officials say the zoo staff found her badly mauled body in the cage of a new Bengal tiger. The county coroner could not disclose her identity, nor the cause of death at this time. The tiger, the newest animal at the zoo, arrived from India last week to replace Tom, the University of Memphis mascot, who died of old age last year. Zoo officials could not say how the woman came to be in the cage with the tiger. They did say that she is not an employee of the zoo. Officials went on to say that it was too early to determine the fate of the new tiger because the cause of death of the woman remains undetermined. We'll bring you more on that story as Action News Five continues."

Becky and Greson stood dumfounded. They looked at each other in disbelief. "Kelly is dead!" Becky looked at Carl. He was fast asleep.

"I'm in shock. I mean, my boss is dead."

"I know, I can't believe it either, but I can't say that I'm sorry. Wonder if the police have found out who did it?"

"I think I'll take a few personal days away from the

office. Things are sure to be crazy and I could spend the time with Carl."

"Good idea, Becky."

"What about Carl? Will he get his arm back?"

"No."

"I didn't think so."

"I'll get the neuro docs to have a look at him, but I'm not optimistic, Becky."

"Okay, I'll wait around here for the day. Kelly's dead, I can't believe it. Who would do a thing like that?"

⚎   ⚎   ⚎

Later that day Dr. Greson entered Carl's room. Carl sat alone and quiet. Greson walked slowly to his bed.

"Hi, buddy," Greson said as he touched Carl's shoulder.

Carl looked back at him. "It won't be long for me now, Paul. I can feel it. I'm ready."

"Don't talk like that. I won't have it, Carl," Greson said, even though he realized it sounded stupid.

"You remember, Doc, that first time we went shooting and we talked about Vietnam and my buddies?" Carl spoke weakly.

"I remember, Carl. What of it?"

"I told you then that those two buddies of mine were closer than family. I offered my life for theirs, and they would have done the same for me. Well, you are like those guys to me. I have gotten closer to you than any man since those Vietnam days. You are really a dear friend," Carl said sincerely.

Greson began to cry. He put his arm around Carl's neck and hugged him. "I'm glad you're in my life, Carl. You are my dear friend, too. I love you, Carl."

"Paul," Carl spoke weakly. "I did it. I took care of your problem and Becky's problem and a lot of other people's problem."

"What do you mean?" Greson asked, pulling away from Carl and trying to look in his face.

"I killed Kelly."

"You what?" Greson shot out. Suddenly he felt like he was losing touch with reality. "You did what? When? How?"

"Early this morning. I snuck out — had everything ready — and waited on Kelly to come back from his jog. Then I killed him." Carl was barely whispering now.

"Why?" Greson asked. Upset and confused, he put his hands to his face.

"Because it's my duty to protect my friends from the enemy. Kelly was the enemy. I would give my life to protect you and Becky, just like a Marine is supposed to. Besides, I've got nothing to lose. I'm gonna take many souls with me when I go, Doc. I've killed lots of men — bad men. And Kelly was just one more — just like the Red Major. That's why he haunted me so long. I hadn't finished the mission. Now, I can go in peace."

"Carl, you're talking crazy," Greson floundered.

"What are they gonna do, put me in jail for life?" Carl tried to laugh, but coughed instead. "What a joke! I wouldn't last through the ride downtown. Go on now, I'm tired, I want to rest." Carl motioned to Greson to leave the room.

Greson stood. He looked at Carl, lying there now with his eyes closed, resting. He couldn't believe it. Greson reached down and touched Carl on the shoulder. "I'll come back after rounds, buddy. You rest." Greson walked out of the room and closed the door slowly.

A knock on the door opened Carl's eyes. "Come in." George appeared. "George?" Carl called out.

"Yes suh, it's me. I come to get ya' now, Mr. Wheat. We be goin'," George said softly, standing at Carl's bedside.

"Where's the stretcher?" Carl questioned.

"Oh, we don't need no stretcher this time. We gonna take a trip where they don't use no stretchers," George said, taking Carl by the hand.

Carl felt strength return to his weakened body. He stood. George turned, leading him by the hand to the doorway. "Where are you taking me, George?"

"I'm takin' you to see the Mastah. He sent me to bring you home," George replied in a slow, clear voice. The room began to fade away. Colors like the rainbow appeared where once there had been walls. The doorway disappeared and Carl and George walked hand in hand into the peaceful light.

Several weeks after both funerals, Becky returned to her job for the first time, even though she was sad and weary. She did not know of Carl's secret mission. The police, likewise, knew nothing. Greson told no one his secret. The murder file of Marion Kelly remained open in the unsolved cabinet. Everyone presumed it was the mob. To Becky, things seemed quiet and unreal. She was numb from shock.

Kelly's office door had remained closed since the morning of his death. Mr. Gregory approached her desk. "Becky, I know it's been tough on you lately. We're glad to have you back. I'm real sorry about your husband. The firm has asked me to speak on their behalf. If there is anything we can do? ..."

"Thanks, Mr. Gregory, I'm okay for right now, but I'll let you know," Becky replied, looking up with swollen eyes.

"When you get time, Becky, if you could box up Mr. Kelly's things for us. Just leave them out in the hallway and I'll see they get taken care of."

Becky nodded. She moved through the day slowly with little interest in her work. Carl remained on her mind. Alone again. No. She couldn't think of it or she would start to cry all over again. Maybe if she busied herself. She entered the closed door of Kelly's office, taking several boxes with her and closing the door. She felt very sad, but not for Kelly. She wanted to be alone. As she stacked items in the boxes she couldn't keep her mind from drifting back to Carl and her boys. It was not only she who had lost someone twice, the boys had too. Becky began to cry. She seated herself in Kelly's chair and wept through half a box of Kleenex.

After her long cry, she noticed it was past 6:00 p.m. She needed to go. Becky moved several items away from the doorway. Behind them sat Wilson's briefcase. She had put it in Kelly's office when Wilson was taken away by the ambulance, and then had forgotten about it. Kelly had never returned from the courtroom, and the hospital said that Wilson died of an overdose of tranquilizers before he reached the hospital.

Becky curiously placed the briefcase on Kelly's desk and flipped open the latches. She gasped. The case was filled with money. Nervously, she locked the door of the office, returned to the desk and slowly reopened the lid. Becky's heart pounded in her chest. She hesitatingly touched it and then shut the case like it contained a viper. She opened it again and looked out the window. It was snowing.